The Little

Cover artwork by Kathleen Harryman

Kathleenharryman.com

For more information, please contact: magic79.jb@outlook.com

© Jeffrey Brett 2019

The Little Red Cafe

First Published April 2018

Revised Version January 2019

My Beautiful Jenny

Love Always

The Little Red Café

Introduction

Every so often that interminable demand which we call life can run amok and be unforgiving. Going past all of us at such a rapid pace it can be difficult looking back and wondering why, where and when we were actually part of the grand plan.

And before you know it something else has come along, taken precedence and become even more important. The danger is that if you don't press down hard on the stop pedal, steal a moment for yourself and take back control you are at risk of meeting your own shadow on the return journey.

A long time ago I learnt my lesson the hard way in prison, discovering the Zen to my existence was finding a balance and taking each step in time with my heartbeat. A friend once told me that to be in tune with yourself was like having the car serviced. Every so often you need an overhaul, replenish the fluids and decoke the engine. I think he was referring to my soul.

At my last visit to see the doctor, she asked if I was getting regular exercise to which I replied, that I filled my lungs with fresh air every day walking to and from work, keeping my mind active, recalling memories of the past and believing that the future would invariably be that much better.

With a nod she agreed. 'Fate and destiny Mr Brand is the only luxury that the government have not yet taxed.' Damn if she wasn't right.

The hard lesson I mentioned will appear from time to time in the book. I cannot say that I am proud of that era, but leaving prison, I left with a different outlook. I was ready to drift along on the tide of human existence, accept that everyone is different and not rock the boat. I also believe that for every problem there is a solution.

Confucius once said *'a man not in step with the tortoise, is in danger of falling over.'* It took me some time to work through that proverb, but his philosophy works for me. Maybe slowing down and accepting your lot will help you also, you should try it sometime.

Before The Little Red Café came along I was always tripping over myself and constantly getting it wrong. The prison officers who walked the landing would remind me that I was there to serve a penitence for my crime and that the three years that the judge awarded my case, meant that I should look upon the sentence as rehabilitation.

'A short holiday at the expense of Her Majesty will undoubtedly help you retune and find your psyche.' Said the judge.

Sitting there in her wig and red robe she added a slight chuckle at the end of the trial just to show that she had a sense of humour. As I have said we are all different. The day that the prison guards unlocked the cell door, gave me back my personal effects and shut the front gate was the turning point in my life. From that day forward I have never looked back and I will never go back, a promise I made to myself.

Professional mystics who write for a living and subscribe to several well-known daily tabloid newspapers align the moon, the stars and the cosmos, bringing them together to inject a little conjecture to my morning breakfast cereals. Duped into believing what I read, the horoscopes say that I will profit from walking a righteous path, that my health will improve and most importantly romance is drifting into my life with the incoming tide. I just need to be there when it arrives.

Every morning, after rising around five fifteen I leave for work and arrive before six thirty. Now very few know that on the back of my bedroom door I have a poster of Sophia Loren, my dream woman, seductively Italian and with dreamy intentions. If the horoscopes prove to be right, then love is just around the corner.

Perhaps, now would a good point to introduce myself. Christened Spencer Marlon Brand, obviously not of my choosing, I am in my mid-thirties and the proud owner of a little red café which can be found in Oslo Road, London. A divorcee, I found myself with nowhere to live after prison, so returning home with my tail between my legs I live with my mother once again.

As you've no doubt gathered she is in love with Spencer Tracey and Marlon Brando, hence my name. Whenever a film of either man is being shown at the local cinema she will disappear for the afternoon

6

accompanied by Vera, her best friend and neither will leave until they had seen the re-run or until the projectionist turns out the light and heads off home.

As time went by natural development took me from being a headstrong teenager into manhood, not that I had matured as I quickly took the wrong path walking into a life of petty crime. But, god bless her my mother was always there for me. So often too she would remind me: *'Spencer Marlon Brand if you want something in today's world, then you go out there and work hard for it my boy. Nothing comes to you on a plate and achievement is only rewarded to those who give in the first place.'*

The morning that I exited the solicitor's office with the deeds of ownership in my hand was one of the happiest days of my life. At last the little red café was mine and although I'd had no intention of owning a café when I had walked through the prison gate, the prospect of actually owning something was a buzz difficult to describe, other than wonderful. Had the mystics who predicted my future been right, it was hard to judge, but with the café I had changed my stars and I was prepared to let destiny carve out my future.

Unlocking the front door and stepping inside the first thing that hit me besides the walls being painted red was that the place felt right. What was overwhelming was the peace. I can still recall closing my eyes and letting the ambience wash over me. I would change very little, if anything.

Now when I walk down the street early in the morning and I see the café proudly ensconced between the bookshop and the florist I take a

7

moment out to realise that I have arrived and that life does hold a purpose despite the ups and downs.

Located near to the junction of Oslo Road and Denmark Street there is in my opinion no finer establishment this side of Newington Green, a stone's throw from Convent Garden and south of Kings Cross. A good many of our regulars tell me that they come to the café because of the magic that they feel lives within. Some say that they always feel better for having been inside.

I never doubt what they say because like them I too I have felt a presence many times. Should you be cynical enough to not in such phenomenons then why not pop along and see for yourself, try a slice of Vera's best home-made lemon drizzle and believe me you'll think you're in paradise.

A back street café we might be, although surrounded by residential houses and many of London's finest tourist attractions we tend to get our fair share of unusual visitors, interested individuals who have heard of our menu, our service and our enchanting magic.

Vera our full-time cook rarely makes an appearance beyond the kitchen leaving the running of the café to a young, but very capable and delectable young woman, who at the tender age of seventeen goes by the name of Danielle.

Quite rightly you might ask why I do not run things as the owner. The answer however is simple. Three years in prison gave me an understanding of society. Fundamentally, we are outnumbered by the fairer sex, as such we should be tolerant, admit defeat quickly and whenever possible take a step back only by and large the women do a much better job. My role as I see it is to ensure that the coffee machine, a Fracino Contempo no less is always clean and ready to produce good quality coffee, whatever your taste. On the quiet I fondly named the coffee maker *'my old lady'* because it has never let me down, is loyal, never argues back and produces excellent coffee every time. Pinned proudly to the wall next to the counter is our licence to operate.

Now I use the Fracino Contempo every day so you would think that by now I'd be accustomed to the belching noises that the machine makes as the temperature of the steam reaches maximum pitch or the fresh ground chocolate coloured beans rattle, shake and roll around the glass bowl, but every time I would say that the noises are different. Danielle believes that our coffee maker connects with the customers in a spiritual way. Personally I think that she's as mad as I am, although many that know us say they come to the café because being in the café is better than being at home, so who are we to argue.

Set between the book emporium and the florist shop we are nothing grand and we could never compete with any of the other fine coffee houses in and around the city, but we have a beating heart unlike some of the other more elaborate establishments who can offer padded velour seating and fine bone china tea sets, but our café has an atmosphere that you couldn't bottle. At a pinch we can squeeze in forty eight customers.

We accommodate all manner of children's events, christenings, birthday and Christmas parties and we have even been known to cater for a wake.

The door opens at six thirty and we close somewhere between three thirty and four depending upon how long the last customer takes to finish their order, although there is no obligation to hurry. We value everybody who walks through the door and the motto over the front door is very aptly worded: *'let the world rush on by, inside the cafe time stands still.'*

Here at the little red café we invite all to join us, so please pop in for breakfast, a lunch or afternoon tea. We want a traveller to pin a postcard of their adventures on our advertisement board or have a lonely nun enjoy a teacake and later say a prayer for us.

Robert Styles our local vicar often comes at least once or twice a week believing that here at the café he can think, find answers and enjoy Vera's delicious range of cakes. Upon leaving he will wish us well and tell us that we're a slice of heaven. If that's not recommendation enough, then I don't know what is.

We have our busy periods where we see office workers, labourers from the building site, delivery drivers, nurses and postmen plus many more too numerous to name. They all come because our prices are reasonable, we always smile and here you can bring your troubles and leave a different person. If you want to just sit quiet and be at peace with yourself then we respect that as well.

And what of Spencer Brand, sometimes just plain Spence depending on how well I know them. I would be the first to say that I like a good chat although I have been known to possess an effective listening ear as well. I am no leading authority on any particular subject, but I will if asked offer advice on politics, crime, religion and most daily issues that seem to present a challenge. I will also listen to what others have to say and offer, as learning is part of life and I believe Robert when he tells me that ninety five percent of what we believe, we think and we say is nothing more than common sense, the remainder you can read in books.

Talking of books, the emporium next door belongs to an eccentric elderly man named Bartram. He has a wealth of knowledge about books and what he doesn't know isn't worth knowing. He can lay his hand on a copy of a rare book without raising so much as a sweat. He will never divulge his source and I have never seem him use a computer and yet some of our customers tell me that he survives because of his on-line ordering service.

A word of warning though should you enter his emporium, Bartram does resemble a Dickensian character, slightly rounded with small circular spectacles, he has little hair covering the top of his head and what he has left protrudes above both ears. He speaks with a rather unusual squeaky voice and he stands with his hands clamped together. Other than that he is as normal as you and I.

On the left side of the café, my neighbouring florist can only be described as serious competition to Sophia Loren. Born Lola Francine

Maria Capella she makes my heart leap and she can stir my tea any day of the week. Equally, if not more attractive than my Italian heartthrob Lola inherited the shop from an elderly aunt and for six days of the weeks produces the most wonderful floral arrangements of colour and amazing fragrances. The shop is aptly named *'Florrie's Flowers'* after her aunt who came to England during the last century leaving behind her beloved Florence. The florist is a place not to be missed.

So there you have it, a small parade consisting of three shops, each with a different service to offer. If you want an unexpurgated nineteen twenty eight edition of Lady Chatterley's Lover by D. H. Lawrence, Bartram is your man. Flowers for every occasion, you'd be daft to go elsewhere other than to visit Lola and if it is refreshment that is your desire, we sit in between.

You may well ask why I should write an anthology of stories about a London café, why not would be my reply. The little red café has changed my life as it has many others, so sharing some of the experiences will no doubt evoke either a memory that perhaps you yourself have experienced or maybe make you wonder about others who tell you about similar events. And sharing is all about wanting to record the mystique.

Those dark days spent in a cell made me realise too that I had not been cheated of three years of my life, but that I had cheated on society. Having the café helps me restore the order and give back what I took. The judge saw something in me that I possibly did not see myself, such was my misguided illusions of the future. Now however as I begin this book I would say that I have been given a second chance and so often that's all it takes to step back on the path of your destiny. Sometimes it just takes somebody else to help give you that little push. That's what I feel the café does, only you never know quite when.

And like our vicar the honourable Robert Styles I have a good many stories to tell, some that are humorous, some thought provoking, others romantic, maybe a little sad, but many an adventure within reach of our soul. So if you have the time to spare I would be only too pleased to share these experiences with you. Why not sit back, relax and have a coffee with a slice of cake and turn over the page and begin.

Trust me when I say that once you have read the first chapter you will want to read on, I know because I did.

A Normal Monday Morning

Overhead the clouds had turned a murky grey culminating like drifting fog, settling for a fine rain and drizzle rather than develop into a full blown storm, the like of which had blanketed most of Scandinavia. In either direction faces dejectedly stared skyward as they hunched their shoulders inside their coats in an effort to keep the chilled air under control. Somewhere up above the clouds the sun however was eager to put in an appearance.

Being a Monday morning it was nothing special, quite ordinary in fact and like the thousands before the weather did nothing to invigorate the spirit of the workers starting a new week. To the less fortunate living on a day to day existence and by the generosity of others the rain meant something different, a chance to wash away the dust and put out some smalls.

Walking as I always did into work that Monday morning I passed a couple occupying the doorway to a shop that shut down a month ago. They were seen as the blight of our high streets up and down the country although truth be known in the struggle after the last war somewhere along the journey we had ourselves pushed aside public spirit, morals and mutual camaraderie. Dropping a two pound coin in their hat I walked on by, believing it was just enough to get them both a hot drink.

Life whatever you think will throw hard knocks your way and when you least expect them. I had, had my fair share although I believed I might just have turned the corner. There was life wherever you looked, in the people walking by, architecturally designed buildings, advertising billboards and down here on the streets, even the traffic was a major element of our society. If it had not been for the Greeks, Monday's would not be on the calendar.

Arriving as I always did before six thirty I unlocked and took a last look up the clouds overhead. Somewhere inside my head a voice belonging to late grandmother said *'we don't have bad days, just bad moments that can last all day'.* I shrugged my shoulder giving the sun until lunchtime to appear.

Flicking the light switch down the fluorescent strips instantly brought the café to life. It felt good to be back and inexplicably I sensed that we had missed one another. I turned around the sign on the door and told the world that we were open for business. Soon the early risers, the postal workers normally from the nearby sorting office would be the first to arrive, followed by the market traders. I went through to the back powered up the kitchen and hung my jacket, filling the kettle which Vera and I considered to be the most important task of the day.

Striking a match I danced and avoided the blow back from the gas ring swearing under my breath. Within a minute or so Vera would breeze in through the door, hang up her long coat and nudge my arm, stating quite jovially *'here we go again Spence, another week, dollars to be made and*

15

hearts to be broken!' It had always struck me as a funny sort of greeting to start the week although I had never asked for an explanation and in essence I think that I knew to what she was implying as many of our customers came in for advice.

Like old furniture we had grown accustomed to one another, realised one another's faults and put the world to right. The only annoying habit that I had to endure was the ritual of flicking the switch on the wall and filling the silence with the awful, condescending drone of the male disc-jockey covering the early show. I was sure that his driver slipped him some additional endorphin vitamins before he arrived at the studio. Only last week I had seen a photo of him in one of Danielle's magazines, in my opinion it was about that he had his hair cut.

Dropping four slices of white bread into the toaster I heard the front door click shut. Looking up at the clock she was as punctual as ever. A nod of the head, a smile and her coat on the peg she slipped on her apron the one decorated with cats. I waited expecting the normal Monday greeting, but today was going to be different that much I could tell.

'We've already got a customer out front. He seemed somewhat desperate in his expression so I told him that I send out a cuppa. You can't miss him he's the one occupying the corner table.'

I peered through the servery hatch. I couldn't miss him, he was our only customer. Beneath that ample bosom Vera had a heart of gold. Generally she saw the good in everybody providing that they didn't mess with her cat. For the time that we had known one another, there had been very few heated discussions and with a right arm as solid as her frying pan, most times her word was gospel.

'I'll make us our normal and add an extra to the pot for him as well.'

Now as you know my name was usual and as you would guess, especially the time serve at school wasn't an easy passage. I had heard all the sobriquets scribed into the brickwork of that educational establishment, nicknames like *'Black Rock, the Old Man of the Sea'* not forgetting *'Mr Christian'*. The only one that I did think suited my ego was *'The wild One'*. I saw myself in studded leather and wearing my collar up. With no maternal father to defend my corner since my first birthday most of my adolescence had been spent around older women.

My success with females teenage or the mature type had never been in the league of Tracey or Brando and most only went out with me the once to see if I had any genuine connection with Hollywood.

Vera's surname was Lee although she liked to remind us that some of the customers thought she was Vera Lynn the way that she serenaded her songs whenever they were played on the radio. Me, well out of earshot I thought she sounded like the cats that sit on the garden walls late at night.

Danielle, the waitress was our latest addition to the team having spent almost a year standing in the dole queue. Her radiance, wit and wiggle could melt the heart of any of the men that visited. On the flip side her temper was not to be crossed if any dared cross the line. The bonus of the two women in my life, besides my mother was that one cooked exceptional food and the other served without any fuss. Swearing by the way is taboo, even from me. If Vera hears any cursing she is out in a flash and so is the customer until they apologise to everybody inside.

On the personal front I still live with my mother, I know but the bedroom that I had as a child has barely changed except the length of the bed. I was married once but a spell inside prison ruined any chance of a revival of our lost relationship. My ex-wife's solicitor took great delight in writing to me in prison and asking that I sign the divorce papers. At the time I hit an all-time low believing that the world had been swept from under my feet, now upon reflection if I saw my trial judge I would pat him on the back and say 'thank you!' One day soon I will own another house and move out of my mothers.

Anyway, Monday. The drizzle had become rain changing to a sudden downpour. Up and down umbrellas were battling not to be blown away. In the corner of the café our customer had been given an appreciative mug of hot tea and a slice of my toast, cheekily asking for marmalade instead of flavoured jam. What I didn't know then was that Jimmy Lloyd Robertson hailing from Dulwich had mislaid his wallet in and the casino or the Soho streets. How was immaterial.

It was no wonder that he looked so down in the mouth as I later established he was at one point five hundred pounds up, but left owing the cashier two hundred. Gambling was and always will be a mugs game.

When Danielle walked in just after twenty to seven I had to check the wall clock twice.

'Have you been evicted?' I asked. Normal Danielle she looked over and winked at the man sitting in the corner before passing me by with a look of contempt.

'Sarcasm does not become you Spencer!'

It sounded so trite, so out of place that I could only reply with laughter.

'If you must know, I've came in early to talk to Vera, women's talk so stay out of the kitchen for ten minutes.'

See what I mean, my café their dominance. Looking over at the only occupied table I shrugged my shoulders *much safer not to respond!* He nodded as his toast went up and down in sequence with his chin.

When the moment arrived for his bill to be paid Danielle explained his predicament at the counter. I rang up a no sale and took three pound from the float.

'That should be enough to get him back to Dulwich, from there he must sort his future!'

Taking the coins he stood, kissed Danielle on the cheek then came across and shook my hand.

'Thanks… I'll repay you someday soon I promise!'

It wasn't necessary and three pounds wasn't going to break the bank. He waved goodbye as he left pulling up his jacket collar.

Out back in the kitchen Vera was busy with the orders, adding more rashers and sausages to the two pans. She pushed aside the hash browns, cupping in the eggs and mushrooms. I had always been in admiration of how organised everything looked, had I been in charge it would have resembled one large omelette. In the background where the volume had been turned down the morning disc-jockey made comment that the weather outside was wet. The man was a genius.

Around eight maybe ten past three workmen entered and caught my eye. What I found peculiar was that each was attired in a brand new overalls, you could see that they were new because the ironed pleats still ran the length of the sleeves where they had been machine packed at the factory. What I didn't like the look of was the brown holdall that the eldest of the trio had brought in with him. Call it what you will, gut reaction from having consumed only one slice of toast, instinct or having served time I smelt trouble. His companions were younger than him, the youngest around Danielle's age.

They occupied the window table clearing away the condensation that had gathered. The young man was eager to catch Danielle's eye although his own were furtively following her every move between the tables. I watched as she took their order. The older man ordering for all three, the leader.

'Three teas and an English for each Spence.' I took her tab and passed it through the hatch to Vera waiting on the other side.

'They're an odd bunch...' I muttered getting ready the teas.

'Yeah, I've not seen them in here before.' She looked to where they were sitting 'He's a bit of alright though the one with the spikey looking hair and earring.'

Sending across a copy of the newspaper I wanted to see if any read it. The only that seemed remotely interested was the David Bowie lookalike. He flipped over to read the back page, a typical sports enthusiast. Several minutes later Danielle reappeared carrying their breakfasts. Still watching from behind the cake cabinet on the counter I noticed the older man check his watch with regular scrutiny.

Like one of those American bar girls from the fifties Danielle propped up the counter twirling a curl into a strand of her normally straight hair. I flashed my hand across the front of her nose making her start, interrupting her thoughts.

'A pound for them,' I said.

Her eyes opened wide 'I thought it was a penny!'

'Inflation.'

'They intrigue me Spence, they just don't fit in. We get all sorts in here day in day out, but they ain't right even the young one!'

21

Danielle was at times like most girls her age a dreamer with ambition of adventure, meeting and settling down with a nice man, a white wedding and the expected two point four children, although knowing Danielle like I did, it would be point five. I had the same feelings in the pit of my stomach as she had going through that pretty head of hers. Mine however were based on previous experience.

When the older of the men ordered three more teas it became obvious that they had time to kill and an appointment to keep.

'His name's Martyn,' she purred the ringlet of her hair suddenly lost in thought 'he's a year older, eighteen almost nineteen.'

'You're wasted here you should have worked for MI5.' I added three more teas to the slip that I kept behind the counter for refreshments. For the next half an hour we went about or normal business supplying office workers with their lunch order, cab drivers with a hearty breakfast and even the old men who came in before they went and did the shopping. Ten minutes to nine they put down their mugs for the last time and sent the young man across to pay. He gave me a fresh twenty pound note from the cashpoint around in the High Street.

'Was everything okay?' I asked as we both waited for the till to total up the cost.

Momentarily he appeared distracted as though his thoughts didn't belong to his mind. He looked back putting together the reply.

'Yes... it was good thanks and the food here is top-notch only I couldn't find room to finish it all.'

With a whirr and an internal bell the cash register rung up an illuminated total. There are times in our lives when providence comes knocking on our door. Not altogether judgement but instead a way to help. This was one of those times. I checked to see that the two older men were preoccupied and not looking over our way.

Leaning over the counter I gestured for him to come close too. *'Whatever you've got planned for this morning young man, I can assure you that you don't need to be part of it!'*

Martyn with the spikey hair and one earring paled significantly as though he had seen a ghost.

'That would easier said than done mister!' it was no more than a mumble but I understood. Below his ribcage I could feel his heart thumping hard.

Beyond the front door a red bus went past weaving two parallel lines in the tarmac where the rain had settled. Five to nine the sun broke through the clouds, so much for my prediction. In a few minutes time shops, offices, banks and countless businesses in and around the city would be opening their doors and trading would begin.

I gave the plea one more go *'Think about it, it only takes a moment to change destiny, but a bloody long time to get it all back on track, if you make the wrong decision. Trust me I know!'*

As if on cue a curt whistle came from his table where the older man was tapping his watch. He put a hand and called across *'thanks'* then reached down to collect the holdall. I didn't wave back just acknowledged with a wry grin I knew in which direction they were heading. With a dip of her head Danielle saw one of dreams disappear.

With an encouraging hug I told her 'don't worry something tells me that he'll be back.'

Danielle didn't seem convinced.

'You forget Spence I grew up around these streets, some of the boys in my last class before I left school are already treading the exercise yard at the Scrubs. Those overalls were brand new and that tool bag didn't have any workmen's tools inside, not least the kind that you'd mend a leak in the kitchen sink.'

With trade going slack for the next hour before the pensioners started to arrive I suggested that we went out back and help Vera, it would also keep Danielle's thoughts together.

'Well did he ask you out?' Vera asked.

'He hinted at going out this Saturday, providing nothing else gets in the way!'

Vera sniffed like elderly women her age do as she turned down the gas on the cooker. She was shrewd old bird and never missed a trick. Resting on the side were a batch of fresh baked scones. She really was magic. When Danielle slipped out back for some fresh air Vera leaned my way.

'The two older men were a surly pair and up to no good!'

'Well let's just say that they've not gone window shopping. I did try warning the young man, but I think he felt compelled to tag along.'

*****

Now the sound of ever present emergency sirens is nothing uncommon in any city but when you hear them coming close you feel your Adam's apple jump, at least I do.

When Harry Hambleton walked through the door my first instinct was that he would tell us what was going on. Like a regular columnist Harry was the eyes and ears around here and very little passed by his interest that wasn't worth noting. Licking his tongue across the underside of his top lip he was also a randy old bugger as Danielle reached across an empty table to gather up the empty crocks.

'Usual table and order?' I asked as he stumbled into a chair still watching her cheeks go from side to side as she wiped the crumbs from the plastic table cloth.

Without turning she issued a warning his way 'Harry Hambleton if you don't stop staring at my backside I will take you outside, tie you to the lamppost and have the crows peck out your eyes!'

Feigning innocence Harry looked my way. I shook my head.

'Thoughts like that will make you go blind at your age.'

'Have you heard all the commotion down the High Street?' Harry introduced. Loaded with crocks Danielle approached his table as I took over the newspaper.

'You mean the police sirens!'

'That's it, a couple of blokes just turned over Redgewelles the Jewellers. The coppers have got the buggers though.' He saw Vera standing in the doorway to the kitchen armed with the rolling pin a warning that he was not to swear.

'Well go on you old sod, what happened?'

'Happened...' he repeated 'happened that as they came back out they bumped into an off duty detective. Within a minute Soho and Convent Garden was swarming with uniforms. Right old fight they had as well only old bill won. It was captured on film by a bus load of Japanese tourists. No doubt it will be on the ten o'clock news!'

Danielle weaved a path through the tables and rushed out to the kitchen. Went I went out back she was cradled in Vera's arms and the tears were coming in a torrent. Tapping Danielle on the shoulder she lifted her head from Vera's bosom.

'You missed something that Harry said, that there was only two men involved.'

The sobs shook her chest as her thoughts swam back ashore. Wiping the dampness from her cheeks she smiled. 'That's right, he said two men.'

Just then there was a rapid knocking on the delivery door out back. I went through expecting one of our normal drivers. When I walked back a minute later with Martyn by my side I though Danielle was going to faint. He was still puffing hard where he had been running hard.

Like a gazelle protecting her young Danielle launched herself at him thumping his shoulders. To his credit Martyn accepted his punishment like a man. When the frustration changed to relief she stopped hitting him and instead put her arms around his waist placing her head on his chest.

'Does this mean that we can go out Saturday night?'

'The police... do they know about you?' I asked.

Martyn looked at me, his eyes still full of anxiety but as each moment passed his heartbeat returned to normal.

'No, I don't think so. I shied away from the job at the last minute, I lost my nerve. When I saw Danny and Geordie come back out of the jewellers and bump into that big bloke I knew that all I could do was run. The only place that I could think of was here!'

Going out back in the delivery yard I shut the gate and locked our back door. I told Martyn to take off his overalls and put on a spare set of clothes that I kept for emergencies. They were at least three sized too big, but at least he didn't look like he had been part of the gang. To add authenticity Vera opened her locker and gave him a cook's jacket.

'At least if they come looking here you won't resemble an oddity who just escaped from the local circus.' If it had been anybody else I would have been offended.

'Let's get the story right in case they do come snooping. You been employed here two weeks and you're a trainee cook.' The suggestion made Danielle smile.

'Thanks,' he said 'but why are you helping me you don't know me?'

'Several years back I would have liked somebody to have done the same for me.' I looked at Danielle and this time I smiled. 'This girl means the world to Vera and me, so this is for her as well.'

'Does this mean that Martyn is on the payroll?' she asked, her head titled to the side and her eyelids fluttering like the heart strings of a harp.

You know that moment when your mind works through the permutations of can we afford another member of staff, is there enough room and what would be the benefits. The café was doing very well and business was becoming demanding as was the order book for private parties. The reason that Martyn had come in that day was I believed down to fate.

'I guess it does.'

Danielle flew across the kitchen and hugged me so tight I thought she'd at least crack a rib. Standing beside the cooker Vera smiled and winked my way.

'*Que sera sera.* '

Danielle quickly laid a fourth plate, dished up four scones, added better and jam whilst I checked on Harry out front. I was still behind the counter when Martyn came through from the kitchen, he stood beside me.

'Thank you. Where I come from you don't many breaks. I'll make it up to you Mr Brand.' It was the second time that I had heard that promise this morning. I wondered if Jimmy Lloyd Robertson got back to Dulwich safely.

'The bravest thing that you did today Martyn was changing your stars. The moment that you turned your back on crime you put yourself back on track. The little red café is special and in time you'll come to realise just how special. Danielle is like a daughter that I never had, so if you do take her out this coming Saturday all I ask is that you treat her right and don't hurt her!'

'Thing is I didn't feel brave, in fact I felt sick especially when I heard that Danny and Geordie got arrested.'

Wiping the tubular steam release on the coffee machine I recalled the moment that I had been arrested. Occasionally it would send a chilling reminder down my spine.

'Danny and Geordie will be arrested time and time again Martyn, it is part of their DNA. Crime to them is like a life-blood need and being sent to prison an occupational hazard. Fate put that off-duty police officer outside the jewellers no doubt looking for something nice for a girlfriend or wife. When they come out after this next stretch they'll be planning the next big job only it'll end the same way.'

'Do you think that they'll come here looking for me?'

'No. They'll go north next time. Having been arrested in London they'll steer clear of the city for a very long time. I know I would.' I tapped his chest with the ends of my fingers 'that's where courage comes from not up here.' I said, pointing at my forehead. 'Up there the ideas happen, down there is what makes us tick!'

We never did see a police officer that day or the next and so on. As the days and weeks moulded nicely into one another Martyn developed a talent in the kitchen that seemed to inspire Vera. I never thought that I would see it happen but she actually gave him lessons in baking, even for the secret recipe she kept hidden for the lemon drizzle cake.

I am not saying that she didn't work him hard every day because she did believing that he had sinned just by thinking about doing over the jewellers. She had done the same with me when I was released from the Scrubs. Going about his business Harry Hambleton never once asked where the new kitchen help had come from and to be honest nor had I.

When I locked the front door of the café wishing Vera a good evening I watched Danielle and Martyn cross the road and head towards Trafalgar Square. From the back he looked oddly funny in my oversized clothes, but nowadays to be fashionable you have to be seen out wearing an extremely loose baggy ensemble.

There are times when the likes of Harry consider me to be a cantankerous grumpy old sod, but he wouldn't be without the café and neither would any of us. The little red café is no ordinary eatery and to believe that a certain magic exists within you would to come visit to find out. That Monday morning by whatever means it worked a certain spell on Martyn and had him change his ways. In a few years from now ask him how he felt the day that he came running, puffing back to our yard door, only I guarantee that he will explain it perhaps better than I can.

A Matter of Faith

How many times in your life have you put faith in the pattern left in the bottom of a china cup where the tea leaves predict your future or remarked that the froth floating on top is an indication of wealth, be honest only we've all done it. My mum would say poppycock, old wives tales and that they all came from the book of superstition. My reply would be, well somebody wrote it.

Spiritual comfort however comes from the divine and although mentioned a number of times in the good book needs no such urban myth. Believing however is down to the individual and men like our Robert Styles are there as a sort of sales manager, marketing agent, spiritual guide. They have already offered their soul to the almighty. As for me well I need to complete my penitence before I am added to the list.

Of course religion is one person's preference as opposed to another. I am not sufficiently scholared to say who should worship what. Joseph the Jewish tailor from down the road attends the synagogue whereas Abdul the halal butcher the mosque. Each is as beautiful as our own churches, no more so than St George's in Arbury Street.

Looking up from the counter I was surprised to see Robert Styles wandering back and forth the pavement in a state of uncertainty and confusion. Many was the time that, that good man had talked with me in his vestry, explaining, justifying the reason as to why I had taken to praying when I had been alone in my cell. I had a lot of time for our man of god.

What I had struggled tenaciously to understand was why any man or woman would devote their entire existence to an entity that they could neither see nor touch. A church was as solid as a castle, built to withstand fire and brimstone, be a sanctuary to all seeking help and yet the few times that I been to St George's I had left feeling battered and bruised. If angels were ghosts then they did an excellent job of setting me right.

Robert Styles however was a man of such strong unwavering belief. He told me that he had broadened his horizons as god was everywhere, a good argument. He respected all religions, had no time for prejudice and saw the good in every man woman and child. 'We are walking in the footsteps left by Jesus,' he would passionately tell me 'so we should inherit the earth as was his wish, in peace, love and an accord with all living souls, animal or man!' Robert Styles was a difficult man to break down although he had my admiration.

Pacing back and forth there was something on his mind obviously evident by the lack of jovial waves and smiles that had become his trademark. I knocked on the window beside the counter gesturing that he come in.

Robert chose a table laying down the bible that he always carried. I asked if he wanted tea, he chose coffee. Offering biscuits he asked for a slice of home-made cake.

'You have the look of a man with the weight of the world on his back,' I remarked as I took across the order to his table. He instantly delved down into his waistcoat pocket for his coins, but placing a hand on his shoulder I told him that both were on the house.

Unsmiling he put a hand to his heart and thanked me. 'Your kindness will be one day rewarded Spencer,' he was one of the very few to call me that.

'I was taking a walk away from St George's because I find myself at odds not only with myself today but the lord as well. Early this morning I had been called out to give prayer and to be present when the time arrived for poor Reginald Hollingsworth to take his place in heaven.

Despite my words of comfort they offered little ease to the suffering of those in the room especially young William, the grandson.

Looking at the wall clock it was registering ten minutes to nine.

'Death is never easy Robert, it can be quite exhausting and testing.' He stifled a yawn to support my theory.

Pushing the swing door aside Danielle emerged from the kitchen, she saw me talking to Robert Styles and waved, he responded although it was half-hearted. I recall that Danielle once had a thing for a man in a dog collar wanting to defrock him of his innocence, fortunately before any damage was done Vera had intervened and made her see the error of her ways. Looking down at the forlorn man of Christ he had no idea what a lucky escape he'd had. Without being invited I took the seat opposite.

'I will miss old Reg and so will Vera, she'll be sorry to hear of his passing. Quite often he'd come in for an Eccles cake and strong cup of tea, bringing in young William at the weekend. During a weekday visit Reg would say that the café was the only peace that he ever got.' I detected a flicker of a smile part Roberts lips. Like an angel Danielle came over placing a coffee where I sat and a plate of biscuits.

With his cake untouched Robert picked up a chocolate biscuit and dunked it in his coffee.

'The church will miss him also. Reginald was a regular at St George's where he helped make the annual float for the carnival, working tirelessly in the background for the nativity play and generally sorted small repairs.'

I didn't know any of this, isn't it strange that we see people, make small talk and yet never really know them. At any time say in the butchers you could be standing next to a heart surgeon, an astronaut or a person like Reg who did so much for the community. Collecting another biscuit he scooped it across the coffee froth before devouring the crumbling delight.

'Regrettably I have been present at a few deaths around here sitting beside an ailing soul but never have I been as tested as I was this morning. Today young William just stood the other side of the bed holding his dead grandfather's hand glaring up at me as though it was my fault. I have to say Spencer that the look on his face tore at the very fabric of my faith and heart!'

I grabbed a biscuit before they all disappeared. 'In time William will understand as do we all. Death is still one of the unexplained phenomenons of the universe!'

Robert looked at me, but luckily the sugar from the chocolate had not yet boosted his glucose level. Heaven as far as he was concerned was the pinnacle, the zenith of god's creation. The one assurance that ever had as a boy was that we are created, born, we live in between and we die. Four chapters and we don't always write in the good bits. The unknown was the end, when and where.

'He wanted to know why his grandfather was as cold as ice. Now I'm no doctor although I explained as best I could that at the point of death an angel arrived and took the soul away. The flapping of her wings made everything draughty. William didn't buy it.' I had to say as I put the rim of the cup to my lips neither did I.

Whether it was the subject that we were discussing or whatever I felt a sudden breeze waft through the small hairs on my arm as though somebody's spirit was just passing through.

'Algor mortis or the death chill,' I explained 'the dropping of the body temperature immediately after death.' Robert looked impressed.

'I am supposed to be the man for all occasions Spencer. Baptisms, weddings and funerals. This morning however William Hollingsworth rightly demanded answers that I could not give. God had let this young man down.'

He took the last of the biscuits.

'Isn't that just you feeling vulnerable,' I asked 'I know a good many people in the area that would be the first to say that you do a grand job.'

Robert said nothing, content to listen.

'You don't go ramming religion down our throats, your acts of encouragement is so often appreciated and what you have to say makes sense. You need to remember back to when you were seven Robert. Everything beyond the front door seemed so frighteningly big, even the park down behind the flats. You probably wondered where'd you fit in, I know I did. On the Saturday's that Reg was accompanied by William they would sit and chat for an hour at least. To the little lad his grandad was his mentor, his idol. You did nothing wrong today and if the church had all the answers then history would have to be rewritten!'

'Do you believe that there is a Garden of Eden?' he suddenly asked.

I recall seeing a painting hanging in the Tate by a man named Mahoney. Other than that and Kew Gardens, Eden was somewhere abroad but if Robert was asking then it had to have a religious significance.

'I would like to think that when I died I would end up on a beach where the sun shone all day and night and the palm trees swayed gently in the breeze.'

'I asked because it's the one place that I am not sure about. I read from the bible every day and what I read I interpret differently depending upon page I open the pages at. Educated scholars argue that the bible is a fabrication of one man's imagination. We die and on the wings of an angel arrive in heaven, the Garden of Eden. Even I admit Spencer that it could be a little way from the truth.'

Whoa stop the press. He was Robert Styles staunch believer challenging the word of god, I never thought that I would hear it.

'You preach that god is all around don't you?'

'Of course.'

Remembering my visits to the prison Chaplin another prisoner had asked the same question as Robert. The Chaplin had replied that Eden had been bigger once but god had cut it in half and sent the remaining portion back down to earth for the living to enjoy. We were already enjoying Eden without realising it.

'And you give hope to those in hospices and hospitals where there is little hope?'

'Again I do.'

'Then where do you get your inspiration Robert?'

Placing his hand over the bible he grinned. *'This...'* he replied.

'Then why worry about what educated people think. Most sceptics only like to be heard because they don't know the answer themselves

He finished his coffee. 'Why do you never come to St George's,' he asked 'my congregation would love to hear your argument only it has merit Spencer!'

'The people that attend church Robert are pure of heart and deed, mine has let me down in the past. Perhaps one day when enough oil has re-anointed my sins will I feel confident to come?'

He smiled at Danielle who was gazing out of the window looking at the passers-by.

'The young have an innocence that cannot be bottled or exploited.' He chortled 'before I left the bedroom of the deceased young William Hollingsworth looked at me and declared that all vicars were poofs because we wore black dresses and that Jesus must have been a zombie to have carried the cross up that hill.'

'The trouble with innocence Robert is that it is very short-lived.'

Having moved from the counter to an empty table that had just been vacated Danielle suddenly came to ours.

'My Nan... she floats around somewhere up there,' she said.

I didn't know whether to laugh or leave but Danielle looked serious.

'We know cos' me and my mum, we go over to Aunt Edie's where we sit around her big oak table, dip the lights and listen as Aunt Edie starts up a conversation with the old girl.'

I watched as Danielle discussed the possibilities of talking with the dead with the vicar, I wondered in essence whether she had ever been as innocent as he made her out to be. Never really lost for words Robert had a gentle way of ending a discussion.

'God moves in mysterious ways Danielle. If he feels that it helps you, your mother and your grandmother to keep in touch then that is god's way.' The biggest smile suddenly appeared. 'In hindsight I should have taken you along with me to this morning William Hollingsworth would have appreciated your take on heaven.'

I have to admit that I looked up at the sky through the window knowing what was coming and Danielle being Danielle she didn't let me down.

'God or no god we still ain't found the jewellery that the crafty old bugger said that she had hidden.' I wanted the earth to open up and swallow me whole. Walking towards the kitchen she wasn't quite done, she turned and looked back 'Still with your satellite link vicar if you say a prayer for me tonight you never know the old bird might give up the location!' With that she was gone.

'One day she will make a fine mother,' Robert said praising her resolve. 'Danielle sees things as they should be seen. On reflection I believe that is what I lacked this morning when I was confronted by young William.'

We both looked when a tiny hand tapped on the window adjacent to where we were sat. Robert almost went white when he saw William Hollingsworth staring at him. Moments later the boy entered the café.

'If my grandad is in heaven like my mum says he is, do you think he'd mind if I had his fishing rod, reel and maggot box?'

And that was how young William came to accept his grandads passing. Sitting on the riverbank he still had a link with the man that he loved so much. He copied the casting technique, cleaned the equipment and stored the maggots just as his grandfather had taught him. William Hollingsworth went to St George's accompanied by his mother and he helped decorate the summer float. Every night beside his bed he would kneel and pray. Nobody was allowed to listen but his mum knew that it was a long prayer as he told his grandad in heaven all about the things that he had done that day. When she was alone and had the opportunity the unmarried mother told Robert Styles about the prayers at night. He told me much later that it helped restore his faith.

Around mid-morning in the little red café a man and a boy had come to terms with death and with one another. Robert realised that there was still many things to learn about being a man of god and that sometimes the answer was always forthcoming form high above. Whether the bible was or was not a work of fiction, then that was for others to evidence.

So remember what I said about reading tea leaves or counting false money. Nothing in life is certain except death. And before I end this chapter Robert Styles and I felt it our duty having known Reginald Hollingsworth to follow the maturing of a young boy called William as he grew into a man. Twenty years from now he would take up a position in a famous London children's hospital, where his skills and bedside manner as a paediatrician would save the lives of countless patients.

When the time comes to say goodbye to a loved one it is never easy because none of us ever really want to accept change. I believe even to this day that young Robert wasn't so much not accepting that his grandfather had died, he just wanted answers as to why. Answers that none of us can really give.

Robert Styles rightly still believes that when the time arrives it is because of god's will. He purchased a print of the Garden of Eden from the Tate and has it on his study wall. Whenever he has moments of doubt he told me that the garden adds the missing bits.

Now I am not going to disclose in print whether or not I believe in ghosts but one Sunday when I was fishing down by the river I could sworn that I saw William sitting with a man at his side further down the embankment. It made me smile seeing him at peace with the world as they fished together. It also proved that we never really lose the ones that we love because they will forever live on inside our heart.

One last anecdote, despite Robert Styles saying a prayer for Danielle that same night she is still searching for her grandmother's lost jewellery.

The Avengement of Cyril

'Ignorance can be blind to a man who wishes to see nothing beyond the end of his nose, observing merely the shadow of his own importance.'

I could very easily claim that the words of wisdom had originated from none other than Confucius himself, but I would be accused of deceiving you all only to be honest the phrase belonged to nobody else, but me.

Long ago I had made it an unwritten rule never to involve myself too deeply in the affairs of other individuals as delving into private lives could not only involve pain, but possibly heartache not just for them but me also.

My second rule was that everybody had the right to involve whatever they deemed important to make the day go better, as long as it was legal, above board and it didn't involve me.

Having said that and with both rules firmly imprinted in my mind I have to contradict myself by saying that as members of the human race we are naturally a curious creature.

Vera was without argument the backbone of our little café. She was punctual, rarely took any time off for herself, would inevitably struggle through a day despite being under the weather and generally she would bring to the place a certain calm, something possibly hard to describe, but you know everybody no matter who is entitled to a secret or two and some secrets can be painful even after so many years. Quite by chance I happened upon her secret only last week when I let Danielle and Martyn get away early so that Vera and I could prepare for the following day.

'That was unusual of you.' Vera said pulling the plug from the sink.

'What do you mean?' I replied.

'Letting the youngsters go early only you normally keep them both here till four.'

I took up the tea towel and began drying the crocks.

'Well Martyn has fitted in nicely since his close brush with crime and Danielle's worth her weight in gold so maybe now and then it doesn't hurt to show some latitude.'

'That's what I mean, it's unusual!' Vera added.

Filling the kettle I added 'and it gives us time to have a chat. Do you fancy a quick brew before we leave off?'

Vera eyed me somewhat suspiciously and with good reason, ordinarily I was keen to clear up, shut up shop before getting away as soon as I could.

'What's this,' she asked 'the lull before the storm, are you working up to giving me notice to quit Spencer Brand?' removing her pinny she flexed her arms ready for the fight. It made me laugh although she wasn't amused.

'Don't be daft,' I replied switching on the kettle 'I was lying in bed last night thinking about you and although we've known each other for a good many years there's little I do know about you!'

With the rolling pin next to the flour board it was handy in case she needed to use it.

'Are you getting desperate, I'm old enough to be your mother you know.'

I sat down to show that there was nothing physical in my admitting to thinking about her whilst I was counting sheep. Dropping two tea bags into the mugs I poured in the milk.

'I was only thinking about you Vera because I couldn't do without you. I was actually wondering if you'd like to buy into the business, become an equal partner and take a share of the profit.'

With a clunk the rolling pin was dropped into the drawer.

'Is that all,' she took the seat opposite mine 'It's a really nice offer, but I am happy doing what I do best. I come to work do my bit for the café and then go home without any worries. If it's alright by you, I'd much rather leave it that way!'

Dunking the teabags in the hot water I conceded and handed over her tea. Vera was right, she was happy and I admired her honesty.

'You said that you didn't know much about me, what do you want to know?'

'Oh, I don't know,' I began 'there must be some interesting bits like where you were born, where you went to school and what you've done with your life besides working here at the café. Things like that I guess.'

Sniffing, she replaced the lid of the hand cream slipping the jar back into her handbag. I watched knowing Vera only ever did things if they had a purpose.

'I'll tell you something about me otherwise you'll only be like a dog with a juicy bone that is unable to get through the gristle, but you have to promise me that you won't let on to Danielle or Martyn.'

I promised.

'I was born in Stepney a stone's shot away from the Royal London Hospital only instead I had a home birth delivered by the midwife. Times were hard but like many families living in the area we made the best of a bad thing. Despite the poverty I had a good childhood and never regretted a single moment, not like some I could mention.

'My father worked on the railway until old age caught up with his body and physically forced him into retirement. Mother was a char lady for some fancy West End actress. My school was called Fife Manor only you would never have known as it was a long way from Fife and most certainly it was no manor house. From what I recall it was tall, dark and dingy, like the houses that you see in those horror movies, not that I really watch them.

'Leaving behind a full-time education at fourteen I went straight into service, employed in a large house over Hampstead Heath way where I scrubbed floors, cleaned bathrooms and made the beds every day. It was hard work, but I thoroughly enjoyed it. After a couple of years I was promoted to kitchen assistant and hey ho it's where I learnt to cook. Blandford Hall was a grand house, a happy place and as staff I laid many a banquet during my days there.

'The master of the house was a lord something although he was never around much and I could never remember his name. A footman once told me that his lordship spent most of his time at Westminster, getting Brahms and Liszt some say.

'Things however went bottoms up one night when some of the silverware went missing from the dining hall. The police were called to deal with the furore which turned out to be a young decorator who had been working in the west wing. Not only had he taken a fancy to his lordship's daughter, but the family heirlooms as well. Deservedly he was sent to Pentonville and she was sent away to some posh finishing school in Switzerland. In a way she had the best of both worlds, first the decorator and then second escaping the clutches of the old lord.'

I opened the biscuit barrel that we kept for kitchen purposes only allowing Vera time to get her breath and prepare herself for the next instalment.

'So what happened next?'

'Well...' she continued 'after the hullabaloo of the burglary I decided it was time to spread my wings and work elsewhere. I landed a position in a high class London hotel where I became a trainee pastry chef, it was where I met my Cyril.'

Now this was a revelation as I had never known Vera as romantically attached.

Reading my thoughts, she smiled 'Cyril was the garden room concert pianist and anybody that saw him play should consider themselves privileged. His fingers would dance up and down those ivories as though he was skating on ice.' I noticed a slight shine to the corner of her eyes where a tear was forming.

'Mum never ever mentioned Cyril.'

Taking a handkerchief from her pocket she scrunched up the corner and wiped each eye.

'I don't suppose she has only it's not something that we talk about often. You see things didn't work out as we had planned.' Vera took a biscuit from the barrel and dunked it in her tea.

'Cyril was a handsome, upstanding man. Admittedly no movie star to look at but he would stir my insides like nobody else. Even when we kissed goodnight and parted I had to uncurl the end of my toes. If I had known what was to come I would have spent every moment of every day with him. We were very happy, me in the kitchen and he playing for the guests.' Vera sighed lowering her head.

'But like all good things, not every cloud has a silver lining. On the way over to attend a gala evening at a local children's charity event my Cyril was crossing the junction near Marble Arch when a lorry for no good reason other than the impatience of the driver jumped the red light heading straight at Cyril. The driver tried to brake and avoid a collision but the lorry skidded and poor Cyril never stood a chance. The policewoman who came to see me told me that Cyril didn't suffer, although I didn't believe it at the time. After the accident I could no longer work at the hotel any longer. I did try but as expected the hotel hired another pianist, but hearing his melodies ring out from the garden room was like a slow torture.'

I left Vera to her tears going through to the rear cloakroom where we had our lockers. Taking a small bottle of brandy that I kept for medicinal emergencies from my locker I retuned. This was a good enough emergency to crack open the top, pouring us a measure each I handed Vera her glass.

'And the driver of the lorry did the police establish who he was?'

Vera nodded back at me. I noticed the sudden change as her eyes went steely cold, staring ahead as though she was walking through a hazy vision.

'Fortunately a policeman on foot patrol noted the registration number of the lorry as it left the scene of the accident. The driver was arrested later that evening.'

She swallowed her brandy clearing her throat in the process. I was aware that her free hand was bunched tight into a fist as though ready to hit out.

'There was no way that I was going to let the bastard get away with killing my Cyril.'

'The police, they took him to court?' I asked expecting no less.

Without being asked she poured herself another tot from the brandy bottle.

'Turned out that he was a foreign motorist, driving over here without the proper documentation. The judge gave him four and half years.' She swallowed the remainder of her brandy in a single gulp. 'Not anywhere near long enough in my opinion, but I counted down every day, biding my time until he was released.'

The brandy hit my stomach with a warm glow although for some reason I sensed a cold shiver run down my spine. It was the look in her eyes.

'What did you do?'

'I was across the road, waiting and watching for the door to open knowing that it was where they released the prisoners. His face etched in the memory cells from when I had last seen him being sentenced.

'As soon as Trybor Droboslav appeared, sheepishly stepping through the door to freedom, I could feel my heart begin to race and the sweat appear on my brow.'

Wringing her hands over and over she was slowly reliving the moment as the blood was drained from her fingers. I swallowed the last of my brandy feeling the tension mounting. Looking straight at me her eyes were set hard.

'And...' I asked, waiting patiently 'what happened?'

'It was raining that day so I had gone armed with an umbrella. As Droboslav made for the underground entrance I followed keeping him always in my line of sight.'

Four and half years is a long time when you're inside, I knew, only I didn't tell Vera.

The story continued.

'I doubt had he seen me following close behind that he would have recognised me. Down on the platform Droboslav stood near the edge waiting for the train. For some odd reason it was icy cold down underground as though an ill-wind was approaching.

'As the vibration from the train wheels thundered down the track I could feel the spirit of my Cyril beside me as I moved forward with my umbrella inverted so that the curved handle was resting next to his ankle. Feeling something brush the skin of his lower leg Trybor Droboslav turned to remonstrate with the owner, but when our eyes met I think in that split second his mind made the connection.

'Quite by chance the umbrella became entangled by itself and it was he who stepped back, whether by recognition or shock, I cannot say. Taking my umbrella with him, he fell backwards losing his balance, moments later the train arrived, but it was already too soon for Trybor Droboslav. Other commuters up and down the platform rushed over to the sounds of his screams and to give assistance but as quickly as my Cyril's life had been taken, so had the tube train ended Droboslav's.'

As I poured myself another brandy the expression on Vera's face began to soften once again. I poured her a third measure.

'I walked from the underground station as calm as a millpond knowing that I had avenged the love of my life. Later that afternoon I went to the cemetery where he is buried and laid a wreath of flowers at his grave. One day, when my maker calls for me I will want to be laid to rest beside the man who stole my heart. Maybe, when that day does arrives the pain of his loss will finally go away!'

This time I finished the glass in one go. I had served my time and paid a penance for something I considered quite trivial. That experience inside prison had changed many aspects of my life. I sat opposite Vera wondering if Trybor Droboslav had any idea what awaited him when he had walked through the door that morning heading for the nearest underground station. I doubted it. Vera picked up my empty glass taking both over to the sink.

'Now you know why your Mum has never said anything to you about me.'

Walking up behind her I placed my hand on her shoulder.

'I'm glad you told me and just so you know it doesn't change a thing and the offer of a partnership is there if you ever want it!'

She forced a smile but it was half-hearted.

'Many's the night Spencer that I have laid in my bed unable to sleep going over and over in my mind whether or not I should have gone to the police and confessed. Whatever anybody thinks I am as much a killer and no better than Trybor Droboslav.'

I shook my head quite fervently, definitely not in favour of her going to the police. Confessing to an accident which it was, I did not see Vera as either the assassin or responsible for what took place down in the underground.

'You said yourself you did not apply any pressure. Droboslav stepped back, tripped and fell. Summary justice for what he did to Cyril. The way that I see it Vera it was an eye for a tooth and all that jazz. Going to see some rookie cooper on the front desk will serve nobody any good purpose.'

'But, he would not have fell had it not been for my umbrella.'

'Accidents happen every day Vera. Was there an inquest?' I asked.

'The coroner, a very nice lady, recorded Droboslav's death as accidental.'

'And there I rest my case. The official verdict as documented by the authorities brought an end to a very unhappy affair. As you said it was raining when he stepped out of the prison, so the soles of his prison shoes would have been poorly maintained and it being wet and with so many commuters traipsing up and down the platform it would inevitably have made the surface perhaps perilously slippery.'

Vera surprised me by coming over and hugging me. It was a rare occurrence but as I held her close I could feel the years of tension ebbing from her body.

'Thanks Spencer. You know if I didn't think that you'd understand I wouldn't have told you.'

'Maybe the café had something to do with that.' I added.

That coming weekend we both went to see where Cyril was resting peacefully. Watching her lay down a posy of flowers on his grave I admit that I felt somewhat contrite towards Trybor Droboslav. He had done wrong jumping the red light, taking the life of another but in the end he had suffered in his own way. Destiny had a funny way of catching up. I also believed that Droboslav would have had many moments alone in his cell where he had wished that he had never jumped that red light.

At the beginning I had said that ignorance was blind and so was the man that didn't know all. That afternoon I had not meant to pry into

Vera's private life, merely want to know about the woman whom I admired and worked with. Maybe in my ignorance I now had something that I had to live with.

Come the next morning Vera was back to her normal jovial self as if nothing had been said and when the opportunity presented itself and we found ourselves alone she told me that she had not slept so soundly or peacefully for such a long time.

Later that day walking home from work I could not be sure but I thought I heard a feint echo as Cyril ran his fingers along the piano keys. One day although not yet a while Vera would hear him play again as well.

Hearing her story made me realise how good it was to unburden the soul and share secrets with trusted friends. Talking is easy, listening as important but being there for one another is what really counts.

Standing alongside Vera at the graveside I was pleasantly surprised to hear her include Trybor Droboslav in her prayers. Closure had somehow found a way to bring about a peace between Vera, Cyril and the driver from Poland. It was a fitting end to a painful and tragic era and that night as I lay in bed I hoped that wherever the Droboslav family lived, they too had found a way to be at peace with the tragedy.

Not often, but when I do let Danielle and Martyn go early I share a mug of tea and a few biscuits with Vera learning a lot more about Cyril and the short time that they had spent together. For such a long time Vera has been part of my family and the more that she tells me, the more

I feel closer to her. Hearing her story made me understand why she had been so kind when I had also walked through that door and regained my freedom.

The Unexploded Bomb

Arriving a little earlier than usual I stood outside of the florists not unduly surprised although in awe of Lola as she busied herself cutting, trimming and arranging the early delivery from Holland. It wasn't quite six and although the sun was up the pavement seemed to be awash with a mountain of assorted empty cardboard cartons. I knew that the flower delivery was early but Lola must have arrived around four to have achieved so much in such a short space of time. Coming over the chimney tops the sun was casting shadows up and down the street.

Amazingly, whenever *Florrie's Flowers* received a shipment of blooms, petals and exotic flowers the street seemed to come alive as did the weather. Since the weekend the clouds have loomed grey without any promise of a respite and yet lo and behold here we are two days away from the end of the week and things have improved. As I watched Lola darting to and fro I was sure that it had something to do with her and her Italian influence. Oddly enough when the flowers arrived so did a surprise!

Lola saw me looking and waved. Being that much early I offered to help with the last few boxes using the opportunity to get to know her better. I tried my best but had to admit that flower arranging wasn't one of my best attributes and I thought that I caught her looking my way once or twice, not sure if she was checking on me or whether she was just genuinely interested in my ineptness. Whatever the reason her eyes were mesmerizingly magnetic drawing me in. With most of the boxes empties she offered a mug of coffee by way of a thank you for my efforts.

'That would certainly make a nice change from my usual brew!' I said accepting.

I had arrived early with a view to making some minor alterations in the café before any of the others arrived but conceded that this was just too good an opportunity to miss and spend time alone with Lola. When she placed two mugs of hot coffee down on the preparation bench adding a plate of freshly baked soft Italian almond biscuits the smell alone was enough to transport me to foreign shores.

'Pasticcini di Mandorle' she said inviting me to try one. 'I guarantee that they are the real deal and my Aunt Bella baked them for me only last night.'

Crunching through one half of a rounded delight the texture of the biscuit melted immediately inside my mouth infusing my taste buds with a sensation of exploding honey, almonds, butter and baked dough. It was like no other biscuit that I had ever tried before. 'Buono per Bella...' I replied wiping the crumbs from my lips.

Lola seemed surprised 'The pronunciation was good, have you spent any time in Italy?' she asked.

'No... although I aim to visit one day. We just happened to have an Italian boy in our class at school, so we each picked up the odd phrase here and there!'

My honesty amused her as she pushed the plate over my way encouraging me to take another. *'Mamma ha sempre detto che la strada verso il cuore dell'uomo era attraverso il suo stomaco.'*

'There you've lost me!' I admitted, breaking another Pasticcini di Mandorle in half. Lola laughed and translated for me 'Mama always said that the way to a man's heart was through his stomach!'

The biscuits were very good and better than anything I served in the cafe. 'Then mama knows best.' I said wiping the crumbs from my lips for a second time.

Every so often the sun coming the rear window would catch the side of a galvanised bucket and leave a shimmering shadow on the floor. One the side of the bench lay a multitude of stemmed flowers, white lilies, coloured chrysanthemum's, red and yellow tulips and many more that I could not name. Lola's world existed of an infusion of colour and scented aroma's that were extremely pleasing to the senses.

Looking up at the clock I suddenly realised that the last half an hour had simply vanished. Not wanting to overstay my welcome I thanked Lola for the coffee and biscuits and invited her to join me early one morning in the café making her aware that the biscuits would not be as good, but the Fracino Contempo did make a decent cup of coffee. Lola accepted although we didn't make it a date. I left feeling that I should have said something else although men are always being accused of never picking the right moment.

Vera was already outside when I took myself next door and her expression needed no explanation.

'So, I've been stood up by the competition… I thought it would happen one day!'

Looking at her doubting looks she reminded me of Helen of Troy from my history lesson. Vera was lovely in a motherly sort of way, but her face was never going to launch a thousand ships. Inserting the key in the lock I let her in first.

'Sorry, but I thought that I would help with an extra-large early delivery.' She virtually pushed me through the door as Lola waved.

'You've been like a cat without cream for the past week going outside and gulping air. It's about time that you introduced yourself and made your intentions known. Even Danielle said the other day that you've been standing at the counter like a dog with its tongue hanging out needing an extra-long drink. You have to realise Spencer that the young look to you as an example!'

I saw my day being a series of peaks and troughs. I had part climbed Everest in the florist shop, but landed deep in the icy chasm on the return journey. Vera had obviously been spying on me.

'You know full well that I've already had my bridges burnt,' I insisted 'and it stung like hell.'

Vera, however being Vera was never one to let the small detail like marriage and divorce dampen her spirits or the argument.

'That was so far back Spencer I can't remember what happened.' She slipped into her pinny and filled the kettle. 'You need to be thinking about the future whilst you're still young enough to grab it.' Turning around she pointed a straight finger my way 'Remember what I said recently in that it only takes a moment for happiness to be snatched from your grasp!'

Since the day that we had stood beside Cyril's grave there was not a day went past when she didn't mention him when we were alone. I looked upon as not grieving but a sort of healing process. Since then she had been on at me to sort my sex life.

'Living at home with your mother won't improve it none!' she would remind me.

Pushing aside the two way door Danielle missed nothing.

'Improve what?' she asked.

'His language.' Replied Vera.

Hanging her coat on the hook she wasn't as easily convinced.

'You sure it was just his language and not Lola from next door!'

I was about to say something when the bell over the door chimed out front.

'Shouldn't you see to the customers?' It was lame but the best I could do in the circumstances. Behind me Vera was laughing.

'There are no flies on that girl.'

With that Martin came hurrying through armed with a box of mushrooms that he had promised to fetch from the market.

One by one out front the regular early morning drifters had started to come in wanting their normal eat-in breakfasts, take-away rolls and coffees. Looking beyond the window the delivery from Amsterdam had brought the sunshine out and everything looked rosy until a representative from the local water board stood before me and announced that the supply was about to be shut off any minute due to ruptured main. I asked for how long but as they had not found the leak it could be an hour, two maybe or even the entire day.

As a café we could not survive without water, we filled every empty vessel that we could find. Thinking of Lola and her flowers I went next door and made sure that she filled as many empty buckets and vases that she had.

Twenty minutes later the vibration and drone of a pneumatic drill carved a hole into the tarmac a street beyond our own. In the kitchen out back Vera was awash with containers of all shapes and sizes.

'It's like a bloody ships galley in here!' she exclaimed as she wrestled with the frying pan and saucepan on the stove.

Surprisingly the custom in the café had doubled since the water had gone off and many of them elderly, local residents having been caught out by the sudden lack of water and in need of a cuppa or a coffee. That was the thing with the people of Britain everything else could come to a grinding halt but as long as you could heat up a brew everything else seemed immaterial. An institutional way of life. For the next hour the till never ceased to ring, although from out back I heard the occasional curse.

Sometime around mid-morning we heard the familiar two-tones of the fire brigade as they arrived nearby. It was difficult to say where exactly but they had stopped somewhere around Denmark Street, where the water board were digging up the road. A few minutes later Robert Styles came in through the front door having made quick his escape from the local old people's home.

'The lord has delivered us a real calamity this morning!' he stated as he ordered two rounds of toast and strong coffee.

'Well so far he's done us proud,' I said, spreading my arms wide to emphasize the crowd that we had in.

'Did you not know about the bomb?' he said as I took over his coffee.

'Bomb, what bomb?' I asked bringing to a halt several conversations nearby.

'The one in Denmark Street. The water board were mending a leak when one of the workers unearthed an unexploded bomb from the last war. The fire brigade are on scene as are the police and the ambulance service. The police have thrown a cordon around the area, just in case. Thinking that I be entombed in the Henry Miller Centre I managed to escape before the cordon was put in place.' Looking around me a lot of the customers were from Denmark Street.

Martyn and Danielle wanted to go have a look, but Robert advised against it stating that the police was letting nobody anywhere near. Taking a respite break from cooking Vera suddenly appeared.

'Martyn tells me that those silly buggers from the water board have uncovered one of the Luftwaffe's bombs!'

Robert Styles who liked Vera occasionally seeing her at his church smiled as he swallowed a mouthful of toast. 'I understand that it is a rather large bomb, at least five hundred kilogrammes.'

Vera sniffed as she walked to the door 'They was sending over so many at a time, day and night that the roads were littered with UXB's.'

She noticed the blank expression coming from Danielle.

'Unexploded bombs. My father was friends with an air-raid warden and he reckons that at least half a dozen still lay underground around here, ticking away!'

I looked at Vera as she winked my way, the melodrama was meant for Danielle but other sitting nearby looked on anxiously.

Pushing his empty plate aside Robert Styles clamped his hands together 'The lord moves in mysterious ways.'

Vera laughed 'Well, if the bomb goes off and it is five hundred kilogrammes then I guarantee that you'll see some in here move faster than they've moved in years. Mysterious or not!'

The vicar looked skyward raising a hand 'Remember Vera, the good lord see's all from above!'

'If that's the case father...' called an Irishman sitting near the back, scrutinising a copy of the day's racing paper *'perhaps the good lord could tell me the result of the two o'clock at Chepstow!'*

The café erupted in laughter, however Robert was unperturbed and as always his faith was unwaveringly strong. 'Be sure Mr Murphy, be it man or beast the good lord favours neither one nor the other.'

Shamus Murphy crossed himself being the good catholic that he was although the confessional had never favoured his interest in betting. Dropping his focus back down to the racing paper he looked for a horse with a religious connection believing that divine intervention could be worth something on the course.

Scanning the faces of our customers my attention was drawn to a smart looking gentleman sitting alone at the corner table. He had joined in when the others had laughed obviously enjoying being part of a crowd. Making my way between the tables I asked if wanted a top-up as the tea and coffee had been flowing quite freely since the news of the bomb had filled the café.

'If it is no trouble another would be grand,' he replied.

At the counter I made a small pot of fresh tea as I watched with intrigue our new visitor. Sometimes although not often you look at a person and see something that everybody else misses. There was an air about his presence that I found engaging. Although I could not explain how, he gave me the impression that he had been places, done things that others dare not contemplate and somehow he made his dreams come true. Danielle agreed to watch the counter as I took over the pot and two fresh mugs, one for myself.

'Would you mind if I joined you?' I asked, equally delighted when he gestured that I could sit opposite him at the table.

'It's not often that I get the chance of company,' he muttered not wishing the remark to be overheard 'although it is rather full in here today!'

I thought his observation slightly odd as I could not recall ever seeing him in the café before today, but with so many visitors it was possible that I had missed his being there on another occasion.

'Have you heard about the bomb?'

'Aye, that I've heard about although there are still plenty hidden about these old streets.' Confirming what Vera had already conveyed earlier.

'How come?' I asked pouring the tea.

'I was a fireman in London and on duty the nights tenth and eleventh of May, nineteen forty one. Nights that I will never forget when hell came to London. Between Hitler and the Luftwaffe they despatched so much explosive force upon the city that I believed come the dawn we would see a skyline of nothing but burning rubble. There was however one thing that Herr Hitler had not banked on and that was our fighting spirit. Whatever he sent across the channel we were determined never to give in.'

'So the shell in Denmark Street is from the war?'

'Aye lad, one I suspect that didn't want to go off. Many of the shells had been packed together so fast that some of the timers were misaligned or faulty. If the hun got it right in the munitions factory a single bomb could destroy a whole terrace of brick houses. I've seen men, women and children buried under the rubble and others that didn't make it.'

'And after the war, 'I prompted, fascinated to be in the company that had been part of home front effort 'did the borough engineers not take into consideration the bombs that had failed to detonate?'

Sipping his tea he considered his reply.

'For those that survived the years thirty nine to forty five, the priority for councils was housing. People and families needed a roof over their heads again and some of the heavier bombs that fell had buried themselves deep underground. When a shell found a niche in which to hide the earth would cave in and keep them buried. Denmark Street is a good example.'

'Until seventy years later the water board unearth it!'

He grinned. Totting up the years in my head I reckoned that the old fireman was at least in his early nineties, although for all that he had experienced his skin was remarkably unlined or marked. Offering a hand across the table he shook mine.

'The name's Albert Stanley.'

'Spencer Marlon Brand.' I replied.

'Like them movie film stars!'

As usual I just smiled 'my mum's fault only she had a crush on both men.'

Albert seemed amused 'my dear mother was keen on Douglas Fairbanks junior although for some reason she named me Albert after the Prince.'

'Where were you stationed?'

'Friern Barnet, not that station names mattered only you went where you were needed. The Luftwaffe didn't give two hoots where they dropped their load and most of the bombers had instruction to hit the docks, the railways or our factories. I suppose we did similar not that it really shortened the inevitable. Rather than take a bomb home they would drop some indiscriminately. That's how a good number of civilians got caught in the blast or ended up buried underground.'

Listening to the old timer recollect his harrowing exploits, I recalled my mum telling me that her uncle was a warden in the war and often he would join a gang of rescuers to go rummaging through a bombed house searching for survivors. In similar circumstances I had no idea how I would cope.

Quite out of the blue he suddenly leaned across the table and announced 'one of those *left over* buggers probably from forty one, a two hundred and fifty pounder plum landed down the middle of Oslo Road.'

I tried not to look too vague as he shook his head.

'Fell down like a fat bird landing on a tree branch only it hit smack dead centre taking out three houses on one side and damaging the buildings opposite. I was off duty that night in the city having a drink with a mate, but word soon spreads like wildfire when something bad happens.

'When we got the word, Charlie and me we ran as fast as our legs would carry us to Oslo Road, but where there should have been three houses was instead a bloody great big gaping nothing. At the back in the rear garden stood a big oak tree, defiant to the last. You know the one I mean, the big oak back of number twenty four.' I knew the tree.

'Later that morning I was called upon as relief to the crew that had been working through the night. Despite an extensive search we never found any bodies assuming that they had all been blown to smithereens.' He looked directly at me 'it happened you know!'

At that point he lent a little closer 'Thing was two bombs dropped that night, one hit the target whereas the second went deep under the rubble.'

'So did they find it?' I asked, my mouth dry with suspense.

'Oh yes... a local police sergeant saw fit to stand guard a constable nearby all night until it was light enough for the bomb disposal officer to arrive and take a look.' Sipping his tea he licked his lips 'you have to be slightly unhinged to be a Royal Engineer and tampering with somebody else's bomb!'

'So you were there when the bomb squad arrived?'

'I was and so was Charlie.'

Quite annoyingly there was a commotion out back in the kitchen as a pile of dirty saucepans slipped from the drainer down onto the floor. I excused myself to investigate stating that I would be back soon. To my surprise when I did return the table was empty and Danielle was clearing away our used crocks.

'When did the old man leave?' I asked.

'I'm not sure but it must have been when we were helping out in the kitchen.'

Holding out her hand for me to see she four old pennies in her palm. I took them and flipped them over reading the embossed markings *George V - 1923, 1927, 1929 and 1935.*

'Saucy old sod,' Danielle chuckled 'he comes in here has his breakfast before disappearing, leaving these as payment.'

Going to the window Albert Stanley was nowhere to be seen. I had a feeling that he wouldn't be there but I needed to check for myself. The texture of the copper between my fingers felt good, not manufactured like the coins of today. I remember having some in my pocket as a boy.

'Never mind, we'll keep these at the back of the till as a sort of good luck charm!'

Danielle's expression was one of amusement and instead of asking why she just accepted my eccentricity, shrugged her shoulders, turned and headed for the kitchen.

Having locked down the café for the afternoon I waved at Lola as I went past having had our water restored around lunchtime and the bomb removed without further incident by those brave men and women from the Royal Engineer Corp.

Walking home I deviated from my normal route going instead to the local library where I asked the librarian if she had any records relating to the last war and especially concerning dropped bombs. Scrolling through her microfiche archives she managed to find an old newspaper report.

The image on the front page was of a policeman standing near to a large crater where there had once been three houses. What interested me more was the inset images of two firemen who had been present the next day. I read the report feeling my heart race having recognised the face of one of the firemen. Drawn to a particular sentence, I read it twice.

'With regret, during the clearing up operation in Oslo Road London, Albert Stanley and Charles Hawcroft, both members of the London Fire Service were critically injured when a large bomb that had failed to detonate on impact exploded as it was winched to the surface. They later died in hospital as a result of their injuries. Constable Albright who had been standing nearby was slightly injured although after receiving treatment was fit enough to return to duty the following day.'

I admit that it was a slow thoughtful walk back home that afternoon as I contemplated the article in the old newspaper. It was obvious that Albert Stanley or his spirit had come back to talk to me about the day that he and Charlie had died. Looking up at the sky I smiled remembering that he did say he had been before.

Of course the most puzzling conundrum was why he had chosen today to visit. Was it because the water board had unearthed an old bomb or because he happened to be in the area or simply that I would never know the reason why.

I wondered if ghosts had memories but I guess they did. Inserting the key in the door I could only surmise that Albert had graced us with his presence because he had a connection with the area and the café. It was what I liked about the place, the mystery and romance and as Robert Styles would say *'everything happens for a reason'*.

Closing the door I called out that I was home before asking if my mother had ever heard of a man called Albert Stanley, a hero from a bygone era.

The Diary

It was Danielle who found the diary in the street. A beautifully leather bound chronicle which had somehow become detached from the owner. On examination it was clear that the book had been a treasured possession, bound together by a deep red leather sleeve where one corner of the front cover was engraved in gold leaf bearing the initials *A.S.* and alongside the lettering sat a small posy of flowers, altogether enchanting.

For over a day and a half Danielle had been fervently turning the pages rooting through the private memoirs of an unknown contributor, fortunate in that we were experiencing a quiet spell in trade giving her the free time to be doing little else. Naturally I blamed the weather. A really hot, sunny day would have our regular customers visiting the big parks central to the city, boating or walking alongside the lake. Some going further afield where they could dip their toes in the cool waters on a sandy beach. Carefree day's where nobody really wanted a cooked breakfast or hot lunch.

I was out front sitting of the café enjoying the sunshine when I heard what sounded like a commotion in the kitchen out back. Pushing aside the swing door my first impression was one of surprise. Locked together in an unusual tug-o-war Vera and Danielle were arguing over the book as Martyn quite sensibly had decided to have no part of the affair standing well away by the sink.

'*What's got into you two?*' I demanded bringing a halt to the proceedings.

Seemingly vexed Vera explained 'It's wrong to be nosing through somebody else's private memoirs. There could be any number of intimate, personal secrets inside that the owner didn't want anybody to know about!'

She was of course quite right.

'I ain't doing no harm,' replied Danielle, her eyelids fluttering like a hummingbird over a water fountain 'I was just looking and it's not as though I know them is it?'

She also had a good argument.

I could however see that if I did not intervene the matter would escalate into a full scale war and as a small unit we could afford tension, especially not between two of our most valuable staff members. Reaching out the book was handed to me.

'Just out of interest where exactly did you find it?' I asked.

'It was just sitting there on a brick wall outside one of the houses further down the road. I had first noticed it when I arrived for when and when I left off it was still there so for safe-keeping I thought it was best that I took it before the rain destroyed it or somebody threw it in the bin.'

Danielle if nothing else was honest and had the heart of an angel.

'I was only looking through the diary because I thought that there might be something inside which would help identify the owner. It's really interesting though!' she poked her tongue out at Vera who did the same, the flames of their squabble abated.

With indifference Vera folded her arms across her chest amusing Martyn. She knew me well enough also to know that I had a soft spot for Danielle and that I would always protect her as best I could.

'Perhaps...' I proposed 'for the sake of keeping the peace I should hold onto the diary until we can establish to whom it belongs.'

Begrudgingly and with a drop of her shoulders Danielle relented.

With a wink aimed for her only, I asked. 'What you read, did you find anything to help?'

'I was getting there when old droopy drawers interfered!'

I stood between them as mediator as Danielle continued.

'Why don't you give it a try Spence, you'll see what I mean.'

With a ring of the bell over the front door Danielle went through to serve. Holding onto the diary I was left to confront Vera.

'That girl has you tightly wrapped around her little finger!' she said pointing a finger at my nose.

'She didn't mean any harm by it Vera, she was doing what anybody would do in similar circumstances.'

Unclasping her arms she went back to the cooker looking across to where Martyn sensibly had his head hung low 'and don't you dare say a bloody word or you'll get the big end of a saucepan around your lughole!'

The poor boy looked at me for backup but I left laughing realising that there were occasions when a man needed to retreat. As usual Vera had the last word. When I closed the door saying goodbye to the three of them I sat alone with a cold coffee and the diary.

Danielle was right, what was written was indeed captivating. Not just the memoirs of the owner but their soul as well. The first entry was dated the 25th of December, 1968 and by the numerous entries of a man named Jakub, I assumed he was the diarist's boyfriend. I was surprised to find that the entries were over forty years old.

Wednesday – as hard as I tried I couldn't slip away to see Jakub. They watch me like a hawk but they cannot read the thoughts that I store inside my head. Happy Christmas Jakub x

*****

Thursday 26th December 1968 – I spent a restless night thinking of you and wondering how you were holding out. I wish that you had not gone to the meeting. I hope that the authorities are lenient!

*****

Sunday 29th December 1968 – Michaela came today and told me that Stephan had also been arrested by the secret police. We are praying that you are both together and that you will stay strong.

*****

Tuesday 31st December 1968 – New Year's Eve. Friends want us to go to their house to celebrate the New Year, but I have made excuses. I will not celebrate without you Jakub. I will pray instead for your release and safe return. Happy New Year x

*****

Wednesday 1st January 1969 – New Year's Day. I finally managed to sneak out of the house without being challenged. If my parents knew where I was heading they would lock me in my room. Michaela met me at the Staromestske Namesti in the old quarter of the town where we had coffee together and planned our strategy.

Putting my finger in the page so that I didn't lose the sequence the place name stirred a memory in my head. The diary was as Danielle had described, compelling reading. Maybe it should have been handed in to the police, but I decided against it as they were always keen on asking questions.

I decided to read on remembering that the Staromestske Namesti was an ancient square in the heart of the Czech Republic in Prague. Drinking the last of my cold coffee I turned the page.

Friday 3rd January 1969 – We have heard that some of the prisoners are being transferred this coming Saturday afternoon from the police station although the destination is as yet unknown. The student union is meeting later to discuss what can be done. Have hope Jakub. Help is coming. I miss you x

There was an additional note which was ringed, evidentially an important entry.

A protest has been arranged for the time that you are moved. I hope that the information proves accurate and I will pray for you all tonight.

*****

Saturday 4th January 1969 – I had to say that I was spending the night with friends as my parents have heard whispers about the protest rally which will take place today outside of the police station. I do wish that they were more accepting of you Jakub.

Almost certainly I had read about the protest in a newspaper where during an era of apprehension the Cold War was extremely prevalent. I remembered reading about a group of student prisoners who had escaped custody during their transfer from a police station their destination unknown. The jostling effect of the large crowd that had gathered outside the building had afforded the young men precious seconds in which to make good their escape. The downside was that several others protesting their innocence had been arrested and hurt in the melee. As expected worldwide condemnation of the event had heavily criticized the Russian and Czech authorities.

Reading the story made me think of my own time in prison and Wormwood Scrubs. World pressure or common sense, who knows but days later every prisoner had been released without charge and a peaceful solution was found to quell the unrest.

Sunday 5th January 1969 – We are hiding out at a friend's house. We have Jakub and Stefan with us but none expected the protest to turn so violent and so quickly. I know some were hurt but we do not know their names or how many were involved. Jakub has promised me that he will not participate in any future demonstrations. He showed me his bruises and the scars. I am appalled but at least he is safe.

Surprisingly there were no entries for the following three weeks after that date and the subsequent pages remained blank as though fate had intervened and what had taken place in between had been too sensitive to record. The next entry was Saturday 25th January 1969.

Stefan managed to find us a truck. The four of us drove across Czechoslovakia until we reached Bratislava. The Lesny forest was very dark when we arrived which proved an ideal place to abandon our transport. We proceeded from there on foot crossing the border and into Austria. Somewhere down river we took a small boat sailing along the Danube to Vienna where we stayed for a further two nights. I will greatly miss my parents, my home and my country but now my life is with Jakub. In my prayers I will pray for my losses.

The following pages were full of entries as to how they lived hand to mouth on a meagre existence, determined to enrich their lives. The generosity of strangers helped maintain that dream although perilously there were others willing to offer them up to the authorities. Life as I read was not easy and there was danger everywhere. Sitting alone in the café where it was warm and safe and the sun was still shining it was difficult to image the hardships they must have endured on that journey.

By the time I did decide to go home I had made the conscious decision to take the diary to Robert Styles. Some might question my reason but I believed that rather than give it to the police what had been written would be better addressed by a spiritual leader. Robert in my opinion was an educated gentle soul and in touch with many religious denominations. Through his sources he would know of a representative of the Czechoslovakian church. Considering also Danielle and Vera's interest I thought my decision would appease both.

The next morning arriving early and with the diary safely deposited in my locker I had intended giving Robert a call later. In return for his help I would add an invite to sample some of Vera's lemon drizzle cake, confident that it would please his palate and soften the task ahead. When the bell over the front door chimed I was surprised to see Lola walk in accompanied by two people whom I had never seen before.

'Spencer...' she introduced 'this is Mr and Mrs Moravek.'

Inviting all three to take a table I shook hands with our foreign visitors. Danielle who had arrived soon after me and before Vera watched from behind the counter where she prepared four coffees. I was surprised to hear that both Mr and Mrs Moravek spoke good English. When she brought over the refreshments I asked Danielle to join us.

'You are very kind,' said the woman her native accent still noticeable. 'I should begin by introducing ourselves properly, I am Adela Moravek and this is my husband, Jakub!'

Gently extending my hand out I closed Danielle's mouth which had opened emitting no sound.

'Would you please excuse me for a moment,' I implored 'only I have something that I believe belongs to you!'

Moments later I returned. When Adela saw the red leather diary she swallowed the lump in her throat placing her hand over her mouth. Taking it immediately to her chest she was without doubt the genuine owner.

'I thought that I had lost it forever!' she whispered. 'It has no value to anyone else but to me this little book is part of our lives, a priceless heirloom!'

Jakub Moravek who had been sipping his coffee put down his cup.

'We are indebted to you Sir. The diary is how we came to be in England. You see Adela would write everything almost every day. Our grandson who rents a flat not far from here was devastated when he found that he had mislaid it.'

'Danielle was the one who found it!' I explained. Jakub Moravek took the back of her hand and kissed it.

'You have the face of an angel young lady and we are indeed indebted to you!'

Danielle who had never had her hand kissed blushed.

'It was nothing, I found it on the wall.'

'How did it find its way to England?' I asked.

Instead of giving me a reply Adela opened the diary at the fourteenth of June, nineteen sixty nine where she had me read the entry.

The four of us have been travelling for so long we are tired. Stefan is ill and needs medical attention. We were sitting at the side of the road when a lorry stopped. The driver, an Englishman offered to take us to where we could find food and drink. His kindness paid for our salvation. Smuggling us across on the ferry he brought us to England where Stefan saw a doctor.

I asked if I could read on going to the next entry. Adela had no hesitation in allowing me access to the fifteenth day.

We only knew the man as Sidney although without his help we would all have suffered. We surrendered ourselves us to the authorities and claimed political asylum, where to our surprise we were shown kindness, offered accommodation and help. Sidney vanished from our lives almost as easily as he had arrived. We each owe him our life.

When I looked up Adela continued.

'When we stopped for food we talked. I told him of our plight and he in turn told us of how he had been held as a prisoner of war. He knew what it was like to be held under a restrictive regime and have his freedom withdrawn. When he saw me writing in the diary Sidney he told us to get ready for the crossing. He was a very brave man.'

'I confess that I read some of what you had written.' I apologised.

Adela placed her hand over mine 'We have only ever found kindness in this country and nowadays it does not matter who reads what is written inside. It was a very long time ago, not that I am suggesting we should forget our history, but time heals wounds.' As she smiled so her eyes sparkled bright 'our grandson had hold of the diary because he is studying European History and needed something factual for his thesis.'

'He had a good subject matter for reference!'

Jakub Moravek nodded 'it was also important that he understood what we had gone through to make this world a better place.'

Sitting alongside Lola, Adela looked first at me then back at Lola.

'Mr Brand reminds me of Sidney, a good man, handsome and with an honest face. You would make a lovely couple!'

The good looks I accepted but honest, maybe that was stretching the imagination too far.

'Given the circumstances I think that what you both encountered, overcome and achieved was remarkable. I am not sure I could have done the same.' I saw Lola smile at me and agree.

Without thinking Jakub held his wife's hand and squeezed it very gently.

'We were all young and headstrong back then. I was foolish to have retaliated and on reflection I placed not just myself but Adela and our friends in a lot of danger. I am a lucky man that she stood by me so loyally. Because of me she has lost so much.'

Still holding her hand he lowered his eyes so that we could not see his shame. Adela Moravek however had no recrimination against her husband or their perilous adventures.

'If we had to do it all again Jakub we would and together.'

It did not need to be written as it was obvious to the three of us bearing witness to this amazing couple that their love went very deep and had never diminished down the years. Survival of a harsh regime and living under the constant threat of imprisonment or worse had only made the bond stronger. I was glad that Sidney whoever he might be had stopped that day beside the road and shown them mercy. Robert Styles too would have approved of Sidney believing that he was one of the good men left in the world.

Adela clamped her hands over Danielle's and affectionately said 'you did right taking the diary from the wall and if you read what was written inside, remember that love will conquer tyranny whatever the price. You will always be our friend. Do you have a boyfriend?' she asked.

Danielle nodded 'he should be here any minute!' she replied.

You could see that Adela approved by the look in her eyes.

'I was about your age when I was courting Jakub. I hope your boyfriend is not as reckless but that he will stand by you as my Jakub has stood by me!'

Danielle grinned 'he'd better!'

'There is one thing that has always concerned us,' Jakub admitted 'the authorities could still have a record for the truck and the boat that we stole. Do you think that it would still go against us after all these years?'

I shook my head replying with a short chortle. 'I doubt that anybody remembers back that far Jakub. The owners probably claimed and received ample compensation. Desperate times evoke desperate measures.'

I saw Lola frown wondering how I knew such things.

'The journey took us through some beautiful countryside between Prague and Vienna.' Added Adela as she let go of Danielle's hands.

'I hear Vienna is lovely!'

The frown disappeared quickly replaced by a questionable smile 'almost as beautiful as Rome I hear,' Lola quipped, 'with Florence equally as inviting where the city boasts many bridges and fountains, history and romance.' I spread my hands advocating my support not that I could claim to had been to either, surprisingly Lola had something else to add before she was done with the tourist pitch.

'Maybe, one day I will show you how beautiful!'

'Then you should go,' Adela advised 'only Jakub and I married in Vienna.'

Sitting alongside me Jakub winked 'it is where I found out that my wife was pregnant with our twin daughters, Anna and Natasha. It is Anna's son who has moved into the flat at the end of the road.'

Adela blushed with both pride and embarrassment at Jakub for giving away such a private moment and how and when their daughters were conceived. 'We can never forget Vienna as it holds such wonderful and sad memories.'

'Why sad?' asked Lola.

Jakub responded first saving his wife the pain of answering.

'Years later when communism had fallen into decline allowing us the opportunity to return to our homeland we had agreed to meet Adela's parents in Vienna, only her father regrettably died before our plane landed. Her mother believes that it was the excitement of seeing his daughter again that stopped his heart.'

It was sad although fitting that he died somewhere so beautiful and not in a land where bitter memories could have tarnished the occasion. Holding up the diary Adela told us that the last pages were dedicated to her father.

'And your mum,' asked Danielle 'is she back in Prague?'

Adela clearly liked Danielle as she stroked her cheek. 'No, she has a little house not far from where we live. My father is buried in Willesden only a bus ride away. We are sure that he rests peacefully in his sleep and that one day we will all be reunited.'

'And your grandson,' asked Lola 'will he travel when he finishes his studies?'

I saw a very familiar look in Adela's eyes that I had seen in Lola's as she spoke of her homeland.

'Andel is so like his grandfather, a little headstrong but so brave. He has Jakub's heart and longing for life. London however is different from other countries, here you can express your views without fear of reprisal. A rebel Andel has the talent to paint his own history be it here or abroad. I would want our grandson to see the world and judge it himself.' She paused momentarily. 'He does possess one thing that I hold dear besides that of my family and that is he also keeps a diary. I told him of the comfort that it gave me through the difficult years. One day perhaps he will show it to his grandchildren and have them revel at his exploits!'

Adela laid her head on her husband's shoulder.

'Here, hopes, dreams and prayers are answered!'

'Andel, that's a really nice name.' Lola exclaimed.

'In Czech it means angel. We thought that it was apt for our first born grandchild and at the christening I said a silent prayer for Sidney, our saviour!'

Just then the door opened and in walked Vera and Martyn, they seemed surprised to see that we already had visitors. I introduced them to Adela and Jakub, stating that Adela was the owner of the diary. Minutes later they insisted on leaving realising that other customers were arriving. I wanted them to stay a while longer but Lola also had to get back to re-open the florist.

As we watched them walk back up the street Lola said that they made a beautiful couple. We had arranged a date for them to come back when we could all get together with the invitation extending to Andel and his great-grandmother.

'Do you know Spencer, special things happen in your café, lovely things?' Lola squeezed my arm then went back to *Florrie's Flowers*.

Do you know she was right and although I was never able to explain how the magic was always present. Later that morning I popped my head around the door of the florist shop as I had a question to ask.

'So you want to show me Florence!'

Lola who was as calm and radiant as a rose turned to look 'maybe keeping your passport valid would be a good idea!'

'It's in date, I assure you.'

We talked for a few minutes when trade was slack and I told Lola that I felt humbled to know the Moravek's. It is not every day that you meet such interesting, courageous people. Individuals who had a real story to tell.

I was about to leave when Lola suddenly laced her arm through mine. 'In Italy there is an old saying *'ascolti ma non parlare, toccare ma no agrie perche la storia e scritta'.*

It *means 'listen but not speak, touch but do not act, because history is being written'.* I am sure that we will see them again soon. London is their home now and the future of the Moravek's lives at the end of the road. Through Andel, Adela and Jakub they will live on forever.'

The Blind Man and his Dog

Generally the trade on a Saturday afternoon varied depending upon what sporting events were taking place in and around the city, not forgetting the odd carnival adding to the frustration of the motorists trying to get from home to their chosen destination.

Feeling generous I had let Vera, Danielle and Martyn go after lunch so that they could watch the procession of floats travel down the high street convincing myself that I could manage the café for the rest of the afternoon.

Since their departure I had not had a single customer not until the bell over the door chimed at five past three. Now as part of our hygiene ruling and customer preference we do not allow any animals inside the café, unless of course they accompany a registered blind person. Coming out from the kitchen I was immediately befriended by a beautiful honey coloured Labrador and his owner who politely asked if it was acceptable that they occupied a table.

'Why of course,' I replied 'please chose whichever you think appropriate and I'll be right over to take your order!' Grabbing a pen and pad I went around the business side of the counter.

As obedient as his training the Labrador immediately lay down beside its master, its soft rump laying gently over the man's foot so that if he got up, so would the dog. It had always amazed me how the bond between dog and man or woman could be struck so quickly. Of the few that I had spoken too before today they had claimed that the dog was not only their eyes, but in many cases their soul.

Kneeling beside the Labrador I stroked the head and neck looking down upon resting eyes. Having put his stick over the adjacent chair the man offered his hand and introduced himself and the dog.

'This faithful friend is Jack and I am Colin... Colin Steele.'

'Spencer Brand.' I replied shaking his hand.

The man smiled looking directly to where my voice had reverberated.

'Your name,' he claimed 'has an air of mystery like you could have served time with the overseas intelligence service?'

I laughed 'MI6... god forbid I'm anything but, secretive. I own the little red café and serving food is about the level of my risk.' Looking down at Jack he was silently watching my every move.

When I asked 'Can I get a bowl of water for Jack?' his ears pricked up.

Colin replied 'if it's alright, Jack actually prefers warm tea. I'll pay of course!'

Recording his request on the order pad I thought it would amuse Danielle when she checked the slips Monday morning.

'As for me, a coffee please,' Colin pondered 'and I hear that you do a special lemon drizzle cake, have you any left?'

'I'll check in the chiller as our cook has already left.'

I was about to pass through to the kitchen when Colin called over.

'If there's enough for two, would you do me the honour of joining me, my treat?'

Armed with two generous slices I returned, placed them on the counter. Made Jack his tea and Colin and myself a coffee from the Fracino Contempo. Hissing steam Jack checked that everything was okay before laying down his head again.

Filling an old baking tray with luke warm tea I put it down where Jack could drink without leaving his master's side. I added a packet of digestive biscuits so that he wasn't left out of the afternoon treat. Fetching our coffees and cake I sat opposite Colin.

Easing back in his chair my guest appeared quite at home in the café.

'It's quite unique,' he exclaimed 'how such a simple celebration as a carnival can clear the back streets and yet bring together so many people in one place. The high street is very busy so Jack and I thought it would be ideal time to visit. We've been meaning to come in for some time but there is always something else to do.' Colin placed his hands on the table feeling for his cup. 'I remember a time when I would happily mingle with the crowd and watch the parade go by. So much changes when you lose your sight!'

Thrown into a world of eternal dark I could not begin to fathom what it would be like to have everything stolen from you, colour, shapes and faces.

'I am sorry... was losing your sight, due to an accident?' I asked.

He shook his head. 'No. Our family suffer a hereditary condition called Retinitis Pigmentosa. I knew that at some point in my life I would lose my sight.' Surprisingly he smiled. 'I am however grateful for the years that I did have sight and of the things that I did see. Those are the memories that I see now. In the distance we could hear the sound of a steel band.

'Sounds exciting,' Colin remarked as he cut a piece of his cake and offered it to Jack.

'I let my staff go early so that they could watch the parade,' with just the three of us it did seem quiet 'although I have to admit sharing time with somebody new is just as engaging as seeing the floats go by.'

Colin cut another slice of cake for himself and then Jack 'this is really good cake.'

'The memories that you have,' I asked 'were they from here or abroad?' I was always interested to listen in people's exploits when they had been travelling.

'Mainly abroad before I lost my sight. Ironically I was a travel writer and my passport was almost full of exotic locations, recording where I had been. Somehow, perhaps luckily there was a story for every place that I visited. It really was the most amazing adventure!'

Pushing my empty plate to one side I asked where he had been.

'Most places really, taking in all the normal tourist destinations and at the same time lapping up the sun, the sand and the ancient churches. The two places that did not interest me were either pole as I don't like the cold. My travels took me as far away as New Zealand, Scandinavia, Australia and the Americas. I did especially liked the colonial countries where the people are very friendly respecting and quite rightly proud of their indigenous cultures.'

'And Florence, have you ever been there and is it as beautiful as they say it is?'

He grinned. 'Beauty is in the eye of the beholder and you see what you want to see. I would often struggle writing about a place that I had visited believing that what I wrote did not do it justice. It is the hidden gems far from the tourist traps where you find the real beauty of this planet.'

Licking the baking tray Jack had almost finished his tea.

'Florence is undoubtedly a beautiful city, full of old world charm, gemstones of Tuscan red terracotta and pockets of renaissance art. The famous, Michelangelo, Boccaccio and Leonardo di Vinci must have thought so too because they left their mark on the city. Oddly enough I had been drawn to Florence many times and although I had never really understood why, some of my happiest memories have been left ingrained in the stone. Why do you ask and have you been?'

'I have an invite to go one day!'

'Then you should and without delay only you never know what's around the corner.' He covered his eyes with his right hand to emphasise the point. 'Once you breathe in that Tuscan air you will be transported to another world and you have the company of a lady then it becomes even better. I suppose when I reflect it was the enchanting atmosphere of the place that had me visit time and time again.'

Gently patting Jack on the head I was enamoured with the Labrador 'he's a good looking dog!'

Colin reached down and immediately Jack licked the back of his master's hand.

'I will have to take your word on that as I have only ever seen Jack through touch. We had a special bond the moment that we met and we get along fine intuitively knowing how the other feels when we wake. I do however sometimes forget that Jack needs moments alone to be by himself as he is no different to a human and there are times when I feel that I am a burden and that he should really be with a family who have children.'

I had never owned a dog and never felt the desire to need an animal companion. I had however heard that dogs and cats could tune into the vibes of a place or person. Watching Jack saunter between the chairs I wondered what he had seen or heard.

'Once you become adjusted, being blind is a mere inconvenience. Others see it differently but I think that they have lost all perception. Losing your sight you gain or finely tune other senses.' To demonstrate he lifted his cup from the saucer then skilfully placed it back down dead centre.

'How is that possible?' I asked.

'Everything in my world now sounds, smells and feels the same, the only difference is that I have to attune my reflexes to what comes my way.'

'Like a physic would see the future?'

He laughed. 'A good example, although we are not magicians.' Staring straight at me the brown pigment of his pupils held mine as the thoughts raced around inside his head. 'You carry inside a secret for which you are not sure of the outcome!'

During my spell in prison I had heard voices calling in the night, some coming from the inner self others from grown men. Prisoners who were scared of the dark or their inability to understand or accept the loneliness of a cell. I was not spiritually aware of my hidden secret so I pursed the matter.

'Has your loss of sight, helped you see into another's soul?'

He shook his head 'I'm no clairvoyant if that's what you mean, although I pick energy. I can pass a man or woman in the street and know that they are suffering, through drugs or alcohol. Other energy I pick up is people who are lost, searching for a way to better their life. Losing one's sight is like cleansing the soul. I see things different to what I did before, much better, much clearer!'

'I was married once although a spell in her majesty's prison ended that particular journey. Nowadays I use my freedom wisely with my family and friends. The café keeps me on the straight and level.'

Wiping the crumbs from the side of his mouth with a paper serviette Colin tapped the side of the chair and immediately Jack appeared by his side.

'Like you Spencer, I too I was married although my marriage went in a different direction once my visual impairment worsened. I could not really blame my wife as she wanted so much more that I could no longer provide. At night I would wonder if I let her go too easily. Perhaps on reflection I should not have persuaded her to marry me in the first place knowing the eventual outcome but we do things on impulse.'

Rubbing the underside of the dog's chin it was clearly evident that they had a strong bond.

'Nowadays I reserve my affection for Jack. He offers no opinion or regret. He accepts each day as it comes and is always there. What better companion could I have asked for and in a way we are tuned into one another.

'Sometimes on night walks I've heard an owl swoop from a tree to snatch a mouse or heard a baby cry when all around is silent. Things that I took for granted. Take a look at what you really want in life Spencer and go grab it before the opportunity passes you by!'

Hearing what he had to say I wondered if his visit had been meant. Had somebody invited him to come knowing that I would be alone, I made a point of asking.

Colin responded with a laugh.

'Nothing as sinister I assure you. We happened to be out for a walk and headed this way. The café comes highly recommended from friends that I still have. Sat beside the florist I would say that with the lady's infusion of flowers and your home baking that you have a winning combination!'

There it was again, that sixth sense.

'So you met Lola before you walked in through my door?'

'We did and how delightful she is, she also recommended that I visit and sample the lemon drizzle cake. Is she attractive?'

'Very...'

'And from her accent originally from Florence!'

'Yes...'

Sitting upright in the chair he smiled.

'And she is the reason why you cannot sleep at night?'

Being blind had certainly given him an insight into people's souls.

'Part of the reason.' I replied.

'Then you should do something about it before it's too late.'

I looked first at Jack then at Colin. I'd heard that dogs can resemble there owners and visa-versa. Strangely enough they both had brown eyes.

'You wouldn't by any remote chance be related to a man named Albert Stanley would you?'

'Not that I recall, is he a friend?'

Considering my answer carefully I responded. 'I'm not entirely sure. Albert was in here a week ago and just as we have enjoyed sharing a coffee and cake, so did he.' Lying across our feet Jack was falling asleep.

Tuned into my wavelength Colin replied.

'During my travels I saw many wondrous things, some mystical some that I didn't quite know how to describe. Feeling that they should remain as such I omitted them from my guide books. What I did write about was fact although the unknown, mystical bits kept me thinking, kept inviting me back.

'It's true that were just out walking today although I did feel compelled to pay you a visit. I can't say Jack brought me to your door as he goes where I go. There is something remarkable about this café and to some extent the energy within is like what I felt in the places that I omitted to write about.

'I sensed the lady's beauty next door albeit I could not see her, but I can tell from the way that you answered you feel strongly about her. You need to tell her how you feel. Don't be like me Spencer and have the future creep up on you. Surprises can have a nasty way of backfiring.'

With that said Colin got out his wallet to pay but I placed my hand over his wrist before he could extract any money.

'Promise that you'll come back another day and we'll call any payment quits!'

Putting away his wallet he thanked me and said that he and Jack would return. Pulling open the door we shook hands and I watched as Jack skilfully guided his master up the road avoiding any oncoming obstacles. From the high street the bands were still playing loudly.

I had just shut the door when Vera suddenly appeared. She immediately took herself to the first available chair and sat down rubbing the underside of her feet.

'It's alright for the youngsters they can stand for hours whereas my plates are almost worn thin.'

'I didn't think you'd be back?'

'I hadn't intended coming back but I had a feeling that you'd still be here. Who was the blind man that I saw leaving the café, I've not seen him before?'

'A travel writer named Colin Steele.'

Vera frowned 'what's he do consult with a spiritualist before he gets on a plane?'

'He wasn't always blind.' I explained.

'Oh,' she seemed ashamed for having jumped to the wrong conclusion. Looking over at the table where we had sat she saw the baking tray. 'Did the dog use that?'

'Don't get upset as I will buy you a new one. Although I'd like this kept as they promised to come back soon!'

Disappearing into the kitchen she reappeared moments later in her pinny.

'I'll finish off out back then pay your mum a visit. I can tell her about the carnival, give her a knitting pattern I found the other day and arrange an evening out for next week.'

I was washing down the counter top when ten minutes later she stuck her head through the serving hatch.

'By the way, have you seen Lola today?'

Now I was suspicious. The interest in my love life and Lola had me thinking that there was a conspiracy in the air.

'I know that she's next door,' was all that I was prepared to offer. 'Have you ever heard of a Colin Steele?' I asked.

'No… why, should I have?' she replied.

In Vera's world there was no grey, just black and white. She did not dilly-dally with speculation preferring hard facts instead. If she said she didn't know him, then I had to accept that it was the truth.

To keep the conversation going I told her about Colin's adventures and of the places that he had visited. As a tit-bit I mentioned that he possessed a strong connection with other people's energy. Looking at the clock I realised that it was almost four and time to lock up. Coming back out front Vera was almost done clearing up.

'Men never notice an opportunity even if it was to lie down in front of them,' she began 'I must have been one of the fortunate one's only with my Cyril he saw his chance and took it. I should have stuck to him like glue.'

I must have looked puzzled and more so when Vera went across to the window looking left down the road.

'You know we're about done here, why don't you lock and go next door and lend a hand. Saturday is a busy day for a florist and I'm sure Lola would appreciate the help.'

I admit that I just nodded. There were times when I either didn't know or times when I didn't question, what I could not see, smell or touch. Was it the magic of the café, Colin's visit or Vera's intuition that set me thinking. Several minutes later and kissing her affectionately on the cheek I asked that she give my mum a message, telling her that I might be back late.

Knocking on the framework of the preparation area where the countertops were awash with water, cut stems and petals I offered my assistance. Lola seemed pleased to see me. Pushing aside a lose wisp of hair from her brow she looked like she could do with a drink.

'I'd appreciate a coffee,' she replied 'as I've not stopped all afternoon.'

Filling the kettle I washed out two mugs and got everything ready.

'Did you see the blind man and his dog earlier?' I enquired.

'Yes, nice man and such a beautiful creature. Labradors have always been one of my favourite dogs.' Seeing the steam from the kettle she pointed to the biscuit tin. 'You'll find more Pasticcini di Mandorle in the tin.'

The next two hours were spent sipping coffee, nibbling a biscuit when we had the time and clearing away. We talked and decided to grab a pizza at a new restaurant that had just opened near to Convent Garden where we talked some more, getting to know one another.

A week later Colin and Jack surprised us with another visit much to Danielle's delight. She and Jack got on famously and from then the pair became regular visitors. Colin always appeared just after three when trade was ebbing away for the day knowing that for the next hour I had the time to share a coffee, a slice of Vera's best lemon drizzle cake and provide Jack with tea and biscuits.

The master of discretion he would never talk about Lola unless I raised the subject but suffice to say that we have become good friends. Their visits are always so captivating and we love to hear of Colin's adventures. Being blind has not stopped Colin sharing his love of the world and I truly believe that I am a better man for having known him.

Whatever the reason that he and Jack visited that Saturday has always remained a mystery but there are some mysteries in life that you cannot unravel. Lola believes that the little red café is magic and that's good enough for me.

Nun on the Run

I have always considered the café a place where you could come and meet friends, participate in good conversation or if the mood dictated just sit by yourself and watch the world go by. There was never any pressure to do anything else but appreciate a nice frothy cup of coffee courtesy of the Fracino Contempo or sample something from our menu.

The female customer who I noticed had been sat at the corner table for the past hour had made her coffee last just as long. Holding the mug in her hands she had continued to stare towards the junction outside, her thoughts as intense as what I believed she would see arrive any moment. Making her a fresh mug I took it across.

'We have a policy here that the second cup is always free.'

I added a smile to promote that we were a friendly bunch at the little red café although when she acknowledged my presence beside the table it was greeted with a half-hearted, troubled and furrowed expression of apprehension.

'Thank you for the coffee, it is extremely kind of you. I had not realised the time and that I had been here that long. I am very sorry!'

Looking over at the clock I dismissed the time as it was of little consequence.

'We only have the clock over the counter for the convenience of Danielle, myself and the customers. We close when the last customer leaves and not before so you stay as long as you like.'

I noticed the redness around her eyes where she had either been crying or rubbing them in an attempt to expel the exhaustion in her face.

'You seem troubled, is there anything that I can do to help?'

She looked up gently shaking her head not so much a refusal but more that she didn't know herself how to resolve the issue. Sensing that an answer was not forthcoming I tried a different approach.

'Sometimes I think of the café as a bolt-hole where I can hide away from all the madness in the world. It's warm, friendly and a good place to be in times of trouble!' I thought of Martyn out back in the kitchen. He would support my theory.

'That's a very reassuring, thank you. Would you mind if I stayed a while longer?'

'You stay however long you want. Now is there anything else I can offer you besides some peace?'

I heard her mutter the word 'peace' before she put down her cold coffee.

'Do you know the coffee here is good, it helps me think.'

Sensing a presence at my side I watched Danielle take the near empty mug.

'Have you eaten?' she asked.

The woman shook her head although I guessed that food was the least of her concerns.

'Well give me a shout if you do want anything, I'm about!' with that Danielle was elsewhere, a whirlwind without a storm.

Letting go with a sigh the woman watched Danielle flit between the tables serving other customers.

'She so young and yet so vibrant and confident. I was like that once,' she smiled 'I would like some toast, buttered no jam, if that's alright?'

Within earshot of the order Danielle called across 'no problem' before she spun herself around and headed for the kitchen. I left the woman to her thoughts following close behind.

'She alright,' Danielle asked as she slipped two slices of white bread into the toaster 'only she seems lost?'

'There is something troubling her,' I agreed fetching over the small pots of jam that we had for such occasions.

When the toaster threw up the heated slices Danielle added butter, a knife and two napkins to the plate. 'I won't be a minute,' she said using her hip to push aside the swing door.

Returning to the kitchen a couple of minutes later she obviously knew something that none of us did but being Danielle she couldn't keep it a secret. 'She's a nun!' she announced.

'How do you know?' I asked.

'Simple, I asked what she did for a living.'

Now most of the nuns that I had come across wore a long back cloak white hood and had a cross draped over their chest. They resembled a penguin. The woman out front looked nothing like either.

'Anything else?'

'She seems a million miles away. I had to repeat myself twice before she answered.'

There was definitely something troubling the nun and I had a feeling that I was about to find out what. I knew that there was a convent somewhere in the area although I wasn't sure exactly where. Vera told us that the only one she knew about was over St Pancras way. It seemed apt. Poking her head through the servery hatch Vera retracted it a second later.

'The poor woman just needs time to think.'

'How do you know?' asked Danielle.

'Call it intuition... a wiser head on older shoulders!'

'Maybe she's a nun on the run,' Martyn introduced adding his bit of humour.

Before the quips started in earnest I left going back out front. Passing between the tables I made sure that everybody was satisfied with their order. When I arrived at the corner the toast and jam had put some colour in her cheeks.

'Did you want some more, like the coffee it's complimentary!' it wasn't but what was two slices of bread in a crisis.

She politely declined although complimented the service 'this is a friendly café and everybody is so cheerful, is it always like this?'

'More or less most times.'

I got the impression that whatever had been troubling her, she had worked the solution through in her thoughts. Without being invited I sat in the seat opposite hers, she watched but did not object.

'Danielle, our waitress tells me that you're a nun. I have to say Sister that we don't get many of your order in here!'

'I admit that I don't feel like a nun, least not today.'

'The mother superior giving you a hard time?' I asked. The question was out before I had thought through the implications.

'Not she but me. I am the one causing her problems. The poor woman.' She looked at me as thought it had been a long time since she had been so close to a man. 'I haven't talked, really talked to anybody for such a long time. Would you mind?'

I guessed that it could be difficult in a convent with so many restrictions. I was however only too pleased to help. When Danielle came to the table she had with her an extra coffee.

110

'On the house Sir!'

She smiled at the nun then went over to the table where some workmen were waiting to give their order.

'She never stops smiling,' said the woman 'I used to do that a lot when I was her age.'

'Danielle has more energy than the England football team put together.'

She looked across to where Danielle was engaging the workman in conversation as she scribbled on her pad.

'Do you know that her name in French means *to be judged by God* and like Daniel who was thrown to the lions, nothing daunts her. I've been watching as she manoeuvres herself between the tables. She moves with the grace of an angel and confidence of a lion.'

I had often admired how Danielle dealt with the workmen earning their respect. She was confident and had good strong character which would serve her well in the future. An angel, probably and I knew that I'd be lost without her.

'If god were to judge her, I'm not sure that he wouldn't have a headache after!'

She laughed, the first time that she had seemed anywhere near happy.

'God does not judge albeit good or bad for we are all treated as equals. Our day of reckoning deems where we go from here!' In my case it was good to hear.

'Where do I go to pay?' she asked about to rise from the table only I caught her arm and persuaded her to stay a while longer.

'We don't get busy until around lunchtime. Why don't we talk some more, it could help!'

She seemed hesitant expecting somebody to walk in through the door bringing with them the wrath of god.

'I really did not mean to bring my troubles to your door,' she insisted but I was having none of it and for every problem there was a solution.

'A nun in trouble, it sounds like the beginning of an intriguing book!'

'Is it that obvious?' she asked.

'Sister I've been where you are now and believe me sometimes two heads are better than one.'

We declined Danielle's offer of more coffee and I waited for the nun to offload her problem.

'A few months back I suddenly found myself in a grey place having emerged from the darkness, where I had put my faith on hold. For a long time I had been questioning the reason that I had become a nun and whether I was prepared to devote my entire life to the lord.

'Please do not judge me harshly when I say that I have not lost my love for my faith, only examining my resolve. The convent gives us a purpose only I see more to my existence than prayers and gardening.'

I held my hand out across the table 'I'm Spencer.'

Taking my hand in hers she replied 'like Tracy the movie star, how enchanting. Mary Elizabeth Matthews.'

'Regally like the queens,' I added. Having told me who she was she suddenly appeared calmer, less agitated.

'That's the first time that I have called myself that for a long time, I have to admit it felt good, normal.' She looked around the café at the brightly coloured counter and the customers listening to their conversations. 'There's a certain something to your little café spencer, something that draws you in. I had no idea where I was heading when I left the convent last night but something drew me here, something special. Oddly because I don't really know this part of London I feel safe here!'

'You are,' I replied.

She watched Danielle help an old lady open a jam pot.

'This café,' she spread her hands 'it has life within the walls, unlike the convent. There you have to give so much with little reward in return. It is probably the reason for my recent uncertainty and I feel that I have wasted my years that I have been part of the order.'

113

'That much I guessed for myself,' I replied 'you see Mary, I know what it feels like to feel trapped. Not too long back I did something that I deeply regret only god and a criminal judge gave me three years in prison to think over the sins of my misdemeanour. Freedom means everything to me so I sympathise over your dilemma.'

Pulling a small crucifix from beneath her blouse she kissed the head of Christ.

'I have been a nun since I was seventeen, a lifetime ago or so it seems. It started with me being a headstrong teenager and in a fit of madness and having argued repeatedly with my parents I had it in my mind that I would join a convent.

'Twenty years ago I left in the middle of the night when they were asleep and walked out of the family home and into the arms of another family, serving the lord as his servant. At the time of my leaving I was the only child although through various sources I have since learnt that I have two younger siblings, a brother and sister. I have never seen either. I wonder if they ever think about me.' She again kissed the crucifix before continuing.

'The week before last a visitor arrived at St Michael's convent and asked to see the mother superior. The visitor was my younger sister. She was told that visits were not permitted but she was insistent. Danielle reminds me of her. So strong and confident.'

'That took some courage!' I said looking at Danielle standing behind the counter.

'Yes although they made my sister leave in the end without seeing me. Last weekend my sister climbed the wall of the convent and waited for me after mass, she recognised me from a photograph that she had found in an album under mum and dads bed.

'Sitting in the bedroom we talked all night before I helped her climb the all again before she we were found out. What we talked about is immaterial but that night set me thinking. Her visit and seeing my younger sister pricked the walls of my conscience. For day's I could not concentrate or think of anything else but my blood family. I put the lord aside and wanted nothing to do with my fellow nuns. For days I prayed for guidance but nobody could offer any answers to the pain that I was feeling.'

'That's some dilemma,' I whistled softly through my teeth 'and have you arrived at a decision?'

I could see the tears coming again.

'Every night Spencer I would look up at the moon and the stars and beg help but the only person who could help was myself, nobody else. The day before I left I was called to the mother superiors office where we had a long talk. As I cried I poured out my heart to a much older and wiser woman than I. As a consequence here I am, sitting in this lovely café, still equally as confused.'

'Did your mother superior not offer you any advice?'

'Only that I pray to the lord and accept his judgement on the matter!'

I looked at her thinking she looked so lonely amongst a café that was almost full of happy, contented customers. I so desperately wanted to help.

'Yesterday, I went to see the mother superior and told her that I wanted to leave the order. She tried to talk me out of leaving and asked that I take a few more days to think it over. Last night I turned back the clock twenty years and climbed the same wall that I had helped my sister climb. I am free and yet I don't feel it. I was sitting here waiting for god to judge me!'

Her explanation at least explained to whom she had expected to walk through the door.

I did consider sending Martyn around to St George's church and have him invite Robert Styles back to the café to help but I quickly dismissed the notion as not a good idea. Robert was an intelligent man although serving Christ his judgement might be clouded. Instead Mary needed good solid guidance. With a click of my fingers I had a brainwave. Before I could execute and put it in motion there was something that I wanted to say.

'You know Mary life is an odd entity and in our younger years we do and say things that we regret later. I know that personally I wish I could turn back the clock but I had plenty of time in a prison cell to wonder why we followed the wrong path or made mistakes. My dear mother still tells that it is all part of the learning process. I often think to myself, what a process.

'The evening that your sister broke into the convent and came to your room. It took a lot of courage and conviction to do what she did. Her love for a sister that she did not know was so strong that nothing was going to get in her way the night she climbed the wall of the convent. The pain of not knowing you was too strong a bond to dismiss and the pain that she left behind in you was only natural. I know that if I had siblings I would feel the same as you both do.

'The blood that courses through your body your parents gave you as they did your siblings. Nobody can deny your faith but a blood bond is stronger than anything else. God is not going to walk through our door nor any other door and he will not think any less of you for loving your family. Think of this way if you must, if you go back to your family, your mother, father, brother and sister, it's four less that he has to worry about only he will know that they are in very good hands.'

When she put her head in her hands I knew the time had come to get help, special help. Before I got up to go Mary told me that the pain she had caused was tearing her apart.

I had one last bit of advice to offer.

Reached over I took her hands in mine. I was surprised at how cold they felt.

117

'What you feel right now is isolation and alone but once you walk through that door I guarantee that you will not be alone, you'll have friends to help you. Soon the light will shine again and when you look back up the darkness will have disappeared.'

Through her tears she nodded. Within a minute I was back with Lola. I made the introductions and sat silently beside Lola as she listened to Mary's story. Although I didn't see it, the pair hit it off almost instantly. When Mary reached the point where we had left off her eyes were dry holding back the pain that she felt inside.

'When I was a teenager in Florence I had a similar discussion with my papa. I was his oldest daughter and a Roman Catholic I felt my duty as a woman was to serve Christ. Initially my papa was upset but being a devout family man he took a deep breath and instead of arguing took me for a walk around the city where he pointed to the buildings, the people and the birds flying freely in the sky.

'During the walk observing things that I had always taken for granted he explained that god was everywhere, that he saw everything and heard every conversation. Papa gave me the option to either join a convent or stay at home and worship Christ, showing him what I could make of my life. I think for the first time ever I realised what I had not noticed before. That day I made my decision and I have never regretted a single moment.
'

'I wish my father had been that understanding.'

Going around the table Lola sat beside Mary so that she could support her physically as well as emotionally. 'Oh don't get me wrong, there were days when papa and I did still argue but I never ever stopped loving him for what he had done for me. Down the years I have experienced good and bad times but I've never judged god and I don't expect him to do the same. You've served him well for a good many years but maybe now it's time to take some of that love back.'

'You really think so?'

Lola looked confident when she replied 'I know so. Grab what's out there whilst you are still young and beautiful. The world is waiting to embrace you and give back what you have given to others. Not too long ago I came to this country to take over my aunt's florist shop and show my papa that I could share my love here. At first it was a wrench but in time he understood, god will too!'

'It's that simple?' asked Mary.

'Taking one step at a time, it's that simple.' Lola said encouragingly. 'Does your family know about your decision to leave the convent?'

Mary shook her head 'Not yet, although I promised my little sister that she'd be the first to know!'

'Did she give you way in which you could make contact?'

'A mobile number.'

'Then why don't you come next door and give her a ring,' Lola looked at me and smiled 'only it's quieter than in here and a little more private.'

I knew Lola would help. Before going next door Mary offered to pay for the coffee and toast but I told her that I was still in judgement and taking payment from a disciple would not go down well with the lord. Somehow I knew that we would see her again.

Clearing the table I joined Danielle at the coffee counter. She was deep in thought.

'A penny for them?' I asked.

'I was just thinking how beautiful she is Spence.'

'Who... the nun, Mary Elizabeth Matthews?'

'No... you fool Lola!'

Danielle was right Lola was indeed beautiful not only on the outside but inside her soul. Her papa had been right telling Lola that beauty was all around and that you didn't need to hide yourself away in a convent or a monastery to prove your love to god. You could show the depth of your faith anywhere, even next to a little red café.

An hour later I caught sight of Mary and a younger woman who I assumed to be her sister walking past the café arm in arm, she smiled and waved but then both disappeared. Later that afternoon as trade slowed I went next door to see Lola and invite her around for coffee and a slice of cake. Not that it was necessary she told me what happened when Mary's sister had answered the call. She said that there were lots of tears both ends of the phone but much joy at the same time. In between eating our cake she called me a wily old fox adding that without my intervention things might have turned out very different for Mary. That afternoon I felt the love all around.

Two weeks later Mary Elizabeth Matthews walked back into the café to pay for her toast and coffee but I was having none of it. Instead I took her out back into the kitchen so that she could be properly introduced to Vera, Danielle and Martyn. There was a radiant glow now in her complexion and coming from her eyes. She told us that everything had worked out just fine back at home. Not the home that she had been resident of for the past twenty years but her real home.

Mary had been back to St Michaels only not returning as a nun but a free woman. Spending a morning in their presence she had thanked the mother superior and other nuns for their kindness. They said that they would continue to pray for her.

Walking her to the gate of the convent mother superior had said her goodbyes to her lost lamb stating that Mary had not really lost her faith only found another flock to care for. I thought that in the circumstances it was both touching and a generous sentiment. It showed Mary that like Lola believed love could exist wherever you laid your head.

I know Mary still prays every night and god has not deserted her. Lola offered Mary a position in the florist shop as an assistant and now together they take in the weekly delivery cutting and arranging accordingly the flowers, laughing and talking like two old friends. Occasionally I am invited around for coffee and to help myself to freshly baked Pasticcini di Mandorle.

Watching them together working in harmony like sisters I am in awe of how the breeze blew Mary Elizabeth Matthews to our door and once again the magic had been worked to resolve a problem. We had all gained a new friend and Mary had been reunited with her family. Things happened for a reason although at the time the reason might not be that clear.

I know that if asked Mary would say that god had sent her to the café and as I had no evidence that he didn't I had already lost the argument. Whatever something did. Over the coming months we also got to know Anna, Mary's younger sister only when Danielle and Martyn took a week's holiday, Anna would work in the kitchen or out front serving the customers bringing to the little red café her own style and charm. I would watch as she danced between the tables smiling at the customers. It was a brave thing that she did climbing the wall of the convent although no braver than her sister in leaving.

Taking a minute to think about the moral of this chapter, sometimes a little faith in yourself can go a long way and life is full of surprises. Not everybody shares those views but believing will make it easier. Sometimes we deviate from the path of our destiny but there's nothing to stop us turning around and getting back on track. If you've a problem right now remember there's always a solution out there somewhere and if we can help, we're only too happy to sit and listen although with a little courage you'll probably get there in the end by yourself.

Thomas 'Rainbow' Jones

In either direction of Oslo Road we are still fortunate to have symmetrical rectangular pavement slabs instead of the boring patchwork of black tarmac that so many other inner London boroughs suffer.

Considering myself to be a traditionalist I sympathise with the constraints put upon councils and their budgets although I have fond memories of us as children playing the game *'London to York'* where using the toe of our shoes we would nudge a single stone down the pavement slabs. Nowadays this would be almost impossible because of the long patches of uneven, unsupported, worn-down black pitch. The fact that we still had this design of pavement was the reason which first attracted Thomas 'Rainbow' Jones to our street and why he came visiting the café.

The more that I became acquainted with Thomas the more I found him to be an agreeable man, quietly intelligent and undeniably thoughtful. On initial impression you could forgive his bohemian appearance, sporting a thick mop of tousled hair which hung limply down to his shoulders almost definitely a throwback to the sixties as was his clothes.

However beneath that disguise his eyes were bright and ocean blue, forever alert and attentive like the fox. Whenever Thomas spoke his dialect had a slight echo of the Welsh valleys as the words flowed effortlessly from his mouth. Getting to know one another better he told me that he originally hailed from the Vale of Glamorgan where archaeologists had discovered the *Red Lady of Paviland.*

My first encounter with Thomas was one Monday morning just before the eight o'clock administrative rush which Danielle had aptly named because it was when all the office workers arrived for their take-aways. Thomas chose a table beside the window where he considered the light was best. He had brought with him a fair-sized wooden box and blanket quite an unusual accompaniment and the most peculiar that I had ever seen. To complete the oddity his jacket was an array of colour, not dirty but as though he had been dipped in a paint tester.

'He stands out in a crowd,' whispered Danielle to me as she picked up the order pad and pen.

Moments later she was back with his order 'one ordinary coffee, easy on the milk and a bacon sandwich. He does have a dreamy sort of voice,' and with that she disappeared into the kitchen.

Because of that first encounter we nicknamed him *rainbow* believing that it suited his general demeanour not that we amused ourselves doing the same to others that walked through the door, but in Thomas's case it seemed appropriate. In fact the only person that had such was Robert Styles the vicar of St George's who we often referred to as the *Dragon Slayer* for obvious reasons.

Having delivered his order to the table came back over to where I was stood watching.

'He's a street artist,' she whispered discreetly 'and he wants to know it of would be okay to draw on the pavement outside of the café?'

A street artist, I had not seen one of those since my childhood. I found them fascinating creatures the way that they could create a beautiful picture from seemingly nothing but what was in their head, many resembling the good pieces that you would find hanging in an art gallery or exhibition.

Looking over to his table our sixties fashion icon gave me the thumbs up to which I responded by raising my coffee mug. Shortly after our artist approached the counter to pay. He was not as I had imagined although up close he was really quite ordinary except for his eyes which were soft and so very blue.

'We've not seen you in these parts before,' I enquired 'are you just passing through?'

'I'm not really sure, London has a unique magic in the under belly of the noise and commerce. For some reason I find myself I'm drawn here by an unusual force!'

Up close he reminded me of Dylan from the Magic Roundabout. I gave him his change which he pocketed without checking that it was correct.

'If you don't mind me asking, what do you draw?'

'Anything and everything with no preference other than what the mood of the day dictates, unless I get a request from an interested passer-by then I will do my best to honour that person's wish.'

I had never been gifted with the ability to draw, paint or sculpture pottery. I could work Fracino Contempo but that was about the limit of my artistic prowess. I was in awe of anybody with the talent to produce art.

'I would very much like to see your work when you've finished,' looking at the sky beyond the window the weather looked favourable 'you picked the right day.'

'That helps.' He replied looking at the clock thinking that it was time to make a start. 'Have you a favourite picture that you'd like drawn?'

He caught me quite by surprise and although there had been days when I had visited the Tate and honouring other galleries with my presence the question was a little difficult to answer. I admired the artists although truth known I could not identify a Van Gogh from a Rembrandt to a Gaugin. What I found pleasing to the eye was the subject matter, colour and simple definition. Modernist art left me mystified wondering quite what was going the artists mind when they were covering the canvas. If I had to choose, I would stick close to home and about the only two names that I did recognise, Turner and Gainsborough. The pictures that I had seen, Turner had vision others found difficult to appreciate and Gainsborough's wide open spaces reminded me of the countryside, cows, churches and rolling fields.

'A mix of Turner with a Gainsborough!'

Thomas nodded as he smiled 'I think I can conjure up something with a blend of both.' He retrieved his box and blanket, thanked me for the breakfast then went outside.

The door was no sooner shut than Danielle was alongside the window to watch him work. With very few tables occupied I joined her.

'Look at all that chalk Spence,' she remarked when Thomas pulled open the box. There were chalk sticks of various sizes and colour. The box resembled a confused rainbow and that was how Thomas acquired his sobriquet.

Realising that he had an audience he gestured for Danielle to join him outside. I watched as she knelt down beside the Welshman and followed his fingers as they scribed a pattern on the rectangular slab. Danielle had the same expression as when I had been a boy watching the pavement artists down on the Embankment. When the picture was almost complete she came back in full of admiration for Thomas 'Rainbow' Jones.

'Wow Spence... you really need to see what Thomas has drawn, it's amazing!'

I was about to go and see when I noticed Mary from the florist approach Thomas. I refrained from interrupting as they were obviously getting on and conversing like old friends, laughing and discussing the drawing.

'Maybe I'll take a butcher's in a minute,' I said 'when Mary's finished.' Danielle went out back to the kitchen to tell Martyn and Vera about our artist. Stepping back from the window I followed.

'He's gonna do me a picture, just for me!' she told Martyn. He asked what but Danielle said that he would have to wait until it was done before he found out. Going to the front window wanted to see who had Danielle so excited.

When Mary went back to the florist shop, I took my opportunity taking a complimentary coffee. The drawing was how I had imagined it would be, colourful and vibrant although with serene rolling hills.

'Do you know, I could walk across those fields right now,' I said as Thomas stood to take a stretch.

'Thanks, it has the mystery of Turner and the depth of Gainsborough.' He placed the coffee down beside his box. 'I said that I would do a picture for Danielle, she's really quite fascinating!'

'And Mary?' I asked.

Rubbing his hands clean on a torn piece of rag he smiled 'more than fascinating!'

I took another look at my picture it was good, very good.

'Do you intend sticking around for long?'

Thomas pursed his lips together ruminating over what I had asked. 'Until today I hadn't really given it any thought I like the area and the people here are very friendly. Probably I will. Is there a reason for you asking?'

I held out my hand 'the names Spencer.' He took my hand, shook it and told me his.

'I was thinking of getting the café decorated soon although seeing your artwork has given me an idea. If you're going to stick around, how would you fancy a decorating project?'

'Do up the café?' Thomas asked.

'Yes, only with a difference. The big blank wall at the back, could you do a mural like what you've drawn here. You could sign it and in return, besides paying you I'd make sure that you got recognised.'

Thomas looked down at his cap where he had only collected a few odd coins.

'The money would come in handy,' he pondered 'and you say that I'd get recognised, how?'

'When it's complete I'd advertise the mural in the local paper, it's bound to draw customers in and get you noticed!' We shook hands again signifying that the deal was struck.

'Would that include a free breakfast until the job's complete?'

I chuckled, I liked his cheek. Pointing down at the pavement I replied 'produce this again and I'll throw in lunch as well.'

'You want it in the same theme?' he asked.

Seeing two faces appear at the window of the florists I had a thought.

'Not quite, maybe something a little cosmopolitan with blue skies, bright coloured buildings and when you walk down the cobbled streets you can feel the warmth of the sun. Autumn will be here soon so the mural will keep alive the spring and summer in the café. I'm sure the old folks around will appreciate it!'

'I could begin the moment that you shut working into the night if you'd let me have a key?' It was an attractive proposition and would not affect our daytime trade. We had a spare for unusual emergencies.

'That sounds ideal.' I was happy with the arrangement and it wasn't as though Thomas was going to run off down the road with the Fracino Contempo, it took two men to deliver and install it.

He handed back the empty coffee mug stating that he had better get on with his other requests. Danielle's I knew about but when I asked who the other was for he smiled and waved at the two woman watching from next door. 'Mary.'

In the short time that he had arrived his popularity was growing. He drew a beautiful brown mare with a gold coloured mane standing beside a foal and for Mary a girl praying beside her bed. By midday he had also drawn a clown and big top for another customer.

Danielle took a photograph on her mobile of all the pictures with May asking if she could print her drawing of the little girl. Winking at Lola when we all gathered outside to admire his work it was obvious that our ex-nun was not just in awe of his artistic genius but Thomas as well.

Handing over the spare key Thomas made a start on the inside immediately after we closed. He insisted on rubbing down the walls, doors and timberwork covering the tables and chairs, counter top and coffee machine with dust sheets. When I arrived the next morning the first coat was already dry. Later that afternoon and evening he started to sketch our mural. Where he slept during the day none of us knew.

Around four everyday he would turn up as punctual as ever his hands covered in dry chalk. Vera made sure that he had a supper to eat when he chose but with each day we would arrive amazed at his progress. Like a ghost Thomas 'Rainbow' Jones would work into the night and when the florist took an early delivery of flowers he would be there to help, leaving before I arrived.

Initially I had been concerned that having the place decorated might interfere with the ambience of the café worried that it would chase away the magic. My concerns however were unnecessary as I found out when I arrived earlier than normal the following Monday so that I could catch Thomas before he left.

Together we folded the dust sheets and I washed down the tables.

132

'There's something strange about the café,' he begun wiping them dry 'not eerie or haunting but quite reassuring. Several times when there's been nobody about I have felt something brush past. I've called out but received no reply. There's an enchanting spirit here!'

I could only agree 'I believe that the café has a special magic of its own.'

Thomas nodded and went on 'well whatever the magic Spencer it certainly seems to approve of what I am doing. On several occasions I have turned out the light to rest my eyes and allow time for my mind to catch up although when I open them again I instinctively know what should come next. This café has a beating heart!'

Besides the mural what was also amazing was that Thomas had at some time visited the barber and had his hair trimmed, washed and conditioned. His clothes although speckled with paint splashes were also not so loud, not so psychedelic. Standing beside the door we looked at the wall at the back of the café. There was only a few more touches to add and it was finished.

Quite poetically he announced 'when I'm painting here all alone I sometimes think of this place as a harbour where you can tie your boat from the storm and know that the stone walls of the quayside will keep you safe until everything's calm again.'

I liked his appreciation of the café and how he thought the place had atmosphere.

'A café with a heart,' he nodded to himself as he looked around the inside 'that's an apt description of this place and walking through the door you can almost feel it beat!'

'Where do you go when you leave here?' I asked.

'Everywhere, Trafalgar Square, the Embankment and across some of the bridges that span the river. The commuters and tourists look upon me as a tradition that they expect to see when visiting the area. In the past when I have been in London I have been photographed for travel brochures and posed for a bus load of Japanese. Art is free expression and not meant to disappoint so it's important that I am seen around.'

Thomas had an easy way of understanding everything around him. We shared a coffee together and several slices of toast to help start the day.

'Do you live nearby?'

'I've digs in a bed and breakfast around the corner although the landlady gets up late so normally I am gone before she is up and about. I could help myself to breakfast but I find the generosity of the early morning commuters quite adequately fills any hunger pains!'

Since leaving the convent Mary had also moved herself into a small although very comfortable two bedroom apartment that she shared with one of Lola's other friends. The arrangement suited both women and it was close to Mary's family, however more significant was the sense of freedom that she enjoyed, coming and going as she pleased. Working at the florist was as important as Mary loved holding and being part of nature. Within weeks she had moulded nicely into our community becoming a favourite amongst friends and customers alike.

Topping up our mugs Thomas told me about Glamorgan, his family, where he went to school and of his ambitions. Without doubt he was an incredibly fascinating individual, as interesting as I have found Mary when at the end of the day I would share a coffee with her and Lola.

As the day went on long after Thomas had gone I was near the door to the kitchen when I happened upon a conversation between Danielle and Vera about the decoration.

'That Muriel's coming on a real treat,' said Danielle as delivered another of used crocks.

'Mural...' Vera corrected 'it's a mural, a wall painting Danielle.'

'Yeah, that's what I said, one of them things!'

On the other side of the door I smiled to myself.

'And that painting of the horses is great. I'm getting a print made for my aunt on her birthday as she like horses.'

Vera looked across and shook her head approvingly 'there are times Danielle when you amaze me!'

Going over to where Martyn was sorting the sausages she nudged his arm 'what's she mean?' but he had the good sense to tell her that eventually she'd get it. That young man was catching on fast.

The following morning everything was complete. The last of the décor had been added in overnight as had the finishing touches to the mural. When I arrived I was surprised to find Mary already there dressed in a pair of Thomas's paint splashed overalls.

'Knowing my interest in art Thomas invited me along to help last night and I have to say that the hours just seemed to melt into the coming sunrise.'

Neither looked tired for having spent all night working and if anything they looked remarkably happy. Admiring the décor and the mural it was just as I had imagined, better.

'Well you've done a magnificent job Thomas and you too Mary.'

As promised I took his photograph so that it could hang beside the mural but Thomas insisted on Mary being included. Overnight the bond between them had weld stronger and together they looked very happy. When Lola arrived early to open *Florrie's Flowers* I called her in so that the four of us could share the moment together and breakfast. Opening the fridge I removed the bacon, sausages, eggs and mushrooms.

Standing beside me and waiting for the toast to pop up, I whispered 'so did you know about our two love-birds out front?'

Lola raised her eyebrows as if to demonstrate that men never ever see anything even when in front of their face.

'Of course,' she whispered back 'women share secrets!' I wondered how many times I had entered into their discussion.

Breakfast that morning before anybody arrived was very enjoyable, the company delightful and for the amount that the décor had cost me I was very pleased. With Mary's help, Thomas had done a grand job. I later found out that she had spent Friday and Saturday night helping. The café looked different, vibrant and cleaner and many of our customers had already said how good it was.

Lola was so impressed that she immediately commissioned Thomas to do a similar painting on the wall in the florists only with a suggestion of Florence in the picture. When Vera arrived she took a photograph of the four of us sat at the table which I have behind the counter, admiring the image every day where at last I have a photo of Lola.

Similarly with the photograph being sent to the local press to help advertise the café and Thomas's talents the requests for commissions started to arrive thick and fast coming in from all manner of interested bodies, local art galleries, private collectors, even an embassy but most were from ordinary people wanting a nice picture to hang on their wall albeit a living room, a hallway or a bedroom. One man even wanted his bathroom decorated to look like a Roman Tepardarium. At first he was overwhelmed by the demand for his skills but with Mary at his side she helped organise his work and leisure time and a month after finishing the décor of the café, Thomas 'Rainbow' Jones took Mary Elizabeth Matthews to Glamorgan where she met his family.

Upon their return I sensed that some kind of announcement was imminent. Also hovering in the wings was a known art agent willing to offer Thomas an auspicious future but the agent did not know out Thomas, a man with simple needs and a love for life.

As honoured as I was Thomas did seek me out one morning to ask my advice, but I told him that whatever path he chose, it would be the right one if he felt it in his heart. He seemed easier having asked although from what Lola had told me, we believed that wherever Thomas went Mary was sure to follow. Life had certainly changed dramatically for Mary and as friends we were pleased to sit on the fence and bear witness to her transformation.

And as for the little red café well things seemed to go from strength to strength. The half page report in the local paper brought a good many new customers to our door just to see the mural, after which I'd say that they need pop next door and soak up a bit of Florence too.

Thomas was fast becoming a household name and whenever he is on another assignment I often find myself reading the little inscription that he added under where he had signed his name *'I only ever paint with my heart and what my eyes see as my fingers are merely an extension of my soul.'*

Removing the key from the lock one afternoon I felt a sudden draught touch me on the cheek as though I had been caressed. Whatever had inspired Thomas has since inspired a good many others, bringing them to our door and helping change lives. The café has certainly changed mine and I feel sure that there are many more adventures to come.

Butterflies

Sitting quite alone at the table by the window staring blankly at the world outside in his vintage grey flannels and matching top hat that sat on the chair beside his own there was no mistaking the intention of the young man that Saturday morning.

Posing the question why he should choose to be sat there rather than where he should have been caused the occupants of the other tables to wonder too. Like a ticking heartbeat the clock on the wall marched forever onward of ten o'clock.

Having spoken and had coffee with Robert Styles only Thursday I was aware that he was officiating at a wedding booked for eleven that morning. It wasn't rocket science as to who was the groom.

Danielle had already been to his table twice topping up with black coffee and the one slice of toast but his mind and thoughts were else only I conceived not with the coming ceremony. The young man looked tired as though he had been awake all of the last night. Checking with his wrist watch time appeared to be moving very fast.

With a distinct lack of apparent interest in anything around him other customers, the weather or Danielle I decided to take matters in hand. Moments later to prove my point two Saturday girls from the salon in Morton Street walked on by the cafe waved and wished him luck but our groom looked straight through them. They left giggling.

A regular pensioner who came to the counter to pay was intrigued by the man in his tails. 'Is he alright,' he asked 'only he looks lost?'

'Wedding nerves I would suspect.' Although I had to admit that it looked more.

When the pensioner stopped at the door to wish the groom luck, the young man half smiled, but his response was dispassionate. Leaving Danielle in charge of the counter and the till I went over to where he was sat.

'I haven't seen you around here before?' I said holding out my hand as a greeting.

'No, but I'm I getting married in an hour's time.'

'Eleven at St George's, that's right, I know the vicar!'

He smiled struggling to boost his energy levels.

'Is it a case of George fighting off the old dragon?' I asked.

He looked at me quizzically dumbfounded. 'Am I missing something?'

'Many of us have been there before and fallen headlong into the trap. You see when you marry you gain a bride, the woman of your dreams and desires but what many men forget you also acquire a mother-in-law, often referred to as the old dragon. When I was married the former was the easy bit and when you think about it, you wouldn't be marrying your bride unless it was meant to be, but with the package often comes a snarling, unsympathetic, blood-sucking formidable foe, a dragon to do battle with!'

'Oh, really.'

I looked over at the clock realising this could be hard going.

'Wishing the next hour away won't bring any comfort and neither will you find any answers starring out into space.

Unravelling the cuff of his shirt sleeve he told me that his name was David Hetherington.

'Spencer Marlon Brand.' It was a more positive start. 'I've been watching you David for the past hour as you've travelling through the universe looking as though you're searching for a place to hide. Can I help?'

'I wish I was...' he mumbled 'a million miles from here!'

I shrugged. 'Believe me I suspect that there are times when every man wishes the same, trouble is David as men we have to stand and face the challenge. Today is really no different than any other day except the ceremony and the only difference that you'll notice is that when you tie the knot you face the challenges ahead together.' I placed my arms on the table leaning forward 'the bride is she worth marrying?'

I had always considered the best way to resolve a problem was to meet it head-on, rise to the occasion and search for the solution, unless it involved Lola, then it was best just to agree that she was right every time!

142

Standing by the counter Danielle had her mouth open wide with two fingers glued to her temple indicating that I had just pulled the trigger.

'Marianne, she's perfect in every way she always has been.'

'Then what seems to be the problem and what's stopping you from making the short walk around the corner to St George's?'

David Hetherington's expression latched onto my soul.

'I'm not sure that I'll make Marianne a good husband!'

And there it was self-doubt, that old chestnut was worrying the life out him.

'Husbands face that dilemma the moment that they go down on bended knee and when the altar door opens and your bride walks down the aisle, you enter a contract with a simple *'I do'*. You promise to love, care and provide for, forsaking nights out with the boys, watching football on Saturday afternoons and instead going shopping, doing the washing up and occasional ironing. It's part of the deal David and as the saying goes 'practice makes perfect!'

At the counter was shaking her head. I willed Martyn to stay in the kitchen. I sensed that there was something else and he needed to disclose all before he entered into the commitment. 'Besides going shopping, something else troubles you only men never do things by half?'

Aware that Danielle was within earshot he leant forward and whispered 'the mother in law only she's not quite as bad as you made her out to be, although when she find out what I've done, she might be!'

At last the crux of the problem.

'She has the reins pulled in tight and won't let go of her precious daughter?' I asked.

'Sometimes, although this time it was my fault!'

Danielle was trying to stretch herself over the counter to listen.

'*Whoa* there tonto, not so fast kemosabe. First rule of marriage when facing the mother-in-law, never admit that you're in the wrong. The ground under your feet is perilous enough without starting an avalanche. So why was it your fault?'

'Last night was my stag-do...' he paused before going on 'and not that it was planned but I ended up with the stripper after everybody else had gone home!'

'*I knew it,*' exclaimed Danielle as she headed straight for the kitchen and Martyn. Her experience of men like David adding another chapter to the bible of life as written by Danielle. I fought hard trying not to laugh. I waited until the door of the kitchen was shut before I replied.

'A minor indiscretion, we've all had them and what happens on a stag-do should stay locked away in a some deep seated sea chest, padlocked twice then weighted down before it's dropped over the side and plummets to Davy Jones!'

'If only it were that simple.' He replied 'After the celebrations, it wasn't meant to happen but we sort of hit it off!'

At this point I saw the chest bubbling back up to the surface. Moments later it was worse when Danielle reappeared with Vera. They stood behind the counter as judge and jury their arms folded. Across their chests.

'I was very drunk so Monique helped me get into the taxi although I was alert enough not to reveal my address. I forget what I said but we ended up travelling to Bayswater where she rented a flat with a girl-friend.'

I dared not look at the serving counter, this was going to get worse before it got better.

'Only when we got to her flat, her friend was away on a business trip. Anyway one thing must have led to another because around four fifteen I heard a fire engine go racing past the block of flats. I woke to find Monique beside me and we were completely naked. Lying nearby were my clothes which had been neatly folded and placed on the chair nearest the bed!'

The café was virtually silent as David waited for a reaction.

'You lucky bugger...' said a man sitting at a table nearest ours, he had three other men as company *'the only pleasure I get around four fifteen every morning is a bloody alarm call and the last time that I saw my old woman naked was when I could see beyond my belly!'*

The café suddenly erupted into laughter bringing Martyn from the kitchen. Across the table David couldn't help himself as he saw the funny side of his tale of woe. Behind the counter Danielle and Vera shook their heads like a pair of unamused ducks.

'So what happened next?' asked the man.

'I put on my clothes and crept out of the flat without waking Monique. Walking back down the road I managed to hitch a lift with an early morning delivery driver. Somehow I'd lost the front door key to the house so I spent the rest of the night in the garden shed until my family woke up. It wasn't until later when I took a shower that I caught sight of myself in the mirror.'

Now you could have heard a pin drop.

'Tattooed on my right buttock were the initials *'MM was here'* and if that wasn't bad enough I had a line of butterflies trailing down to my nether region!'

Well that was it, I for one could not contain myself and nor could the customers in the café. Tears were rolling down our cheeks and even Danielle and Vera was laughing. The uproar brought Lola and Mary in from next door. They looked slightly vexed as to why everybody was laughing so much. It didn't help when David explained that the stripper was also a tattoo artiste.

Lola looked at me as I tried to hold onto my abdomen because it was hurting so much having laughed so much. Asking Vera why she told them.

'And Monique's initials were MM?' I asked.

'I don't know I didn't look around the flat. The only thing I did see where photographs of her previous clients!'

I thought the laughter would bring down the rafters and when I next looked I saw Lola and Mary had joined in. Mary had certainly changed. It was nice to see.

'What am I going to do,' David pleaded 'it's bad enough that I have to explain this Marianne on our wedding night but her mother is bound to find out and how do I explain a line of butterflies disappearing up my rear end. It's not likely to be only butterflies!'

Through my tears I looked up at the clock seeing that we had twenty minutes in which to resolve the matter. Unable to stay and take any more punishment the four men paid for their breakfast, wished the groom the best of luck and left. Soon after they had left the café settled down again. It was left to me to sort out his mess.

'A good number of grooms find themselves in trouble on their wedding day David.' I went closer to avoid being overheard. Blame last night on your friends. They invariably got you drunk so say that they had you tattooed and in time you'll think of an excuse for the initials. The main thing is to show Marianne how much you love her.'

'And the butterflies?' he asked.

'From out of the darkness emerges light.' I uttered. It was the first thought that entered my head. 'Butterflies represent new life and getting married could equally be looked upon in the same vein. I am sure that Marianne can accept that.'

Sensing a presence by my side I expected Lola to be standing there so I was surprised to see Vera.

'Or you could tell her the truth!'

'If I did that, there would be no wedding.' We both sensed the cloud of doom descend.

Twirling the salt and pepper bottles between my fingertips I saw a vision appear of a bride and groom.

'I think what Vera is trying to suggest is that it might be better to tell the truth rather than live a lie for the rest of your life.' At my side Vera nodded. 'In a way David she's right.'

'You said that you were married.'

'I was once, quite happily or so I thought. The trouble with me David was that I was always chasing a rainbow that was never really there and eventually the dreams of something better were only in my head. I told a pack of lies and they all came back to slap me in the face. Had I told the truth things would not have been so difficult. My lies cost me a marriage, a house and several years of my life.'

David looked shocked.

'I'm sorry, I didn't mean to pry!'

'You didn't but perhaps telling the truth is starting out right.' I paused as I thought. 'How can you be sure anything happened last night with Monique, by the sounds of it nothing did.'

'How can you say that?' he asked.

'Because nobody tears your clothes off in a moment of lust, folds them and places them on the chair beside the bed. You probably crashed out before anything did take place and Monique had the good sense to let you sleep.'

Suddenly the light came on in David's head and he saw things more clearly.

'Christ you're right, nothing did happen!'

I managed to grab his arm before he picked up his hat and ran in the direction of the church.

'Only leave out the bit about the flat belonging to two girls. That could muddle the explanation!'

With that David Hetherington was out of the door and gone.

Still at my side and watching him leave Vera put a hand on my shoulder.

'You know Spencer not all mothers-in-law' are ogres,' she added 'mine, had Cyril lived would have been lovely and she had a son. Mothers can be very forgiving, even supportive of sons or daughters, even in-laws!'

Arriving at the church David Hetherington was calm and ready to face the day, not his demons, but his future wife. In the face of adversity laughter had proved to be the best solution. It was amazing how when you put things into perspective everything seemed that much clearer although I was glad that I didn't have any initials or butterflies tattooed on my right flank. My only reservation as the clock struck eleven was the best man's speech but David would have to get around that by himself.

A month later a familiar face walked back into the café only this time he brought with him his beautiful glowing wife, Mrs Marianne Hetherington. I called Vera from the kitchen where we shared a pot of tea and fresh baked scones. Vera asked about the honeymoon and enthusiastically Marianne Hetherington told us almost everything. The tattoo was never mentioned and I doubt that it ever would be. Some things were best left in a dark place and not seen.

I have been called many things in my time but never a marriage counsellor. David's apprehension were merely no more than many men and women feel on their wedding day. We chatted for almost an hour before they left and they promised to come back again soon.

A short time after the visit I received a thank you note through the post addressed to me personally. When I pulled the card from the envelope it was from David. He thanked me once again for helping sort his problem that Saturday morning, stating that everybody in the little red café had helped. At the bottom of the card there was a brief addendum which mentioned that he had told the truth the night of the wedding only he had slightly modified the truth so as not to spoil the occasion. And 'MM' somehow had been excused as meaning 'My Marianne'.

Quite by chance I happened to bump into Robert Styles a day after receiving David's correspondence and in our conversation I asked about the wedding of Mr and Mrs David Hetherington saying that the that the groom had visited the café before going to the church. Robert seemed delighted to report that the ceremony had been a complete success and that the bride's mother was especially happy with the way that things had turned out.

The vicar added that there was only one awkward moment when the groom had turned somewhat pale when he had asked the congregation 'if there was any lawful impediment as to why the couple should not have been married in holy wedlock'.

'For one awful moment I think he expected somebody to raise their hand!'

Quite clearly having met David's wife the couple were suited to one another.

Standing behind the counter before I closed the café I did wonder where Monique had hailed from and whether she had been in the congregation that day. I also wondered if David's friends on the stag-do had staged her being present knowing the likely outcome. Men can be insensitive creatures when it comes to the pain of others.

A year later down the line Mr and Mrs David Hetherington returned to the café with a beautiful addition to their home, a daughter who had her mother's eyes and her father's hair colouring. I was in no doubt that a grand-daughter would have brought both mother and son-in-law even closer together and although I had no idea who Mrs Longhurst was, if she ever did know about the butterflies she was the embodiment of discretion never letting on. As Vera rightly said some mother-in-law's are really not that bad.

Angus, Amelia and Friends

Throughout life it is rare if somebody declares that they have never been troubled by stress whatever the age. To a young child losing a teddy, a treasured companion, the experience must have left a bad memory in their life as nobody forgets a precious friend. I could not have written this anthology of short stories without including the tale of a teddy bear named Angus.

Wearing little else except a mottled fur coat, more a darkish brown rather than gold and with a pair of engaging brown eyes to match Angus stood proudly upright, draped in his tartan neck scarf. When exactly Angus had come visiting neither Danielle nor myself could tell but his presence certainly caused a furore like no other and would leave a profound mark on my life.

Clearing away the dirty crocks from a table Danielle found Angus sitting on the chair all by himself. She dumped him on the counter top and asked if I was acquainted with the little chap.

'A new helper?' I mocked.

'Oooh he's gorgeous Spence. He was sat at table six all on his lonesome.' Like a tiny tot she waved a hairy paw my way 'and I am calling him Angus.'

It was evident that Danielle was already besotted with the teddy. How she knew that he hailed from the Scottish Highlands was down to her imagination. We placed Angus on the shelf beside the Fracino Contempo where he could be seen by customer and passers-by expecting him to be claimed at any time. We had been extremely busy that morning so it was virtually impossible to say who had sat at the table.

'What's he your new mascot?' asked one customer who thought that the bear was watching everything that went on inside the café.

'No. Angus was found lunchtime, he'll be gone by the time we close.'

Angus however was not claimed not that day, the next nor any other day. After a week of being on the shelf Angus had become a permanent fixture and many that came in asked about him. I told them that he belonged to Danielle, but in turn she told them that his stay was temporary. Every so often just to remind us that he was still there Angus would fall forward until we propped him back.

With nobody claiming Angus, Danielle had resorted to taking him down to the newsagents and having his image scanned with photocopies being made so that we could distribute his find around the immediate area. Within a short space of time Angus was becoming a celebrity and each morning when the school children went by on their way to school they would stop and peer through the window waving at the little wee bear who looked back. In a last ditch effort to find the owner I placed an advert in the local newsagents hoping that the rightful owner would realise their folly and come and collect him.

As the days extended into weeks the hope of finding his owner faded. Every morning I would say hello and every afternoon goodbye. Danielle was convinced that Angus was beginning to look forlorn so to help she brought in one of her teddies so now instead of just the one teddy we have Oscar as well. Sitting alongside Angus in his blue patterned waistcoat and matching trousers the two bears look quite at home together.

When the men from the nearby council yard came in they would rib me about our recent toy collection, promising to bring any that they collected on their rounds. I was against any more believing that our hygiene certificate could be in jeopardy, however as usual my concerns fell on deaf ears and with another week passing by Ted Jarvis our local postman delivered another stuffed effigy that he had found propped against our front door. The regular customers named our latest edition Bashful and that night Vera took Bashful home to have his patches repaired and put through the washing machine.

Instead of a little red café we were fast becoming known as the teddy bear sanctuary. My frustration was further tested when on the way home I saw a hand written poster pinned to the telegraph pole, it said: *'lost and wayward bears, please make your way to the little red café where you're guaranteed to be made welcome'.* It was odd but the style of writing looked vaguely familiar like Danielle's.

Soon the shelf had five teddy bears each vying for space as they huddled next to one another. Unsurprising Danielle had a name for each going left to right there was Angus, Oscar, Bashful, Edgar and Eric. I am still uncertain as to where and when the last two appeared but there was no mistaking they were there sitting proudly next to the coffee machine alongside their counterparts, their damaged clothing repaired with new stitching, freshly laundered and hair combed. I was convinced that Lol and Mary had contributed Edgar and Eric when Mary came to bless our quintet, stating that even stuffed teddies had souls.

Reaching beneath the counter I pulled out the newspaper that had run the advert for Thomas 'Rainbow' Jones. Going outside I called the reporter responsible for his recent success. After explaining my plight Stephanie Steele agreed to visit providing the coffee and cake was on the house.

That afternoon she arrived bringing along a photographer who took a number of photographs from all different angles. I had never witnesses such attention for five little stuffed bears. The next day the newspaper ran the report. Danielle arrived with a copy looking as pleased as punch.

'Look at this Spence,' she said as she dropped the paper onto the counter top and pulled it open at page four. Entitled *'Quintet of Bears Storm Café'* I wasn't sure whether I wanted to cheer or admit defeat. At the end of business I held an impromptu staff meeting invoking the rule that if nobody claimed Angus, Bashful, Edgar and Eric by the end of the week they would all have to go to the nearest charity shop.

'But Oscar's got used to having his friends around each day!' Danielle fought back.

My situation was saved by the bell when Ted Jarvis pushed open the door with the late post.

'You might want to read the top letter,' he said before he pulled the door shut and went next door to the bookshop.

I went over to the counter and picked up the blue coloured envelope, on the front it was addressed to:

Mister Spencer Brand, The Little Red Café, Oslo Street, London.

I flipped the envelope over and noted the type printed address of the back *Saxon House Children's Home, Little Banbury Street, London*. Using a knife along the seam I opened the envelope and took out the single sheet from within.

Dear Mister Spencer

This is an important letter, so please read very carefully. I saw your story in the newspaper the other day about the teddy bear's that you are keeping in your shop. I don't have a teddy of my own as we have to share the different coloured bears that live in the big toy box in our dormitory that I share with Maisie, Sandra and my best friend carol. I was thinking that if Angus has not found his mummy and daddy soon, can I please have him for myself? I promise that I will love him forever and wash him every Saturday morning.

Yours sincerely

Amelia Hart, Room 9

I read the content of the letter twice, then showed it to Vera who read it, passing it on to Danielle and finally Martyn. It hit the lumps in our throat every time that it was read.

'Proper takes your breath away, don't it,' Vera remarked as Martyn handed it back to me. 'I don't see how you can refuse Spencer!'

Folding the letter and carefully concealing it back in the envelope I felt the same. I asked Danielle to cover the counter so that I could take the letter next door and show Lola and Mary. When they read it Mary had a tear in her eye and Lola was fighting hard to control her emotions. Mary made the call and the home confirmed that they did indeed have an Amelia Hart as a resident and that she was just seven and half years old. She handed me the phone going to find the tissue box.

Conversing with a Miss Johnson the manager of the children's home we discussed the content of the letter, little Amelia and Angus. I told her that Angus was still unclaimed.

'She really is quite resourceful,' said Miss Johnson 'and a very gentle little soul. I am sure that if the teddy bear is available she would do exactly as she said promised in her letter!'

When I put the receiver down I had to admit that the emotions tumbling around inside my stomach were never going to settle until I made a decision. A couple of minutes later Mary re-joined Lola and myself having splashed her face with cold water. She apologised but I wouldn't hear of it.

'I thought I was stronger than that,' I admitted 'but the call got to me too Mary.'

'I know of Saxon House and it is full of poor orphans like Amelia. At the convent we would visit all the big shops on the run up to Christmas giving prayers for their generous donations and gift for the children. We saw it as our duty to ensure that every child had a gift to open on Christmas morning. Like the other sister we would visit Christmas morning just to see the joy in their little faces but when the time came for us to leave it would tear the fabric from my soul. That night in prayer I would ask for forgiveness as I questioned my faith and why there should ever be lonely children.'

Looking at the letter I traced the words with my finger.

'Miss Johnson said that it had taken little Amelia a long time to pen the letter and that she had put all of her faith in receiving a favourable reply!'

Pushing herself away from the cutting bench Lola looked very determined. 'Then we must her wish come true Spencer.'

I nodded but I couldn't look either of them in the eye. My emotions had got the better of me. I had rubbed shoulders with hardened criminals, men a lot worse than me but right then I felt like crying, not just for me but children like Amelia. With Mary there Lola looped her arm through mine and squeezed mine tight. 'I like a man who is not afraid to show his emotions.'

I sniffed and cuffed the sentiment with the back of my hand breathing deep.

'What about the other children,' I asked 'what do we do with them?'

It was a problem as we only had five teddies and one belonged to Danielle. Lola as resourceful as ever had the solution.

'Do you think Stephanie Steele would run another article for us?'

'Almost certainly, if it would help sell papers.'

'Good...'

Before I could ask why Lola had dialled the number and asked to be put through to Stephanie Steele. When she heard what Lola had to propose she in turn went to see the editor and he agreed to run free of charge an advert asking for any unwanted toys that could donated in good condition and delivered to Florrie's Flowers. The response was better than any of us had imagined and soon Lola's preparation area was full of boxes and bags, each a good quality toy.

Chipping in Vera had a great idea as well getting the support from Danielle and Martyn. It meant me calling Miss Johnson again but when she heard what we were proposing she was all for the idea.

Come Saturday evening with the added help of Thomas, Stephanie Steele and Robert Styles we inflated balloons, put up streamers and covered the tables in bright coloured paper. Mary prayed for sunshine the next day so that Thomas could decorate the pavement outside with the children's favourite cartoon characters and Robert surprisingly said that he would walk Stephanie home believing that it the chivalrous thing to do.

Mid-morning Sunday the sun was out and Thomas was already hard at work by the time that we started arriving. Danielle, Lola and Mary added paper plates, beakers and more surprises to the tables as Martyn and Vera worked in the kitchen baking quiches and jam tarts. Robert Styles and Stephanie Steele promised to be along as soon as the last parishioner had left the church. I never did the chance to ask if she had attended the service that morning, but when they arrived together it looked very much the case.

To our amazement word had got around fast courtesy of Stephanie and her editor. A local bus company had promised to collect and return the children free of charge using a red double decker and a bakery shop near to Euston had contacted Vera and asked if they could help with additional pastries and the baking of a party cake. The list seemed to go and on and one of the big hotel chains close to Trafalgar Square had offered to supply all the sandwiches, jellies and ice cream adding that for every child there would also be a jamboree bag full of surprises. Of course the manager quite rightly refused to disclose what would be in the bags as they needed to remain a surprise.

With everything in place and ready Michael Parkin, the press photographer arrived. He bunched us together and took a picture of everybody that had helped. Adding it to the wall beside the framed image of Lola and myself, Mary and Thomas we are getting quite a well-known gallery.

Right on time the red double decker arrived with a lot of excited faces looking out of the windows. As this adventure had started with Danielle finding Angus I thought it right that she held open the door and be the first to greet the children. Standing aside we took delivery of our excited arrivals. Watching them clamber into the chairs and tables I could feel my emotions getting the better of me once again, but thankfully Lola was on hand to steady my nerves. As soon as they were settled we poured drinks and began dishing out the food.

Hiring a clown's outfit Thomas had permed his hair with Mary's help. He arrived when nobody was expecting him and going from table to table he helped keep the children amused as we went back and forth to the kitchen clearing empty sandwich plates, before supplying jelly and ice-cream and cake. Around four in the afternoon came a very special moment when a special guest suddenly appeared on the counter top placed there by Mary.

On arrival Miss Johnson had kindly pointed out Amelia Hart to me as she had taken her seat and for most of the afternoon I had been observing the little girl as she enjoyed herself with the other girls sat at her table although once maybe twice in passing I had caught her watching me as I had moved awkwardly around the room trying not to get in the way.

Seeing Angus sat on the counter top I could see her getting excited as she bunched her hands into two tiny fists. Amelia Hart aged seven and a half was the most adorable little girl that I had ever known and I found myself becoming very fond of her.

When Mary called Amelia forward, she offered the invitation to me as well. The room fell into a silent hush as the expectation of the moment grew with intensity and excitement. I could feel my heart beating hard inside my chest as I edged past Danielle and Vera who were already sharing a box of tissues.

Realising that I was much taller I went down on one knee coming face to face with a pair of big saucer eyes that belonged to a very excited, although apprehensive little lady. Amelia stood beside Mary with her hands crossed behind her back coyly aware of why she had been called forward.

Taking hold of Angus, I asked the question. 'I think this little brown bear is looking for a new home and owner, do you know of anybody that could look after him and love him lots and lots?'

Taking a step forward Amelia held out her short stubby hands eager to hold her new best friend.

'I will,' she said looking up at Mary 'and I promise to love and hug him forever!' Holding on as tight as she could to Angus, Amelia pressed him to her chest. He would remain there for the rest of the afternoon.

The moment and passing over of angus was memorably captured by the flashing of camera bulbs as they popped around the room, catching also the arrival of Arnold the bus driver as he stepped in through the swing door armed with sacks full of presents aided by Robert Styles and Stephanie Steele. There ensued a flurry of activity as every child received a beautifully wrapped present. Sitting at the corner table I observed Amelia, noting that she wasn't really interested in what the other children were getting only having already received Angus she was quite content with her little teddy bear.

That afternoon the party was the best that the café had ever arranged. All about there was torn paper where presents had been excitedly opened, some had streamers in their hair and on the ceiling helium balloons had become detached from their string not that any of it mattered as we would clear the place once the children had left. The main thing was everybody had fun including the adults. An hour after receiving their presents Miss Johnson called for order and once again the room fell instantly silent.

'I think children that we should give a big round of thanks to Mr Brand and all the people that have helped make this day so special. This has been the most amazing party and we should thank everybody for all the wonderful presents and food.' She started the applause which seemed to last for ages adding to the occasion. It ended when the clown alias Thomas 'Rainbow' Jones popped lots more streamers. In the corner I saw Robert Styles say a silent prayer for the children and the people that had made the whole party a success. I smiled and gave a nod when he looked my way before Stephanie Steele moved alongside again.

Moving between the tables Michael Parkin kept snapping away as the children played with brightly dressed dolls, armoured soldiers, zoo and farm animals, aeroplanes that could fly and cars that raced trains or pirate ships. Also dancing between chairs, tables and children Lola and Mary made sure that everybody was enjoying themselves. The air that afternoon was thick with laughter, hoops and shrills, whistles and the sound of a recorder that a little boy had found. I was sure that the memory of that party will live inside of me and the café forever.

Finding her way back to where I was stood Lola hugged me tight and kissed me on the cheek winking at Danielle and Vera.

'You've made everybody so happy today, especially the children. You've also made the dream come true for a special little girl as well. One day Spencer Brand I predict that you will have a family of your own.'

I still had my arm around Lola's back when a disparated thought ran through my head. Pulling Lola closer I whispered *'it would be our luck for the real owner to turn up now and claim Angus.'*

Sensing my apprehension Lola pointed to where Stephanie Steele was sat amongst a group of girls and boys.

'Stephanie and Mary went out the other afternoon on a special mission to locate a teddy bear that looked almost identical to Angus. If by any chance a little boy or girl did come to claim the bear we already have a substitute to give.'

'You're amazing, you think of everything!'

From the corner table Amelia Hart smiled and waved at Lola and myself. She was besotted with the little bear. We realised that if anybody did come, nobody was going to take him from her.

Whispering in my ear, Lola asked 'you're quite taken with that little girl aren't you?'

I agreed. 'There's just something special about her that tugs at my heart strings. Up until the moment that I received that letter from Amelia I had never really thought about children, but what she had to say in the letter was very emotional and soul searching. If I was lucky enough to have a daughter one day, I would want her to be just like little Amelia Hart.'

When the time came for the party to end and have the children leave they ran the gauntlet of adults lined up to say goodbye and make sure that each had their present as we wanted none left behind. We each received a kiss and a cuddle and on purpose I had positioned Vera to be the last knowing that she cherish every moment.

Angus the Second as we aptly named the substitute teddy sat on the kitchen shelf beside the saucepans until Vera could take no more deciding that he also needed a good home, so one afternoon wrapping him in tissue paper she sneaked him out and took him home. When I found him missing she told me that Angus the Second reminded her of Amelia Hart and the other children. At night she would pray for Cyril, Amelia the children and all the teddies in the world.

A month after the party we received another letter from the children's home only this time from Miss Johnson and to officially invite for us all for afternoon tea which she should would be served by the children of the home as a thank you for such a wonderful day when Amelia took custody of Angus and the other children received presents too.

And so two weeks on one beautiful late summer Sunday afternoon, Lola and myself, Mary and Thomas, Vera, Danielle and Martyn, Stephanie Steele and Robert Styles, not forgetting Michael Parkin and Arnold the bus driver took ourselves off to Saxon House to be met by a rowdy but excitable bunch of children who were eagerly waiting to show us the place where they lived.

Lola and I was about to climb the stairs when a little hand suddenly gripped tight the two fingers of my right hand, looking down I recognised those unmistakable big brown eyes.

'Would you like to see where me and Angus sleep?' she asked.

'We would love to see that, thank you,' replied Lola as Amelia led the way clutching Angus close to her chest.

On the landing above we followed down a brightly coloured corridor with bedrooms on either side before coming to a room near the end housing four single beds. It was nicely decorated, clean and very tidy.

167

Amelia went to her bed and propped Angus against her pillows so that he could sit up straight.

'He likes it here, she said 'and at night we whisper to one another until the others in the room have fallen asleep. Then we make plans for the day that we intend to escape and of the wonderful places that we will visit.'

Lola sat down on the bed beside Amelia. She took a hairbrush from her handbag and begun gently brushing the little girl's hair.

'Every girl albeit big or little likes having their hair brushed.'

Nestling herself comfortably on Lola's lap they looked so right together and I could feel my heart thumping inside my chest again.

That afternoon we had sandwiches and cake washed down with orange, tea or coffee, an afternoon garden party fit for kings and queens. Come five thirty however it was time to take our leave and let the staff settle the children before bed. I didn't want to go and I felt guilty leaving but we promised Amelia that we would visit again providing Miss Johnson said that it was alright.

Getting into Lola's car we were the last to leave so that we could wave goodbye to little Amelia. We watched as she held Angus under one arm and waved. A short distance from where we had waved Lola stopped the car and turned to me.

'If you could adopt Amelia Hart would you?' she asked. I could tell from her expression that she was serious.

'In a heartbeat…' I replied.

My response had surprised me. Living at home with my mother I had come to accept that my prospects were never going to improve unless I got a place of my own. The little red café was doing well, much better than I had ever expected, but most of the success was due to the people around me. I was never going to be rich not that having a lot of money meant a lot to me, that much I had learnt in prison. As long as I was happy, healthy and content I considered myself lucky and that I had everything in life, well almost everything. Looking at Lola that afternoon then back again at little Amelia standing alone on the drive of the children's home there was room in my heart for others to be a big part of my life.

'Most definitely,' I suddenly added 'although you have to remember Lola that I have been inside so any adoption would be a very difficult ride.'

Lola gave Amelia a big wave calling out loudly *see you soon* before she engaged gear and rolled the car forward again. 'That all depends on whether you marry the right woman Spencer Brand!'

On the drive back home I had a lot to think about. Oh and before you consider asking I never did find out what happened to Bashful, Edgar and Eric as they mysteriously vanished overnight. Danielle took Oscar home, however as for the others they remain a mystery like life.

The Tobacco Tin

London a city which is steeped in a long record of history, mystery and diversity has like many other principal regions home or abroad adopted a cultural difference which is both rich in language and customs. Depending upon what we see, we hear and accept, as a nation or an individual the many changes in society will often demonstrate either our ignorance or understanding. As a man who has been in prison and been part of that change, I was ready to welcome anybody into the little red café.

Such a visitor arrived late one afternoon having come foreign shores and in need of refreshment, food and a friendly smile. The café was there to deliver all three requirements. The individual's reason for paying us a visit will become clear as you read on.

Wilhelm Wendell originally from the small town of Premnitz in the Brandberg State of Germany had travelled to England bringing with him a deep personal and rather emotionally charged purpose, something that for a very long time had been preying upon his mind and affecting his sleep. Safely ensconced in the café he wanted to tell his story, a tale that began in the early spring of nineteen forty three.

As a young man Wilhelm had served in the German Wehrmacht, Group Company C where an uneasy alliance had been formed alongside the Corpo Italiano di Liberazione, the Italian Liberation Corps which was strategically holding back the line on the south west front. It was during that campaign that time Wilhelm had become friends with an Italian soldier by the name of Antonio Lorenzo Capella.

Friendships however formed and especially during the troubles of war are never easy and in the May of nineteen forty three due to the downfall of the fascist government ending the Pact of Steel that had originally been signed between Mussolini and Hitler the two sides found themselves in conflict with one another. Skirmishes had quickly turned into a deadly conflict.

It was during such a gun fight that Wilhelm saw his friend Antonio injured in a volley of cross fire, the Italian being wounded by a stray bullet to the hip. Helplessly Wilhelm watched his one-time friend being helped to safety by his comrades.

With the Italians on the run Wilhelm's company searched for survivors amongst the dead and near to the spot where Antonio had been wounded Wilhelm found a silver tobacco tin engraved with the initials *ALC*. He recognised the tin and knew that it belonged to Antonio. Since that fateful day Wilhelm had kept the tobacco tin safe trying every conceivable way to trace his long lost friend.

Through various sources including the Italian press, military records department and searching out old war veterans, Wilhelm had ostensibly time and time again hit a brick wall and yet like a quest not accomplished the tobacco tin burnt a hole in his soul begging that he find the owner.

Three weeks prior to Wilhelm coming in London and quite by chance a reporter with whom he had been corresponding over Antonio sent Wilhelm a copy of an obituary that he had seen concerning the passing of an old Italian soldier who had served in the same campaign.

Giuseppe Rossini had been one of the soldiers who had pulled Antonio clear from the skirmish, but regrettably Rossini was dead. Wilhelm went to the funeral in the village of Brenner on the Italian, Austrian border hoping that Antonio might have been amongst the mourners but his old friend was nowhere to be seen. Another veteran of that era however told Wilhelm that Antonio had survived the war but that the Capella family had suddenly uprooted themselves from the family home and moved to a district somewhere north of Florence.

Armed with the tobacco tin and travelling to Fiesole, north east of Florence, Wilhelm met with the mayor the Sindaco, only the news was not good. Antonio Lorenzo Capella had passed away not long after moving to Fiesole. He was survived by a wife and two daughters. Following his death mother and daughters had moved on once again, moving in with an aunt in Turin.

What he told me next almost swept me off of my feet. Through other sources Wilhelm discovered that one of the daughters had in time had a daughter of her own and had name the child Lola. Asking around it had transpired that the young woman had since moved to London where she ran a small florist shop once owned by the aunt, named *Florrie's Flowers*.

I was in awe of the ninety year old, as spritely as he had been at fifty. I made sure that his order of hot tea was sweet as he asked and that his teacakes were buttered and warm. Adding a complementary plate of biscuits he deserved a few minutes rest and to realise that his long journey had finally come to an end. Being invited to sit at the table he had been glad to offload his tale.

'Lola is only next door,' I said as he sipped his tea 'why did you not go in and see her?'

Reaching down into his coat pocket he took out a blue cloth and gently unfolded the folds revealing an ornate silver tobacco tin. It was slightly dented and scratched as you would have expected after having gone through such a traumatic ordeal. Staring down at the beautifully crafted metal container tin I was amazed that such a precious trinket could have survived and that the man sat opposite me had sacrificed so much of his own life to see it returned, it really was a remarkable tale.

Caressing the metal lid Wilhelm replied. 'Having searched for so many years, I stood out the florist shop ashamed of my actions the day that we fought one another. We were friends Mr Brand and friends should not fight one another, let alone try to kill one another.' He looked at the engraved initials on the lid. 'Having learnt that Antonio had passed away I am not sure how or what I should say to his grand-daughter. I came into the café to find my courage again.'

Danielle who had been watching and listening was fascinated by the old soldier. She came over asking if we wanted anything else, really it just an excuse to be involved although I didn't mind because she used to people coming into the café, seeking help. Wilhelm smiled at her encouragingly and explained that he had a great grand-daughter her age who gave him so much pleasure. Danielle apologised when called over to another table where she had to serve a lady who had spilled her tea.

'She is so like Lillie, so young and always smiling. War is a terrible thing but if it meant that young people like Lillie and Danielle could live free then I suppose it was worth it.'

Wilhelm suddenly placed his hands over mine.

'I am ashamed now that I once fought against any man, I alone your nation Mr Brand. When I look at Danielle I am guilt-ridden that I could have caused so much suffering. I wonder how my daughter, grand-daughter and great grand-daughter think about what I have done. I wonder at how things might have been different had we won the war, perhaps not like it is today.' He watched as Danielle dealt with the spill.

'You are lucky to have such wonderful members of staff.'

'At times Wilhelm I look upon Danielle as my daughter.'

He pulled his hands back from mine 'such a beautiful sentiment and such things missing in so many ways these days.'

I found it hard to believe that a man as gentle and understanding as Wilhelm Wendell could hold a rifle in anger. He was so mild mannered man, polite and knowledgeable. Instinctively I knew Lola would like him also. I asked Wilhelm to excuse me for a moment whilst I took myself next door. He seemed hesitant that I should go but accepted that the moment would have to be faced.

When Lola walked through the door of the café the pallor on Wilhelm's face changed as though he had seen a ghost arrive.

'Mein gott Fraulein you have your grandfather's looks.'

Like the gentleman that he was he stood and kissed the back of Lola's hand expressing how proud he was to meet her. I let Lola occupy my seat so that they could talk as I re-joined Danielle at the coffee counter only this moment belonged to Wilhelm and Lola and nobody else.

His narrative did not include the moment when her grandfather had been shot and injured but I could tell the mood was solemn when he handed over the tobacco tin along with the blue cloth. Watching I saw Lola tenderly rub the metal lid as though she was stroking her grandfather's heart. Moments later neither had a dry eye. United in grief, the memory and friendship they each accepted his passing. As soon as the last customer departed I locked the door so that neither could be disturbed. Ten minutes after locking the door I was asked to join them at their table where Lola showed me the tin. I didn't let on that I had already seen it.

'It's really beautiful Spencer it belonged to my grandfather.'

Handling the metal container as though it were made of glass I asked if I could open the lid. Inside the tobacco was still dry, untouched, half a century old and still held a familiar odour of crushed, dried tobacco rich leaves. The smell was almost captivating.'

'I know somebody who would also like to see this...'

'My mother.' Lola agreed and so did Wilhelm.

He was calmer now that the ordeal of handing over the tin had been fulfilled.

'Your grandfather and I would sit and smoke his tobacco in the evenings as we watched the sun go down. He would love to hear the birds sing in the trees. They were our happiest memories in a war that was so futile. They are the moments I treasure and I feel are captured within the tin.'

Lola quickly closed the lid so that not too many escaped.

Later as arranged we met Wilhelm at the Corinthian Hotel where he was staying. Lola suggested that we dine out at a favourite Italian restaurant that she knew not far from Covent Garden. Sitting beside her the meal was initially charged with emotion as Lola's mother talked with Wilhelm wanting to know everything about her father and making it known that she held no animosity or ill-feeling towards the old soldier. She was indeed indebted to him for making such a long and arduous journey.

Sipping from the rim of my brandy glass I watched the three of them converse with one another like old friends sitting beneath an olive tree and watching the sun go down enjoying a smoke. Sat beside Lola I sensed an accord had descended and that at last the souls of the dead could rest easy.

Around midnight we saw Wilhelm safely back his hotel where we bade him good night and farewell as he was due back in Germany the next day. Before we left he told us that a great weight had been lifted from his mind and that hopefully at last he could sleep in peace.

We never did hear from Wilhelm Wendell ever again not that any of us really expected too. His last undertaking had accomplished and now it was time that he spent the rest of his life with his own family. As Spencer Brand I felt it an honour that I had known Wilhelm and would always regard him as a gentle soldier with a heart of gold.

Occasionally over dinner when I am alone with Lola we mention Wilhelm and we are all proud to call him our friend. The tobacco tin has pride of place in Lola's front room and sits beside a framed photograph of her grandfather.

I caught myself looking at the table where he had sat a couple of weeks on recalling the day that the humble man from Germany had visited thinking how his brief stay had made us all realise how lucky we all were. Lola had researched the campaign where her grandfather had been shot but there was no mention of either her grandfather of Wilhelm not that expected the record to know either of them.

Life can move as such a rapid pace that at times it is easy to pass a stranger in the street and know nothing about them, about the history that surrounds them or what they have to tell. We take so much for granted, such as watching a sunset or sharing a smoke under an olive tree. Precious moments that are so easily forgotten and yet can be one man's lifelong burden. Looking at where Wilhelm had sat I bowed my head forward and in my head recited the words *'Rest in peace Antonio Lorenzo Capella and one day in the not too distant future, you will no doubt share another ounce of tobacco with a very dear friend named Wilhelm Wendell.'*

Hitting the Wall

London is considered by many to be the hub, a central point of the land, full of posh houses, expensive restaurants, hotels and brightly lit theatres, pavements laden with gold and a city of hope. Teenagers from all over travelled to the capital expecting to find and make their fortune believing that opportunity would come knocking around each and every corner.

Let me put you wise, no pavement slab is impregnated with gold and many that remain where tarmac has not replaced stone are badly cracked and in need of repair. True, there are some very rich entrepreneurs around but the number is a closely guarded secret and rare that you come into contact with one. Long gone are the days of fashionable long hair, wide bottom trousers and free speech. Music has become a monotone of disillusioned, lyrical rubbish and art changes style so fast that it is impossible to see through the fog od impressionism and abstract. I remember walking out of a job Friday only to apply and start a new position Monday without references, a curriculum vitae or any knowledge of what was required.

Nowadays ego gender celebrities top the bill and have a cult-like following, although I would ask is it good to become so mesmerised that you possibly lose all identity yourself. There is however a growing band of men, women and in some cases young adults who struggle to get any recognition. I am of course talking about artists and writers. In a world of marketed commercial trends, written words tend to be provocative, pornographic and bed hopping to satisfy a craving, whereas art is in some cases as seedy and more distasteful. I have seen some examples so bad that they should never see the light of day. Society however is changing by the minute, the day even the year and you can call me what you like, only remember that I see all who walk through the café door.

Alfred Wilson is a scenic artist and writer, a paid up member of this struggling species. A jovial man normally who I have known for quite some time, in fact we went to school together. Alfie to his friends has always attacked adversity with an unwavering upbeat attitude believing that chance will bring down bureaucracy and red tape should be confined to an electrician's tool box.

Alfie would draw and paint from the heart, not be influenced by society or trend and he could be found sitting on the bank whichever side the sun was setting. By night when it was darker he could found writing prose or thin king of new ideas for a best-seller. Many that knew Alfie would say that his life was idyllic and like Danielle was another who referred to me as Spence.

We were well into the autumn season with the winter months knocking hard on our heels as the weather outside grew more grey, wet, cold and gloomy as the daylight hours began to fade fast. A regular throughout the spring and summer I had not seen Alfie around for a good three or four months. I did ask around but nobody else had neither heard nor caught sight of him. Then like a leaf falling from a tree he breezed in through our door one Monday morning promptly ordering a bacon sandwich and a mug of tea as though his last visit had been only yesterday.

'Have you been putting down plans for the hibernation period?' I quipped as Alfie took the table nearest the counter.

'No I've been busy,' he replied warming his hands between the tops of his legs.

'Then you must have hit the big time!'

Alfie looked at me as though I was mad.

'Rumour says there's opportunities out there for the taking only I've never come across any!'

We heard the bell ring out back and Danielle shot off to collect Alfie's bacon sandwich.

'Well then, where have you been hiding yourself?'

'Travelling,' he replied biting into the bacon and buttered bread. I watched his expression change as the food filled his stomach. 'I was fortunate to pick up a contract to go to some of those exotic locations where I could draw and paint, then write about the place that I was visiting. In the evening I would drink wine and into the bargain get paid for every minute that I was away. It sounds great until you crash land again when you return home. Suddenly the landscape doesn't look half as attractive and neither do the natives. Basically Spence my old mate you hit a wall.'

I had heard others mention this condition in business although this didn't sound like Alfie, he was always so upbeat about everything.

'So what comes next?' I asked.

'I am not sure. I told the company that had offered me the commission that I needed to deal with some personal issues back at home but that I would be back on the job within a couple of days. They appeared understanding although I feel they might already have a replacement in mind in case the ideas have dried up.'

On the table beside his mug was his doodling pad which Alfie was never without. Unusually it was still closed. Drumming the table top with his fingers I sensed that something was wrong. When the drumming stopped Alfie spoke. 'Do you know Spence, you're a lucky so and so. You always said that you would never amount to much and yet here you are the owner of a busy café. I envy you, your roots and the man with a permanent smile.'

'Get away,' I announced 'what do I know Alfie, I've only ever been as far as the Scrubs and I owe a mortgage on this place. Unlike you, you've been places and have a nice flat down by the south bank.'

'And you think that my lifestyle has made me the richer,' he fired back 'I've got blisters on my feet bigger than your current buns from all the travelling. Some might see it as fun but living out of a suitcase or my rucksack can quickly dull the initiative and I'll tell you this Spence not every place that I have seen has blue skies and stars out at night.'

'Come on Alfie some must have been mystical, some magical.'

I took my coffee over to his table and asked if I could look inside the drawing book. There were sketches of the Taj Mahal, the Eiffel Tower, the Grand Canal in Venice, the Colosseum, the Pyramids and Sphinx at Gaza and the Statue of liberty. None of them mere schoolboy dreams, instead places that Alfie had seen and written about.

He dismissed the sketches as just memories. 'That's is but a fraction of where I have travelled. My problem now is that I am beginning to miss home and I've hit the wall on my latest psychological journey.' Alfie chewed on his last mouthful of the sandwich 'and that Spence could be a barrier too far!'

And just like when we had been kids at school he sat and licked the sauce and grease of the bacon from the ends of his fingers. I watched until he had finished, Alfie did sound like he had a problem.

'Can't you take a break and do your own thing, something that might not pay, but be just as rewarding, maybe then you'll recharge the old batteries!'

Alfie picked up his mug and shook his head.

'Professional etiquette Spence old chap and my passport is my bible. I need to keep the bugger stamped to prove my worth or without it I would be a has-been. Tourism is multi-national industry that has become the mecca of all trade and the exchange of money made each year is phenomenal. Tourism doesn't just bring in millions, but billions.'

'Why not go and lie around, lapping up the sun and do the least amount possible, surely you could do quite easily Alfie.' It was unlike me to offer such bad advice, but my old friend was looking for a solution to his problem.

'Fabricate the evidence you mean,' he laughed 'I've done that, only at some point some bugger is going to read what I have written and look at the pictures that I have produced and say *'hold on a minute, this place is nothing like what the writer or artist depicts'*. Non-compliance of the small print in a contract is serious business Spence and I could end up losing everything.'

'Surely things and places do change, but the natural features will always be there regardless.'

'Yes of course,' he replied 'the odd cave, rock formation, sandy bay and church never really change, not unless an earthquake hits but for once I would like to write about London, Bath, Brighton and even Edinburgh. Far flung assignments are great but there comes a time when you need to head in a different direction.'

I could see that we weren't getting anywhere fast. Looking at the mural on the back wall Alfie was impressed. 'That's good who did that?'

'A man with a calling from the valleys, he goes by the name of Thomas 'rainbow' Jones.'

Alfie nodded 'Thomas is talented and he tells his story well through his painting.'

'He's due in soon, I could introduce him if you like?'

Alfie saw Danielle refill the cake stand with a freshly homemade lemon drizzle.

'Cut me a slice of that and you can call who you like!'

I wasn't sure that lemon drizzle and bacon would mix well but Alfie Wilson always had a cast iron constitution. Danielle cut him a generous slice as he was an old school friend.

I would have joined him but I was on a diet and losing weight wanting to show the adoption board that I was in good shape to take on a child. Lola and I were going through the administrative process of filling in forms recording our reasons why we wanted to adopt little Amelia. We realised that the journey ahead could be rocky but we were determined to succeed and keeping healthy was part of the plan.

Outside the window the weather had squalled into dark grey clouds with the threat of rain although it was normal for the time of the year. Looking out Alfie was still insistent of being in London.

As he consumed the lemon drizzle I continued looking through his sketch book.

'You know Alfie London is full of history and although times are changing we march on regardless. Why don't you pen something about the old place only we could do with a fresh approach and not just the normal blurb but something really new, something that even we Londoners don't know about. You were always good at ferreting so find something unusual and bring us up to date. Dan Brown did a damn fine job with Paris and Rome, so why not Alfie Wilson reinvent London.'

'Does it really need reinventing?' he asked.

'It does if you are our age. This place had a magic back in the last century only somewhere down the trail some of it has been lost and the youngsters of today are fast losing touch with what's important. Maybe you could tell them and I am sure that there's an agent out there who would support such a project.'

Alfie scrapped the last of the cake from his plate before he spoke.

'Do you know Spence, you're right. Going away did you some good, you found your enthusiasm for life!'

With that Alfie paid for his tea, bacon sandwich and drizzle cake. He scooped up his doodling book and left but not before I had time to reply.

'Come around again soon and I might also have some news!'

Watching him run off up the road I wondered how long it would be before we saw him again. Later that evening going through the forms for the adoption board I told Lola about Alfie Wilson.

'You sound a little jealous of his adventures,' she remarked as she put down her set of guidelines.

'No, that wasn't the life for me although we always knew that Alfie would go far as he had itchy feet all through his school years.'

'And now,' she asked 'do you feel trapped with the café?'

This was out of the blue and unexpected. I wondered if this adoption was causing some apprehension.

'Never, there's no place that I would rather be than here with you, although we do need to discuss our future if we're serious about adopting a little girl.'

My response brought back the smile that I had grown to love and she knew that I meant every word. My commitment was unprecedented although we did need to have an in-depth discussion about the future, our future. Wandering the world was a nice fantasy although in reality being grounded was just as important. I was happy and content just as I was with Lola and in the little red café. Turning over to page thirty six we were nearing the end. Later sharing a bottle of good wine I realised that Alfie had not met Thomas 'Rainbow' Jones.

A week later the door of the café opened and in walked Alfie Wilson. The weather was better than his last visit and so was his mood. He ordered two rounds of sausage and egg sandwiches and a mug of strong hot tea, inviting me over to his table to join him again.

'So… how did the research go,' I asked.

'Better than I thought it would.' He exclaimed. 'I thought that I would start at the bottom and work my way up only it seemed like the sensible thing to do. My quest began at the Burwood Junction Cemetery where I found a headstone belonging to one Thomas Oliver Barringer who passed away in 1779. Reading the inscription he was a man of incredible history: *'A rascal and a bounder of the highway that met his match!'*

'Barringer was a highwayman?' I felt my jaw drop.

'A reprehensible thief who I understand had an eye for the ladies, enjoyed good living and French brandy.'

'Much like you Alfie.'

He frowned although laughed 'maybe two out three although I'm no thief.'

'So…' I said 'going by his epitaph he led an adventurous sort of existence?'

'He sure did, robbing the rich although not quite to give to the poor but them inn keeper, he's a good subject upon which to begin a new book.'

'How does that tie in with London and promoting the capital?'

'I can make a connection between the highwayman and our present government. Looking back, ignorance has sired thieves and rascals, only as the public we're the victims!' Alfie dipped his bread and butter into the egg that had run from his sandwich. He had never minced his words which is what made him a fine writer. The same as he objected to paying taxes believing that the Inland Revenue and the like were the modern day highwaymen.

'So where do you go from the cemetery?'

'The Registrar of Births and Deaths, the press archives. At one time Barringer was the talk of the town and almost as famous as Dick Turpin. Rumour has it that Thomas Barringer's loot still lies buried somewhere in the cemetery near to where he was born.'

I could see a treasure hunt emerging. There was nothing like the lure of treasure to get people fired up and tourists would flock to London just to hear about Thomas Oliver Barringer.

'Surely the treasure hunters have already dug up everything that they were allowed to overturn?'

Alfie held up a single finger. 'Ah that my good Spence, is the beauty of this tale, who really knows. It has been two hundred and forty three years since the old boy staged his last robbery. Myths and legends were made famous around such people. I'm just exploring the myth and adding my slant.'

Alfie was right. Stories did get distorted down the decades and what he said was true it could all be a myth. Thomas Barringer could well have squandered his money on fine brandy, women and good living. I envisaged another bestseller before the end of the year.

'And what about the contract with the travel firm?'

'Somebody else, younger and with more enthusiasm can take that on. I want to stay closer to home.'

'So once you've laid the bait, what happens next?' I asked.

'I continue writing about the legend of Thomas Oliver Barringer. As you said on my last visit Spence, invent some of the legend only who out there can disprove it. I doubt Burwood Council will be singing my praises as they could have a problem with treasure hunters visiting the cemetery, but I am sure that the pubs, bed and breakfast houses, hotels and restaurants nearby will do a roaring trade. In an unconventional way I am writing a travel guide about a traveller, only with a twist. I like it!'

'And pictures, what about the artwork?'

'I'll produce my own. Who knows I might sell a few on the side.'

'So does this mean that you're finally going to be putting down roots here?'

Pushing aside his empty plate he reached for his tea.

'Oddly enough I had a call from a friend last night, who is currently in Peru. He thinks he has a link to a story about some Inca gold and he's asked for my help. Initially i refused but the pay is good and I'm catching a plane out there tonight.'

'And the highwayman, what about the travel guide?'

'Thomas has been buried for over two centuries and waiting for his story to be told. He can wait a little longer and whilst I'm in Peru I can add to the myth. Some of the best pirates were from this mainland and treasure will always be around!'

He promised that he'd keep in touch although you never knew with Alfie Wilson quite where his feet would land. He did write his travel guide along with others and they are on the book shelves. Whether or not what he has written is true, maybe you can tell me.

I never did see Alfie ever settling down, but I was glad that in part I had helped him get beyond the wall and help find that lost fire in his belly. Alfie had a passion for adventure and travel and it would take a lot to stop him.

I did read that Burwood Council had hired the services of a security firm to help keep the cemetery from being invaded, but that as predicted by Alfie other local amenities had profited from the influx of visitors, live ones of course.

Into the second week of his absence Ted delivered a postcard from Peru upon which was a short message: *'Inca's were a devious lot although nothing found but Barringer has let me into a secret!'*

I picked up a copy of *'The Lost Mausoleum'* by Alfie Wilson and read it from cover to cover. It was mysterious, intriguing and beguiling. The illustrations were from paintings that Alfie had produced although quite where he found the time to do them intrigued me.

On reflection I saw little difference between tourism and treasure hunting, it just depended upon which way you started the journey.

On his return from Peru I did tell Alfie about Lola.

He met her and was genuinely impressed that I had settled at last. I wondered if Alfie would ever make the same commitment only he would know that. As for Peru there was no treasure just relics but Alfie was already searching the cemeteries for more headstones. Still it date stamped another visit in his bible.

This story is almost done although I thought you'd be interested to know that Alfie is now in darkest Africa researching the treasure belonging to King Solomon. He has the bit between his teeth although if all else fails I did hear that the treasure belonging to Thomas Oliver Barringer is still missing.

Danielle's Dilemma

Danielle and Martyn were now sharing a flat together just around the corner from the café and I had at last moved out of my mum's house moving in with Lola and sharing her terraced two bedroomed house. The night that Alfie Wilson had left for Peru, Lola and I had talked over the future, discussed our dreams and aspirations agreeing that our main priority was seven year old Amelia Hart.

Lying in bed awake that night I had watched the stars move slowly across the sky realising just how lucky I had been. At forty two I had my own business, a beautiful woman and the possibility of adopting an equally adorable little girl. Seeing a shooting cross the cosmos I considered that it was time that I made an honest woman of Lola Francine Maria Capella.

Waking a little later than usual I was in time to hear Lola singing in the bathroom. I sat up in bed and knew that there was no better time than the present.

Leaving Vera in charge I took myself down to Convent Garden just after nine to purchase an engagement ring. With Lola in the shower I was able to size her ring finger with another ring that she kept in the drawer of her dresser. On the way back to the café I booked a table at Lola's favourite Italian restaurant and set the stage for Wednesday night. All that I needed now was for Lola to accept my proposal.

Looking back over the year the café had seen a lot of extremely interesting people walk through the door. Many had heard of our reputation coming in to sample our menu whereas others had come because they needed help.

The changes that had occurred to us as a unit were hardly noticeable but Vera and I were delighted when Martyn and Danielle had found a one bedroom flat so that they could be together. We have witnessed the change in Danielle, not just in her development growing into a beautiful young woman but the way that she had flourished since she had met Martyn.

There were times when I thought that he did well in coping with her unpredictability as Danielle could be a hare-brained livewire, but her innocence was priceless at times. Despite them living under the same roof I still felt responsible for her looking upon her as a surrogate daughter.

Over the year there had been many memorable moments of tears, laughter and reflection and a good many souls had touched my heart in a way that I would never have expected. Lola brought a love to my love that I never thought possible and little Amelia had made me realise just how much I wanted her to be part our family. There were others like Mary, Thomas, Robert Styles and Stephanie Steele, each as important as the other that made my life so different. I had met ghosts and a people with such drive that I could admire their tenacity, Adela and Jakub Moravek and Wilhelm Wendell, incredible ordinary people, the champions of our world. With the adoption papers back at social services Lola and I were now playing a waiting game.

Many of you will say what about Vera the backbone of our café and of course I could not cope without her influence. She did the most amazing things in the kitchen and without the least amount of fuss. With my mother's help the two of them had organised my move into Lola's house, much to her amusement although I believe the urgency to have me out was so that they could stay out late when they went to the bridge club.

Every day, every moment I thought about Amelia Hart and what she might be doing at the children's home. I wondered if she thought about us wondering if we would ever return as we had promised. Either Lola or I telephoned every day to enquire how little Amelia was doing and Miss Johnson as polite as always was forever encouraging stating that as soon as she had any notification regarding the adoption we would be the first to know. Mary helped, praying for us every night.

I know that I am rambling on but every so often it does the soul good to let it all out. I realise that my life is no different to thousands of others but because we get so engrossed in our own troubles we often miss what is going on around us. When Danielle arrived early for work the next morning with her hands thrust tight inside her pockets rather than holding onto Martyn I sensed an atmosphere. It was to be expected and in the throes of a new relationship they were going to feel exposed at times. Looking at Danielle first then Martyn I felt sorry for them.

The normal routine would be that Martyn would join Vera for a cuppa and once her coat was hung on the peg out back Danielle would join me beside the Fracino Contempo preferring a cappuccino to tea from the kettle.

'Lovers tiff...' I enquired offering a smile as we stared out of the window 'only you've a face like a pair of old leather boots that need new soles!'

Danielle who was always so vivacious and upbeat about everything was definitely down in the dumps. She shrugged her shoulders looking ahead at the traffic going past.

'Just things Spence, things that will probably work out right in the end.'

At forty two she might have considered me past it or not yet wise enough to help but I felt that 'fatherly' approach was required. I placed the cappuccino beside her elbow and nudged her arm.

'You know I am the soul of discretion when it comes to my staff and especially you.'

Danielle sighed long and hard a clear indicator that something was troubling her. I didn't believe that it was just a lovers spat. Taking her coffee mug in both hands she opened up.

'We were awake most of the night going around and around in circles without reaching a solution. After so many hours without sleep the talk got more heated we tried to help one another!'

It happens when two souls lying beside one another cannot see eye to eye, although taking a step back the answer often presents itself.

'Do you want to talk about it?' I asked.

There was only three of our regular customers in that morning and they quite happy talking amongst themselves. We tucked ourselves behind the cake cabinet where we could not be overheard.

'You know Danielle argument never really resolve anything they just prolong the hurt. Somewhere there has to be a compromise before you see no way back. It was like that with marriage only I couldn't see it at the time. Life is like an acorn growing into maturity to become a tree.'

Danielle looked straight at me as she contemplated her response.

'Then Martyn and me, we're stuck somewhere halfway up the trunk Spence, only at the moment we're sitting on different branches.'

The metaphors were flowing thick and fast for such an early hour. Danielle had blossomed and the change was very noticeable. Looking at her then I wondered if she was too much for Martyn to handle.

'Are you pregnant?' I whispered.

Danielle squeezed her eyes shut. I put my arm around her shoulder and pulled her close to my chest. Sometimes you need to let the other person absorb your strength and have them know that you are there for them.

'You know it's really not the end of the world,' I said. 'You have Martyn, Vera and me to help if you need us and then there's Lola and Mary next door. In times of trouble Danielle you need friends!'

Danielle squeezed tight as she battled with her inner thoughts.

'That's the issue here Spence I'm not entirely sure!'

At last the crux of their problem and so easily resolved.

'There's a quick and easy test that will tell you either way!' I suggested.

'A woman knows these things Spence.' It was first time that I had ever heard Danielle refer to herself as a woman.

'And Martyn, what does he have to say on the subject.'

'If I am pregnant he wants me to have the baby.'

I still had my arm around her shoulder for encouragement.

'And what about you?'

'I do and I don't.'

'Because you feel that you're both not ready or that you're concerned about the responsibility that comes with having a young child?' I had lay in bed at night and had the same thoughts about little Amelia.

'A bit of both I suppose.'

Her hands suddenly dropped to her stomach where it was as flat as it had been a month ago. Acknowledging the presence of a new customer I asked that they took a free table and I'd be over for their order in a minute or the specials were on the board.

'If you have Martyn supporting you to have the baby then I think that you're more than halfway there already.'

'You think so?' she said, reaching out for her pen and pad.

'I'll deal with the customer, you stay here!'

I insisted, but Danielle was having none of it. With a half-hearted smile she was already around the other side of the counter and heading for the table. When she came out from the kitchen she had on her coat.

'Do you mind if I pop down to the chemist in the High Street, as you say Spence there's one way to find out for sure?'

Standing before me she was a young woman and not the young teenage girl who had come in for the full-time position as waitress.

'Take all the time that you need. We can manage here for an hour or more. I hit the till and took out a twenty pound note and handed it to Danielle.

'No arguments. Good luck.'

'That's what Martyn just said!'

Equally I felt for Martyn out back in the kitchen. His mind was probably a turmoil of uncertainty, apprehension and misgivings. Whatever the age troubles are always better when halved.

I watched Danielle walk up the road until I could no longer see her then took myself out back to the kitchen to make sure that Martyn was coping although I knew that he had Vera for support.

'Everything alright back here?' I enquired.

Vera looked up from the cooker and Martyn tried putting on a brave face. 'We've been talking,' he said. I asked him to join me out front so that I could watch the front of house.

'There are times in a man's life Martyn when it's best that we're not around and when Danielle returns don't be hurt if she needs Vera rather than you. It's just a woman thing!'

'What do you reckon?' he asked.

I placed an encouraging hand on his shoulder 'It's not what I or Vera thinks but what matters is what you and Danielle think. We are here to help whatever the outcome.'

'Thanks Spencer. I somehow knew that you'd say that. I wanted to tell you myself this morning when we arrived for work but Danielle insisted that I didn't.'

'Women can be strange creatures sometimes Martyn. They need us to be strong for them and yet other times it can take wild horses to knock them down. We could live to be a hundred and still not understand the way their minds tick.'

Twenty minutes later Danielle came back clutching a small patterned paper bag. She winked at me, ignored Martyn then disappeared out back to the staff cloakroom. Making sure that everybody was happy out front we left it ten more minutes before we both went through the swing door.

In the kitchen Danielle was being hugged by Vera. She nodded at us both indicating that all was fine only Danielle needed a few moments to compose herself. We went back out front where I made a coffee and a tea adding extra sugar for Martyn. Several minutes later Danielle poked her head around the door and asked Martyn to join her. Her eyes were still wet where she had been crying.

Leaving the three of them alone I left it a while before I too went through again only this time the atmosphere was much more genial and Martyn and Danielle were hugging one another for comfort. When she saw me standing there she came over and hugged me tight.

'It was negative Spence... negative!' It was barely a whisper.

I gestured for Martyn to join us. Putting a hand on his shoulder whilst holding Danielle I told them. 'When the times right to have a baby then you'll both know and be ready. Why not chalk this up as an experience and for now just enjoy life and being with one another.'

Considering the stress that had been involved plus the lack of sleep I gave them the rest of the day off going next door to see if around lunchtime Mary could help out in the café.

Locking the door around four as the last customer paid and said goodbye, I sensed a calm in the café again. In the kitchen Vera called me through where she had made a pot of tea.

'I suppose that was bound to happen, she said as dried two mugs.

'They're young and they will make mistakes, we all did!'

She smiled as she added milk to the mugs 'In a way I was a little envious only I would have liked to have told Cyril that I thought I was pregnant.'

We shared a brew chatting and catching up. Although I should have left it until I had seen Lola I discreetly showed Vera the ring that I had purchased. Vera said that it was perfect.

'It's about time you settled down again,' she said 'Lola is a good woman and she will set you straight once and for all.' Like your favourite aunt she kissed me on the cheek and hugged me tight. It was definitely a day for tactile emotions. 'Get it right on the night and you'll make an excellent couple.'

When Vera left and I was alone I felt shattered, emotionally drained. It was the first time that I had ever seen Danielle upset and I couldn't say that I liked it. I wondered how I would feel if we were successful in adopting Amelia how I would cope if she came home with a similar problem although smiling to myself there would be Lola and she'd sort the situation and me.

And Wednesday, well I was a bag of nerves all day and as much as I tried to enjoy the meal it kept getting stuck in my throat. When the waiter cleared away the main course I could wait no longer. In front of a packed restaurant I went down on one knee and asked Lola to be my wife. To the rapture of cheers and applause and a complimentary bottle of champagne from the restaurant owner Lola agreed. I am the luckiest man alive.

We have almost come to the end of this chapter although I feel that I can't leave you wondering but that I should tell you that in not too many years from now Danielle and Martyn moved out of the one bedroom flat acquiring a slightly bigger place with two bedrooms as they needed the extra bed for a baby. A girl that looked like her dad but had her mums temperament. You see things do work out in the end just as nature intended.

There was one more surprise before the week was out and it came Friday afternoon when I wasn't expecting it. We had shut the café when Mary came running over and banged on the window insisting that I went next door to the florist. I raced next door thinking the worst.

When I arrived Lola was on the phone looking rather tense. She gestured that I went over and held her hand. I could feel her pulse racing. Lola whispered the name Amanda Wilks our contact with the Adoption Service. I could not hear the conversation although every few seconds Lola nodded as though in agreement. The longer they spoke I felt my hopes fading. When Lola ended the call with *'thank you very much for calling and I promise that we'll be there!'* I had no idea where. A moment later she punched the air with delight and pulled Mary and I in close so that we could both share in her joy.

'She's ours… little Amelia can come and live with us!'

We jumped up and down like demented teenagers the tears of joy flowing freely, including my own.

I have never been one to be lost for words, but right there, right then I couldn't think of anything to say, such was my overwhelming jubilation. When we did eventually settle Lola said that we were to meet Amanda Wilks at Saxon House and that once we had signed the release clause on the paperwork we could begin to enjoy life as a family with Amelia as our daughter. Mary looked towards the heavens saying a silent *'thank you'*, pleased that her prayers were still being heard.

'So when can we go to Saxon House?' I asked.

'Anytime this weekend. Amanda Wilks has already been in touch with Miss Johnson and the home will make any necessary arrangements their end. We have to realise however that adoption is a big thing for such a young child, so they will need to determine that Amelia is ready for the transition. We also have to understand that as much as she wants and needs a family Amelia will be leaving the other little boys and girls behind, that alone will be hard only for some time now they have been her family.'

If I could have adopted every one of the children I would have, but I felt in my heart that once Amelia was in her new home things would get easier.

Watching her discuss the future with Mary I wished that I could have read the thoughts that were going through Lola's mind wondering if she was like me planning ahead. At home that evening we searched the property papers for a bigger house only it was wise to consider all options, just in case.

Before I fell asleep that night I had one last thing left to do. I prayed giving thanks. Thanks for having made things right between Danielle and Martyn and thanks for giving us little Amelia. Thanks for Lola accepting my proposal and thanks for getting me through a week of surprises, drama and uncertainty. Looking up at the stars I would never again take anything for granted although I did believe in miracles.

Fate and Destiny

Armed with a list of properties to view over the weekend and the officialdom of the adoption out of the way we arrived early at Saxon House to collect Amelia Hart and Angus the brown teddy. Parking the car near to the front entrance the butterflies were going wild in our stomachs. What kept us together was knowing that there was little girl inside probably feeling just the same.

During the night I had woke several times in a panic wondering if I had everything ready for her arrival but lying beside me Lola was already awake. She was normally the ultimate in calm and restraint although I know that the butterflies were going just as crazy for her. We had been told that neither of Amelia's parents had wanted the baby and that at three months she had been taken by Social Services. It was a heart-breaking start for somebody so little. Around three we were downstairs having a cup of soothing tea.

'Do you think Amelia will like it here?' she asked.

'I think she'll positively love it!'

'Then why couldn't you sleep?'

'Because I'm too excited. I have always wanted a daughter and now at last I am going to have one.' Lola kissed the side of my neck and made me shiver.

We talked not returning to bed seeing the sun come up making plans of all the places that we wanted to take Amelia, although first we had to go and collect her.

About to knock on the door of the home Lola suddenly turned to me.

'I think I'm going to explode,' she expressed.

Taking her hand in mine I smiled encouragingly. When the door opened we were greeted by a beautiful little face accompanied by a very smart looking brown teddy bear. Amelia ran into Lola's outstretched arms, both crying tears of joy. She asked if Angus could come as well. In the back ground Miss Johnson and Amanda Wilks stood watching knowing that the decision to say yes to adopt had been the right one.

'Only if Angus can share your bed at night,' I replied to which she nodded enthusiastically. 'In which case Angus had best pack his bag as well!'

Amelia hugged and kissed Miss Johnson, thanked her for looking after her and Angus, doing the same to Amanda Wilks. She looked around to see if any of the other children were about but the staff had them occupied elsewhere to save any embarrassing or distressing scenes. We thanked them both and invited them to tea one weekend to see that Amelia had settled in her new home.

Carolyn Johnson promised to visit. She gave Amelia one last hug and told her that she was to look after Angus and make sure that he eat his greens. Picking up her suitcase and rucksack they both seemed very light.

Lola settled Amelia into the child seat in the back of the car and Angus sat on her lap. As we drove out through the gate I sensed that Amelia might be taking one last look slightly apprehensive and saddened that she had not said goodbye to her roommates. Lola looked in the rear view mirror then winked at me to signal that everything was okay. On the journey back home we heard Amelia telling Angus that they were going on a big adventure. Amelia could not have been more right.

Pulling up outside of the terraced house we felt the butterflies reappear, this was going to be a big moment for all three of us, four if you included Angus. Taking hold of Amelia's hand Lola made her put the key in the lock and push open the door as I retrieved the suitcase and rucksack.

Standing on the threshold Amelia with Angus tucked under arm stood with her mouth slightly open.

'Am I really going to live here?' she asked.

'Yes,' I replied 'this is where we are all going to live.'

Lola crouched low so that she was level with Amelia. Taking Angus from under her arm Lola whispered in the bear's ear. Moments later she nodded and gave Angus back. *'Angus say's to tell you that this is your new home and that he would like to stay, as long as you do!'* Amelia too whispered in the bear's ear stating that as they were friends he had to stay as well.

That single, but so important exchange clinched it and the hard bit was over. At last we were home, the four of us just as we had dreamed it would be. Weeks of stress ebbed from my shoulders as I watched Lola take Amelia and Angus go up to their new bedroom. In the kitchen down below I could hear them talking as Amelia explored her new surroundings. Am short time after Lola came back alone.

'She wants to unpack her suitcase and put her clothes in the drawers. I think it's good that we give her time to adjust. Amelia feels safe because Angus is there to help!'

'Will she be happy here?'

Overhead we heard her running back and forth along the short landing and into the front bedroom then back to her own.

'She is already happy Spencer, listen!'

We heard footsteps coming back down the stairs and then a face appeared at the kitchen door of course accompanied by Angus.

'Can I still see some of my friends that I had back at the other home?' she asked. I had wondered when she would broach the subject.

'Whenever you like Amelia. We wanted you to live here with us because we love you but that doesn't mean that you cannot see your friends.' Spoken like a true mother Lola was already watching out for her adopted daughter and taking into consideration her feelings.

'Can they come to my birthday party?'

Scooping her up in my arms I responded 'when it gets nearer the time we'll send out the invites and you can decided whether we have a party in the garden or the house, whichever sounds better.' Whispering in Angus's ear he agreed the garden.

'Then it's settled, a garden party we shall have.' I just hoped that the weather stayed fine on the day.

Her little face lit up now that two important issues had been resolved. They had obviously been playing on her mind but once answered the matter was put to the back of her mind. Children were so innocent and objective that they could switch from one subject to another with random ease. Taking herself back up to her bedroom after I had put her down we heard her talking to Angus *do you think that they will like our new home?'*

Lola fell into my waiting arms purring like a cat 'Amelia's already settled.'

Believing that we would get a yes from the adoption agency and the children's home Thomas 'Rainbow' Jones had help decorate Amelia's bedroom and one each of the walls Disney characters complemented the furniture that we had transformed into castles and fairy grottos. On the bed Lola had found the picture of a princess embroidered into the cotton and even the lamp beside the bed was from a well-known fairy story. The room was not only enchanting but welcoming.

Hearing her run about we went up.

'Did you empty your suitcase,' Lola asked to which Amelia showed her the empty case 'and was there enough room in the drawers?'

To show that everything fitted, she pulled open each of the three drawers. I was shocked to see the empty spaces in each but Lola already had a solution in hand. Taking Amelia and Angus over to the bed she sat them on her lap.

'I think later you and I need go to the shops and buy some new clothes don't you. We'll leave daddy here and he can look after Angus. What do you think?'

'I've never been shopping. Do they have teddy shops as well?'

Lola laughed 'maybe although first let's get you sorted and then we'll think about Angus.'

Sitting on her lap Amelia suddenly went quite pensive.

'Can I call you mummy?' she asked.

Lola cuddled her and told her that from now on we were her mummy and daddy. It was another hurdle overcome, but the most important one.

After eating lunch they both went missing for a good three hours that afternoon and came back loaded with bags of all different shapes and sizes. Even Angus had a different scarf to wear. Seeing them unload their purchases we watched Amelia fold her new clothes and spread them across the drawers filling the empty spaces. Lola had been right, a girl could never have enough clothes. Watching them sort the bags I loved them both more than they would ever know although I was determined to show just how much.

Much later I did the washing up whilst Lola bathed Amelia and sometime between eight and night we tucked her up in her new bed with Angus by her side. Lola read her a story as I sat on the toy box and listened. When Amelia could no longer keep her eyes open we waited a few seconds longer until they were shut before we kissed her goodnight then crept down stairs to where I had ready two glasses of wine.

'Here's to the future!' I said as we chinked glasses.

'Should we wait a while before we go looking for a new home?' Lola asked. 'Amelia really likes it here and looking for somewhere new so soon could unsettle her again.'

'There's no rush and besides I think she's set her heart on having the birthday party here.' It was settled, we could leave looking for another time. Like new parents we checked on her several times to make sure that everything was alright more through apprehension than anything else although we need not have concerned ourselves as Amelia was tucked down warm and cosy and sound asleep.

Sitting on the settee Lola had some other news to tell me.

'Mama received word this morning from auntie and the rest of the family in Florence. They can make the wedding.'

'That's good, has she told them about Amelia?' I asked.

'I don't think she has only it's going to be a surprise, a nice big surprise!' It would certainly be that.

Lola laid her head in my lap. 'I would like Amelia to be my bridesmaid.'

I smiled. 'I had already guessed that, she'll be perfect and so made up that you would ask.'

Lola was happy. 'Together with Mary and my cousin Francesca, Amelia will fill the occasion just nicely. It would also show everybody that she is now part of a big family here and abroad.'

We had permission from the children's home and Amelia's school to let her have a few days off so that she could adjust to her new circumstances and surroundings. On Sunday we went to the park and visited Convent Garden, Trafalgar Square and took her see Buckingham Palace. We didn't want to do it all in one go but it was as exciting for us as much as it was for Amelia. In reality we were only doing what most families did at weekends.

Monday morning we took Amelia to work with us much to the delight of Vera, Danielle and Mary, Martyn as expected was pleased to see her although a little reserved. That Monday Amelia spent the day with Lola and Mary arranging flowers and tying ribbons around the pockets of posies. Every so often she would come next door with one of them and take back sandwiches for lunch or a cake for their afternoon tea. With the sounds of laughter and giggles coming from the shop next door I had no concerns knowing that all three were enjoying one another's company.

Finding five minutes to myself I stretched my aching limbs realising that the fresh air and running about in the park had proved that I was not as fit as I thought I was. Clearly I needed to improve my health now that Amelia was around.

*****

I had known Sandra Ellingham from our days spend at Burwood Comprehensive when she had been one of the girls in my form, a stunner then and just as jaw-droppingly attractive now. As a teenager I had tried in vain to find not just the courage but the right words to talk to her and have our association become something more permanent. The problem however was that at that age very few boys were gifted enough to know the right words or have the social skills to make the approach. At the end of our fourth year she suddenly disappeared and I didn't see nor hear of her again, not until she walked into the café that afternoon.

Sandra as I would find out had made good use of her schooling and progressed nicely through a good airline achieving the echelon of a Cabin Services Director. Surprisingly the moment that she walked into the little red café, it was as though we had known one another forever.

'Hello Spencer, long time no see, how are you?' she asked standing the other side of the counter.

'Grand Sandra and yourself, you certainly look good?'

She smiled then shook her head as though she had been expecting some sort of remark.

'You never did come across and talk to me when we were at school, why not?'

I shrugged my shoulders and made a lame excuse.

'It was a boy thing, nothing other than that Communication gets easier as you get older!'

I wasn't telling a lie. I had been a slow starter although now I could talk for England. I was surprised to see that she wasn't wearing an engagement or wedding ring. Reading my thoughts she held up the left hand.

'I did give it a try once but it wasn't for either of us, so we decided to part before the mud-slinging party got under way. We still see each other occasionally although generally as we pass through the departure lounge. Terry is a pilot for another airline.'

'So what brings you to this neck of the wood, I thought that you'd be grabbing a coffee in Covent Garden or some other up market coffee shop.'

Looking around she heard what I had said but was admiring the interior.

'This is so much better than those over-priced hyped up establishments. Your café...' she paused selecting the right tribute 'it has a heartbeat that makes you feel welcome!'

'Thanks, it's never stopped beating not since I bought it.'

Under her long coat she was wearing her uniform.

'You going on or off duty?'

Sandra hesitated before replying 'in between.'

It seemed a long way from any airport including the dockland airport.

'In between?' I prompted.

'Meaning that I am neither here nor there!'

Her response was a little puzzling but I guessed that she had a reason for being between flights.

Our normal afternoon trade was mainly the elderly, men and women who wanted some fresh air, to get away from the tedium of staring at four walls and enjoyed the company of others. On a Monday afternoon the ones that came in had just left the bingo session which had been held at the nearby village hall adjacent to St George's Church.

'If you're stopping I suggest that you pick a table quick only we're likely to get a rush in here any minute from now!'

Sandra thought I was joking until a few oldies started arriving.

'Do you have time to share a coffee with me... my treat before the masses arrive?' her expression alone enticing me over to her table.

I agreed placing two cups under the Fracino Contempo. Taking them across to the table Danielle took charge of the counter.

'Thanks Spencer, I could do with the company!' She had chosen a table near to the counter in case I was needed.

'I especially like your mural, it brings the outside in without losing any charm.' From where we sat she could see the photo of Thomas. 'Is that the artist?'

'He goes by the name of Thomas 'Rainbow' Jones only he would tell you in person that his fingers do all the work and his heart has the ideas.

Sandra nodded. 'I thought I recognised him, his photo was in one of our in-flight magazines.'

It didn't surprise me, Thomas's reputation was fast growing and his name was on a good many lips here and abroad.

'You always said that one day you would own your own business, I thought you would.'

It was pleasing to hear somebody appreciate our café and the effort that we all put into it. We tried our best to make everyone welcome, give good service and offer the best food for miles around.

I couldn't help but notice how she had developed into a fine looking woman when she removed her long coat and uniform jacket.

'And you've done well for yourself.'

To my surprise she shook her head and dismissed the compliment.

'The uniform makes the job look glamorous although underneath the façade there's a lot of tough times flying.' I sensed an immediate betrayal of confidence in the tone of her voice.

'So what brings you back to this neck of the woods?'

Now would be a good point in the story to explain that although I had never asked Sandra out on a date, with a few others we had skipped school taken in an afternoon matinee at the local cinema and watched a film that none of us really understood. Our undoing had ended quite abruptly when on one particular jaunt we left the cinema early only to bump into the school secretary who had been down to the bank to top-up the petty cash. Sitting opposite I wondered if Sandra remembered that occasion.

'My mum still lives around the corner and I promised that I would call in today, only I forgot that she goes to bingo.'

I recalled Sandra's mum, a tallish lady with fine features and long dark black hair. She had been present when the headmaster had called me into his office to ask about our afternoon spent at the cinema. I remember getting a long detention only I was never party to what punishment Sandra received. Life in those days was so much easier than today.

Like Alfie Wilson, Sandra must have seen a lot of the world. 'I expect that you've seen nearly everything that there is to see?'

'More or less although after a while the tedium of going places tends to blur into insignificance and flying just becomes a job, something that you have to do to pay the mortgage and live.' She was about to dunk her biscuit when instead she stopped 'there are times when I could flip a coin and change everything.'

'Doing what instead?'

'I'm not really sure although it might be fun finding out.'

It then that I heard the alarm bell ring inside my head.

'I'm forty two just recently engaged and Lola and I have just adopted a little girl!'

Sandra laughed. 'Just like school Spencer, you were always quick to defend your corner. I wasn't suggesting that you come with me, I was just advocating the possibility of exploring beyond the inside of an airplane cabin.'

'But the world's your oyster. Surely all it would take would be a few days away to get some of that good old English fresh air inside you and then you'll be as right as rain to begin again.'

Slipping the moist end of the biscuit in between her lips she waited until it was gone before she replied. She looked at me and studied my face.

'You and me, we're about the same age. Other than my flat, I have nothing else to my name.'

I could see the writing on the wall.

'You know Sandra life is full of surprises and you never quite know what's around the corner!'

I told her how Lola and little Amelia had completely turned around my life around. About the day that Martyn joined us, Mary's dilemma at leaving the convent and about Thomas 'Rainbow' Jones and of course Alfie Wilson who she knew. I wasn't trying to promote life but I wanted her to see that there were other choices only some we couldn't see unless we went searching.

'Are they the women that I saw working next door, they seemed very happy!'

'That's them.'

'You see that's what's missing. I've lost that buzz that we need inside to keep going.'

When I told her about my stay in prison she seemed genuinely shocked. 'You can change anything Sandra but your destiny. What lies ahead has already been pre-planned, like the pilots charts. A little breeze can deviate the course but eventually we have to get back on track and follow the path. I believe that the choices we make, we were meant to make.' It sounded heavy but it was true. My going down on one knee to propose to Lola being one such destiny.

Sandra pursed her lips together then licked them with the tip of her tongue.

'Prison was heavy stuff Spencer and it beats flying around in an Airbus A380. I would never have thought of you as a bad boy. Playing hooky was about our limit!'

It proved my point.

'Fate and destiny Sandra. I was in the wrong place at the wrong time. I am ashamed of my past but my future is now more grounded. Who knows, maybe you've reached that point where you need a change and to head in a different direction.' Apt metaphors but each an option.

She wiped the side of her mouth with the napkin. 'Maybe that's the answer. The crews today, they're all so much younger than me and the women don't need as much war paint as I do!'

'Well you still look damn good to me.'

It wasn't meant as a chat up line, that was twenty odd years too late, merely an observation.

'Thanks Spencer.' Sandra scratched the top of her head. 'Trouble is the war paint isn't the only thing that I need to help me get on board a plane these days. Occasionally I down a drink or two to find the courage to climb the air stairs. Something inside has gone AWOL and I admit flying frightens me.'

On the one flight that I had taken to Scotland to attend a funeral it had scared the hell out of me. Somehow I had to overcome my fear if Lola wanted to take me and Amelia to Florence for a holiday. I had never thought of Sandra Ellingham as either a dipsomaniac or suffering from aviophobia. I sensed that there was more to come.

'And what else ails you?'

She frowned 'are you a clairvoyant when the café shuts?'

'Only when a friend comes calling for help.'

I offered another coffee but she declined stating that she'd have one with her mum later.

'One of my best friends, a member of the cabin crew was killed last year whilst skiing of all things. Amanda was the life and soul of any party and game for anything. She was fearless and would tackle anything, men included but her great love was flying. I can't get it out of my head or my system that I am destined to drop down the same chasm. It's awful Spencer I wake with perspiration running down my back having dreamt that I'm in a plane plummeting back to earth.'

I reached across the table and took her hands in mine.

'That's only to be expected after such a tragedy. It's only a state of mind Sandra and coming to terms with losing Amanda, nothing else.'

'That's why I'm in between. If I don't do something soon I feel that fate and destiny will prevail. I have to make a decision soon about my career not only for my sanity but my mum. She would not be able to cope without me being around. She never tells me although I know but more recently she's also been having bad nights and especially when I'm flying long haul.'

'Mum's can be like that and mine is always fearing that I'll end up inside. Maybe now I have Lola and Amelia to think about those fears will be abated. So what comes next?' I asked.

'I've made a start by getting rid of all the drink. I'm not sure why I came here today, to the café I mean but something drew me this way. I'm pleased that I did come and that I bumped into you again. I suppose I have a decision to make and soon. I need some purpose back in my life after Amanda.'

'You said that you and the pilot were just passing ships in the night, has there been nobody else?' Now I was prying.

'There is although I am not sure that he knows how I feel about him.'

'Then perhaps it's time you told him.' I paused as another lot of pensioners arrived but Danielle had everything under control. 'You've already made changes by getting rid of the drink so why not take a leap of faith and let this man know how you feel about him. One way or another, once said you'll feel better for having let it go.'

She shook her head not deriding me but in admiration.

'You were never this confident at school, maybe things would have been different had you been!'

I doubted it and looking across the table I could never ever see myself with anybody but Lola. Not even my first wife had my heart and soul. Sandra Ellingham had been out of my league, untouchable at school. In a strange way I felt that she still was.

'Do I know the lucky man?'

She shook her head. 'Nobody from school. Sebastian is an orchestral musician. I go and watch him perform as often as I can. He sends me places that I have never been!'

'Then tell him Sandra. Have him know what your heart wants you to say, it really is the only way forward.'

Behind us the bell over the door chimed and in walked a tall dark haired lady a lot older than when I had seen her last. Margaret Ellingham was pleased to see her daughter although Sandra seemed puzzled. 'How did she know that I would be in here?'

'Mum's know everything!'

Margaret Ellingham was a sprightly as when I last saw her although the years had taken their toll much the same as they had with my own mum. Sandra stood, kissed her affectionately on the cheek before introducing me.

'I remember you,' announced Margaret Ellingham *'you was the boy that got my daughter into trouble!'*

Several heads including Danielle's turned and looked my way.

Standing up I frantically explained 'we went to the pictures instead of having geography and history one afternoon!'

It amused Sandra and for the first time I noticed the look in her eye that I remembered seeing when she sat behind me in the English classroom. Her eyes had a sudden sparkle as though somebody or something had switched on a light. I offered them both a drink but Sandra said that they had better be going as she had things to do, I guessed what things. They were about to leave when Margaret Ellingham announced.

'I'm glad that I found you dear, only I had a call yesterday from a man called Sebastian. He wanted to know if you were coming home this week.'

At least I had a name only I didn't know any Sebastian. Sandra kissed me on the cheek told me that she would keep in touch, thanked me for helping and wished me good luck for the future. She left arm in arm with her mum more buoyant and happy than when she had arrived.

Standing behind the counter I explained to Danielle that Sandra Ellingham was an old school friend.

'And it was just for playing truant?' she asked her eyes full of suspicion.

'Just for going to the cinema. Nothing else happened.'

I wasn't sure that Danielle believed me but she was willing to give me the benefit of the doubt.

'She did look nice in her uniform!'

I had to agree Sandra was still stunning and yes she did look nice in the uniform although I didn't think that she would be wearing it for much longer. Destiny still had one more surprise for Sandra Ellingham.

Three weeks later Ted handed me a postcard which had a Canadian postmark. Flipping over to the reverse side I immediately recognised the name of the sender.

The message read: *'With my Cello in Quebec to hear him play. Before we boarded the plane at Heathrow Sebastian proposed and I said yes! I talked with Amanda the other night and she told me that she was really pleased. Still not entirely convinced that you are not a clairvoyant. Lola is a lucky woman and one day I hope to meet Amelia too! Thanks Spencer. I forgive you for getting me into trouble. See you at the wedding. Love to you all. Sandra xx'*

A Night in Accident & Emergency

The rapid development and introduction of modern technology and space travel had arrived so quickly that it caught many of us on the hop and before we realised that it was actually happening. The thought of being able to walk on another planet in our solar system was a boyhood dream for many although as I knew dreams could become a reality.

In some ways and maybe somewhere down the age of computers, cell phones and iPads we had lost an important part of our identity. Values, morals and attitudes had changed which in some ways was sad although inevitable. Change will march on regardless of history and change is inescapable to society or individuals alike.

Many years back my mum had hung up her nurse's uniform and accepted pessimistically that after a lifetime of giving to others there was little else to look forward too unless it was bingo on a Monday and the bridge club which she attended with Vera. Truth was I knew that for two half pennies and nothing more she would have slipped back into that uniform if only for one more shift.

Regulars wearing a similar nursing uniform would often come after a long shift rather than just head home and their bed. Food was energy and they needed both for the following night. Watching them arrive Julia Hornet and Claire Richmond waltzed through the taken tables finding one near the window. They looked tired but in need of refreshment. Preparing two good hot frothy coffees I sent them over with Danielle.

In the kitchen Martyn was helping prepare the breakfasts adding four generous slices of bacon to the pan before skilfully cracking open two eggs for each sandwich. As a café we felt it was our duty to keep our blue angels well-nourished as their days and nights could be arduously long and as a public we demanded a lot from such dedicated individuals.

'Busy night girls?' I called over.

'Was it ever!' they replied in unison.

Danielle arrived with their breakfast order her eyes falling on the uniforms and wondering what she would look like in one. Julia and Claire were not much older than Danielle and instinctively I could tell what they were talking about. As I have said many times in the book change is inevitable. Danielle was young and ambitious. She wanted more than just serving at tables and I was resigned to losing her one day. When she came back to the counter she knew what I was about ask only she got there before I could.

'Don't ask,' was all that she said before she crashed through the swing doors.

Danny Deakin, a colleague of postman Ted came in too after finishing off a night shift at Kings Cross where he worked the sorting office. He was also looking haggard and badly in need of something hot, wet and invigorating. Outing another mug under the Fracino Contempo I pulled the lever down.

'Hi girls,' he greeted as he took the table next to theirs 'what a night I've had how was yours?'

'Busy, although it always is Danny.' Claire added another splash of tomato sauce to the egg of the sandwich.

'What made your night so busy?' Julia asked.

'Staff shortages, holidays and a couple off sick nothing much out of the ordinary. So tell me,' he said 'what cranks did you encounter?'

Julia who had already finished her food answered for them both.

'The shift began with a distraught mother who arrived in toe with a young boy and his sister. She claimed that they had been watching a documentary on Africa only finding a pair of large plastic rings the boy had yanked them down over the younger sister's head. When the mother tried to remove them she couldn't. Thing was the boy had done the same only on himself. They looked like a pair of Masaai warriors as they ran around the department whilst the doctors searched for a way to get them off.'

'So how did they?' I asked leaning over the counter.

'In the end we had to call the fire brigade. They cut them off using their specialist equipment only the plastic had a thin membrane of wire running through the middle and none of our cutters would do the trick.'

229

I made a mental note to check the shed for anything similar in case Amelia developed any ideas or watched any such documentaries.

'Blimey,' said a builder sitting nearby 'I could have done with one of those rings for my old woman, it might stop her snoring at night. When she gets going she sounds like a bull on heat!'

'And how would that help?' asked one of his colleagues.

'She might do me a favour and throttle herself in the process!'

Laughter was a common occurrence in the café and I had never yet stopped a customer from enjoying the moment. It all added to the ambience. When the laughter did subside it was Claire's turn to supplement the report. Looking over to where a pair of young female office workers were enjoying a coffee together she offered a warning.

'Our next admission was a young man with a towel over his privates.'

I noticed that the builders had again stopped eating and their ears pricked and next to me Danielle was listening intently.

'Around eleven a man arrived at the casualty reception holding a towel over the front of his trousers. When the receptionist asked why he needed medical help he showed her. We could hear the laughter from inside the cubicles. When sister went to investigate she brought the embarrassed man through. Initially he looked as fit as a fiddle until the towel was removed.'

'*Did it pop out and scare her!*' called out one of the builders but Danielle told him to be quiet and let Claire finish.

'It scared him more than sister and any of us. You see in a wild moment of passion he had fumbled so fast with the packet containing the Viagra tablets that he had taken three instead of one. He really should have read the label.'

The builder who had mentioned his wife pulled his knees together 'Christ, he must have been proud for hours!'

'That was only part of the problem. Having satiated their desires his girlfriend went to work as a cinema usherette so without a car that they shared he had come to the hospital by bus.

By now the café was a writhing mass of laughter again bringing Martyn and Vera out from the kitchen.

'Blimey, you had better get Joe here some of that stuff only his missus is always complaining that she ain't getting enough!'

Danny who sat nearest the girls had tears running down his cheeks.

Behind the counter Danielle looked across at Martyn. I read her thoughts.

Whispering in her ear I told her 'don't worry, it'll be years before you encounter such a problem!'

'So how did you handle that one?' asked another customer as the laughter rippled through the rafters.

By now they could have heard us laughing down the end of Oslo Road. Even Claire was crying as she tried to tell the rest of the story.

'We had to sit the poor sod in a cubicle with an ice pack. After about half an hour the blood had chilled enough to return everything to normal.'

As somebody anonymous called out *'NASA calling Saturn five you can come on down now!'* I saw the door open and in walked Mary and Lola. They looked at the table where the builders were still laughing before looking at me.

'We can hear you next door,' said Lola 'what's going on?'

'Stick around and you might find out.' I said.

'Anymore, before we go back to work?' asked another workman as he drank the remainder of his tea. Claire gestured that it was Julia's turn.

'Alright one more and then that's it only we need to hit the sack and no dirty remarks you lot!' she said pointing a finger at their table.

'Around one in the morning we had a teenage boy in accompanied by his father. Eamonn Doherty had managed to super-glue his right hand to his mobile telephone. Throughout the evening he had been putting together a plastic model for a school project using super-glue only around a quarter to midnight one of his classmates had called to see how he was getting on. By accident and reaching for his phone he had leant on the tube which had then erupted covering his hands. Eamonn answered the call thinking he had time to deal with the call then clean his hands only

232

the tube used was a fast reacting agent. An hour later his father brought to accident and emergency.'

'And what happened?' asked Danny.

'We had to reshape his hairstyle, use a low spirit acetone on his ear and hands. In the process he lost not just his hair but his phone and his pride.'

I knew what was coming next but before I could prevent it from happening, it happened, I cringed looking at Lola and Mary. *It was just as well that it wasn't the same bloke who had taken the Viagra!*

Unashamedly Danielle was the first to laugh followed by the entire café even Mary. I had this vision of the poor man sat in the cubicle doubting that no amount of ice or acetone would have helped his case.

With that both girls stood took a bow and headed for the counter to the sound of applause. Julia winked at Danielle and in return for their making everybody happy I refused any payment. Soon after their departure the builders followed taking Danny with them and the office ladies went soon after leaving just me to face Lola and Mary as Danielle had escaped out back with Vera and Martyn.

'If I didn't know better I would say Spencer Brand that you initiate the amusement in this café!'

I looked at Lola with an expression of hopeless innocence spreading my upturned palms as high as my chest.

'What happens in this café half the time has nothing to do with me, it's this place it attracts all sorts of people from all walks of life.'

Lowering her eyes I could see Mary was amused.

'I should think that that poor soul with the Viagra was extremely embarrassed.'

I was surprised that Mary had raised the subject. Living with Thomas she had completely detached herself from the calling of the convent.

'Let's just say that he will steer clear of anything in tablet form for some time to come!'

Lola looked at me despairingly her long eyelashes trying to cover her eyes. I could read her thoughts. Later she would tell me off stating that with a young daughter in the house I would have to watch what I said and mind my 'p's' and 'q's'.

Going back next door Mary waved and gave me a wry smile. Soon after they left the café emptied leaving me alone out front.

Whatever Lola thought the café thrived on people from all walks of life. They each brought a bit of themselves here and left a bit behind albeit ghosts, artists, treasure hunters, nurses, postmen, builders, secretaries or even the odd air cabin crew manager. I never wanted things to change and with my recent responsibilities I could see myself changing but only where it was necessary otherwise Spencer Marlon Brand was going to be the same man as before.

Looking around the empty room I had a sense of achievement having upheld the tradition of the little red café. People came here with expectation and they left a happy individual, much wiser in some cases, relieved in others. Whatever the occasion we were here for everyone.

I could never see myself doing else but being the owner of a small red café. Each and every day I admired the people like Julia and Claire who saved people's lives, like the builders who built our homes and cities or the men and women who flew to the moon, they each enriched this planet and left their mark.

Popping around to see my mother after work to make sure that she was coming to tea at the weekend and spend time with her new granddaughter I noticed that she had washed and ironed her old nurse's uniform. When I asked why she told me that she was going to do some voluntary work in the old people's home which Robert Styles had recommended. It amused me to think that most of the residents were not much older than her but rather than say anything against the idea I encouraged the intention, after all said and done we each have something to give in life albeit laughter, a smile, love and kindness or hope.

Wedding Bells

Having already been married once you might have considered me an old hand at the experience but when I woke up earlier than normal that Saturday morning, the butterfly's in my stomach were doing a tango followed by the rumba. On other occasion I would blame the beer or the wine but today I could not lay the blame at the landlord's door of The Benbow Arms only my stag party had been on a Thursday night and a very tame affair. Respecting the wishes of my bride to be Friday was out of bounds and alcohol taboo.

Quite naturally as this was her first time at walking down the aisle she wanted everything to be perfect. All week relatives had been arriving coming as far afield as Florence, Sicily and Rome and quite rightly the forthcoming event had been upstaged by Amelia, who Mama Capella had proudly guided her granddaughter through each introduction. It was plain to see that Amelia was going to be a big hit with her Italian aunts, uncles, cousins and friends and there were times when I was concerned that so many new faces would daunt her but with Lola and Mama Capella by her side she faced every challenge with a polite confidence. Lola and I could not be more proud of our little girl. Of course on many of the meetings she was glad to show her new family her favourite teddy.

The wedding was set for one o'clock at St. Mary's the Roman Catholic Church in Lewis Street and Father Michael had kindly consented to officiate at the ceremony with Robert Styles giving a blessing for the

Church of England members in the congregation. I didn't dare tell Lola but the coming together reminded me of an England versus Italy football match.

Vera had promised to stick close to my mother throughout the day as I was sure that at some point of the proceedings she would begin to cry although probably not for me but Lola. With Amelia stood between her grandmothers she looked like a princess from one of her fairy tale stories. Other special guests included Carolyn Johnson and Amanda Wilks. They were both surprised to see the transformation in Amelia recognising that she had put on a healthy weight and lost some of her shyness. When she saw them she ran to give them both a hug.

Holding with tradition whereby the groom could not see the bride the day of the wedding I had stayed overnight at my mother's and been fussed over something rotten.

Lola and her bridesmaids Mary and Francesca, Danielle and Amelia would have their hair done at Mama Capella's leaving me to arrive at the church by myself. Lola had insisted on Danielle being a bridesmaid too which had pleased me immensely and Danielle was over the moon to be asked.

I had asked Alfie Wilson to be my best man but he had sent a polite refusal wishing us well for the future but stating that he was still somewhere in the deepest depths of Central Africa. Personally I think he was lost.

My cousin George from Brighton agreed to be the stand-in at the last minute pleased that he would get to kiss the bride and dance with Mary even though I told him about Thomas. Martyn and Thomas were acting as ushers and looking after the guests arriving at the church. And so at last the day was planned and set, we just needed to turn up on time.

Swinging my legs out and over the edge of the bed that morning the sun was already rising above the rooftops throwing a contrasting skyline of reds, yellows and creams against the blue hue. I yawned despite having had a good night running my fingers through my hair. For some inexplicable reason the day reminded me of my last day in prison.

On the floor below my bedroom I could hear the low hum of a radio coming from the kitchen where my mother was already bustling around and keeping her mind and herself busy. What was pleasing was the way that she and Lola had become close and not just because they were going to be in-laws but friends. Including Amelia, Mary and Mama Capella the five of them had planned the wedding.

Mama Capella was a very attractive woman and had rightly passed on her beauty to her daughter. I admit to having been nervous the first time that I met her knowing how much Lola meant to her mother but unlike some Italians her mother was quiet, thoughtful and reserved in her judgement, only saying what needed to be said when the occasion called for to intervene. I liked my future mother-in-law, it was a good start.

Despite the month of November having a bad reputation for unpredictable weather we had decided not to wait until after the New

Year to get married wanting Amelia to have our family name and have her know that we were a real bonded unit.

Choosing a Saturday near to the middle of the month in honour of Lola's grandmother who had passed away several years back in November we had pencilled in the twenty sixth. Up until the last morning Amelia had crossed through the days marking the day of the wedding as the day that mummy and daddy were getting married.

'I'm getting married today!' I muttered to myself as I looked in the mirror. I never thought that I would again not after the last disaster but today the feeling felt different, right.

Other than the Saturday that I had attended Burwood Registry Office to marry Sylvia Watkins from East Ham the café had never been closed. It was strange and a little disconcerting that today of all days old memories should be coming back to haunt me.

I even remembered going to Billingsgate Market early every Saturday to get my old Nan some fish so that she had it fresh for her supper. It was Billingsgate where I started work as a porter. I laughed recalling that the day I married Sylvia she had complained that I smelt of fish. Had I known then what I know now I would have made sure that I always kept a wet kipper handy. Before going downstairs I took a shower.

When I walked into the kitchen not quite finished dressing in my tails my mum was already crying, instinctively putting my arms around her I asked what was wrong.

'I'll miss having you around,' she snuffled through the lace of her handkerchief 'we've been together for a long time Spencer!'

I wouldn't mind, but I'd been living with Lola for goodness knows how long.

'Think of today as you gaining a beautiful daughter-in-law and that Amelia will be staying with you at weekends when we come back.'

That thought instantly stopped the snuffling and put the colour back in her cheeks.

For our honeymoon Lola had picked the Amalfi booking the places that we would stay on line. We had both agreed that Amelia would come with us as she had never ever been abroad. We wanted her to be part of our life and there was no way that we were going to leave her behind. The school were very understanding and extended their wishes for our special day. Truth known Amelia was as excited about the honeymoon as she was the wedding. To help she and Lola had been going through the travel guides looking at the places that we were going to stay and where to visit. Lola had been teaching Amelia some of the local phases.

Although the tears had ceased I knew that there would be more later in the church and later still when we headed to Stansted to catch our flight. Having been to the doctor he had given me some pills to calm my nerves of flying. I had thought about calling Sandra Ellingham but decided against the idea not wanting anything to interfere with our big day.

Sitting me down at the table like she had when I was a small boy she placed before me a cup of tea. Seeing her wring her hands on her pinny I knew what was coming next, that was something else I remembered from my childhood.

'You've got it all ahead of you now Spencer Brand,' she said adding a slice of bread to the frying pan. 'Lola will make you a wonderful wife and little Amelia is a heaven sent angel.' I couldn't have said it better. 'You just remember my boy that you have responsibility now so you don't go gallivanting around with your head in the clouds. You look after those two girls with your soul, otherwise you'll have me to deal with first and then Mama Capella.'

With the lecture over she dished up my breakfast handing me a tea towel so that I didn't spill any down my front. After we were done she ordered me back up to my room so that I could finish dressing.

Sitting on the end of my bed my legs were suddenly like Jelly. I thought of David Hetherington wondering who I could call to help. It wasn't as though I had done anything wrong the night before like ending up naked next to a naked tattooing stripper, slept in the garden shed or ended up in some strange café seeking solace, I just needed somebody to calm my nerves. Thinking of where David had sought his spiritual guidance I knew the one place that could help was the café.

Picking up the keys I told my mum that I was going for some fresh air and that I would meet her at the church. I kissed her goodbye, thanked her for everything and told her that I would always love her.

The walk to the café was more difficult than I had imagined with so many well-wishers wanting to stop and talk but in the end I had to carry on walking determined to get to my destination calling across or waving as I went by and George had sent me a text to say that his train was due in at Liverpool Street Station with no delays expected.

The moment that I inserted the key in the lock my trepidation disappeared. Sitting alone where I could not be seen from the street I felt safe, much calmer. I experienced what a lot of other people experienced when they came inside. It was difficult to explain but whatever it was real. It was no wonder that we were so popular.

Looking across at the mural painted by Thomas I saw for the first time the small images of people walking down the streets, it was odd because I had never noticed them before. I went over to look closer. What was even more remarkable was the fact that they looked like Lola, Mary, Vera, Danielle and Martyn. There was even a street artist knelt over the pavement to be representative of Thomas but the most amazing figure was that of a little girl running up the road almost identical to Amelia and the girl was holding onto a teddy. Going over to the box under the counter where we kept the emergency key I was surprised to see it there.

'If you're there,' I whispered *'I could do with some help. Make me get it right this time!'*

Now whether you are a believer or not and it doesn't really matter because each to their own but I am I sat there and closed my eyes seeing only the things that I wanted to see mainly Lola and Amelia.

I thought of my father and how I and my mother missed him. His life had been cut short by illness but with my eyes closed I could suddenly see his face as he walked towards me. Taking my hand in his he looked happy.

'Hello son, you've come a long way since I saw you last.'

'Hello dad, is it really you?'

'It's me although not quite in the flesh but next best thing. That's a pretty girl that you're marrying today much better than the last one!'

I laughed and he did too. I wished then that I had known him.

'And the little girl, Amelia she's beautiful. She will make you both proud one day!'

Thanks dad. I love them both so much.'

Then what's to worry about my boy. You've got so much to look forward too. If I had been half the man that you are I would have been a much better father. Take my love with you today and know that I am watching over you every day as I will my daughter-in-law and granddaughter, but before I go which I have to give my love also to your mother and tell her that I am sorry. Somehow I'll make things right one day!'

I waited until the vision had gone before I opened my eyes. It was not what I had expected to happen. Was there a magic inside the café, I believe there was and for the first time I had experienced it myself. Picking up the keys I whispered 'thank you' as I headed for the door. I had a wedding to attend.

Standing outside of the little red café I took a moment to stand back and look. I felt better than I had for a long time, positive, charged and ready to show Lola, Amelia and all the family that I was worthy of being her husband, Amelia's father, a good son and friend to them all. I could not wait to see Lola walk down the aisle with Amelia behind and see her cheeky little face look around her mummy at me. I could not wait to begin out life together as the Brand Family. Giving the thumbs up I turned away knowing that the next I saw the café I would be a married man.

For the next ten days Vera was in charge with my mum helping out and Martyn and Danielle dealing with the front of house. It was something different for Martyn but I had no reservation knowing that he could cope. I had this vision of Vera and my mother in the kitchen together just like the old days when they had run the WRVS canteen some years back.

Walking with a confident stride and purpose towards St Marys I waved proudly at people that I knew accepting their well-wishes, gratefully accepting their compliments that I looked good enough to be the groom. Not too far from where I turned the corner I could see the church spire above the rooftops and chimneys, soon I would arrive as would Lola holding the hand of our daughter. I felt my heart was full of love, it was a good feeling a very good feeling.

With a couple of hundred yards left to go I suddenly came across a young boy no older than Amelia, he was out in the street alone and kicking a football against a brick wall. Feeling compelled to stop I did admiring his tenacity as he kicked the ball wanting to get it right. When he saw me looking he stopped, picked up the ball and came over to where I was stood beside a tree.

'Cor you darn look a right toff mister are you gonna get married or sumfink.' He asked.

Looking down at the smeared green smudges on his cheek, knees and shins where the ball had skimmed over the lawn he looked every inch the urchin from a Charles Dickens novel. Under his shirt the hem of his tee-shirt was hung loose and his trousers had seen better days. Standing there all confident, his head slightly tilted to the right he reminded me of William Hollingsworth.

'I am dressed like this because I am getting married this morning.' I replied. 'What's your name?'

'Kenneth,' he replied cuffing the underside of his nose with the back of his hand as he looked me up and down. 'Have you got time for a quick kick-about?'

I couldn't help but admire his impudence, his innocence a rare delight. Any other time I would have gladly said yes, only not today. I explained to

Kenneth that if I did partake I would be late for the service and that my wife would never forgive me.

'Okay sport,' he responded 'perhaps when she gets bored with you like my mum does wiv' my old man, you can come find me and we'll have ourselves a right old kick-about.'

I was about twenty yards from where the ball was bouncing back off the wall again when Kenneth called out 'and if there's any cake left over, save us a bit mister. I know you from that café down in Oslo Road so I'll pop by and pick some up during the week!'

With that Kenneth ran off kicking the ball high and hard, chasing it before it landed. I watched him disappear thinking that I had better warn Danielle about an unexpected visitor that was coming for a slice of cake. I'd tell her to keep some lemon drizzle back as I doubted he would know any different.

With only a street away to go the bells started to peel, I ran the remainder thinking I could be late but the campanologists were only testing the ropes ready for the main peel. At the door to the church George had arrived early. Handing over the rings I shook his hand and thanked him for stepping in at the minute.

'An honour young Spencer, although you do cut things a bit fine we were all getting worried!'

'Believe it or not George I was waylaid by a street urchin.'

246

We stepped inside and walked down the aisle nodding gratefully at relatives and friends on either side some I knew, some that I didn't not that it mattered because come the end of the evening I would know everybody.

I was pleased to see Sandra Ellingham sitting alongside Sebastian proudly wearing an engagement ring. I was also happy to see on my side of the church David and Marianne Hetherington only when I stopped to say hello Mrs Hetherington looked more rounded around the abdomen than the last time we had met. I would ask later.

With the continuous peel of bells the echo resounded loudly around the inside of the church. I looked back down the aisle and saw a sea of smiling faces just before Martyn and Thomas pulled aside the huge oak studded doors letting the sunshine flood in.

'Are you ready?' George asked.

'Ready George and happier than I have ever been!'

I watched the procession walk down the aisle with Amelia holding Lola's train flanked by Danielle, Mary and Francesca. As expected Amelia looking resplendent in her pale blue dress and tiara scrunched up her button nose and gave me a great big smile. Lola knew to whom I was returning the smile as this was our daughter's day as much as ours. Looking over to where my mum was stood I whispered *'I love you!'*

That Christmas Spirit

Now if Father Christmas had suddenly knocked on your front door rather than coming down the house chimney like tradition said he would you might very well have asked why and had folklore changed that much with the times.

When Santa walked into our café one cold and frosty morning my initial reaction was to ask if he was lost but seeing that he had no reindeer or elves to keep him company I was quick to identify from his expression that there wasn't a lot of festive cheer about his visit.

Archibald Simmons or Archie to his friends was a well-known children's entertainer in the district and with his seasonal side-line as Santa he was a favourite of the children for miles around. Archie was never without a smile and he could be relied upon to cheer any dismal overcast day but on this Saturday the clouds had seemingly descended upon him and him alone.

Dressed in his familiar red costume, wide black belt and polished shiny boots Archie had a natural paunch to fit the tunic requiring no padding and come yuletide his services were in big demand seven days a week at all the large retail stores, children's parties and charity events. And when there were no official engagements he would brave all weathers standing on the junction of the High Street clanging his big old brass school bell collecting needy funds for the destitute and homeless. Archie Simmons had a heart as big as his collecting bucket.

The previous Saturday Lola had ringed a circle around the date on the calendar that she was going to take Amelia to see Father Christmas and every day like the lead up to our wedding she would mark off the day seeing the date get closer. I had tried to recall when I had been that excited about seeing Santa but the memory was blurred, Amelia on the other hand would never forget and besides marking down the days she also had the fun of opening the door of the advent calendar each morning. Christmas was a special time of year for young children.

Acknowledging that I was behind the counter Archie took himself over to an empty table removing his peaked hat, false eyebrows and beard placing them on the chair beside his. Within an instant Danielle appear from out back to take his order. She about to quip *'ho ho ho it's Santa'* when I caught her eye shaking my head. Miming back she asked why to which I responded in similar fashion *'things are not right with Archie!'* Danielle took his order and disappeared into the kitchen giving me time to go across.

'What's up Archie, you're normally so full of life?'

Archie looked up at me with bags under his eye lacking any real lustre. 'I just don't know Spencer. It just don't seem the same anymore... there's something's missing!'

Trying to sound perky I implored 'but you're the one person who brings the season to life Archie and without you the children around here wouldn't have anything to look forward too. Santa's grotto is the big event on every little boy and girls calendar and without you I wouldn't get extra cookies and milk on Christmas Eve.'

Archie rolled his head around shoulders expelling the ache from his bones.

'I know all that Spencer but it's me. Somewhere between last year and this yuletide I've lost the spark inside that sets me on fire.' He looked forlorn 'I just don't think that I can face another season of endless requests and expectant faces.'

Now if the eyes were supposed to be the windows to the soul, Archie had pulled his curtains together and what he said was serious. This was a major problem that needed a radical intervention and fast. As a café we could easily provide refreshments and breakfasts, lunches and afternoon teas, but some saw us the local drop-in centre for problem solving. I took the seat opposite his promptly pulling my chair in close to the table realising that Amelia and a good few many more like her depended upon my getting Archie back on track.

'So come on tell me what's happened between last January and this December?'

Archie appeared tense almost agitated as his thoughts pounded his head.

'I wish I knew, really I do Spencer. My diary was full January to September with kid's parties, school fetes, church bazaars and even the odd family barbeque, but come October when the weather started to change so did my outlook. With the grey, damp and winds came a strange uncertainty as though the spirit within had been sucked from my soul. I struggled through October and November trying to hold it together but the more that searched for the magic formula the more my audience realised that something was wrong and for the first time ever people who had hired me started to complain.'

The problem was indeed serious. I had been to functions and see Archie perform, he was a natural talent and within seconds he could have an audience rolling around the aisles. The problem now was how to put back the magic. As friends we had known one another for years and we trusted one another's motives.

Like me Archie had started as a porter at the fish market where we had carried heavy lade boxes and baskets to and fro, cut the heads and tails off fish and washed away the oily scales. Day or night Archie would entertain the customers and other stall holders telling his funny tales and jokes and soon his reputation had become so well-known that he left the market and went as a full-time entertainer doing the summer holiday camps. However like many entertainers the profession had its draw backs, one being that Archie had never married or had children of his own.

'So when do you think things were right?' I asked. I nodded at Danielle who mimed if I wanted a coffee.

'A good question my friend. July, August maybe September, I'm not entirely sure.'

'Alright, when did you get your first criticism?'

'Three weeks ago when a young boy about ten years of age told me that I was crap!'

There was a definite crisis afoot and I suspected it was around Archie's confidence. Not that I was any expert but I had seen parents in the café trying to deal with the off awkward child. Having a ten year old steal your thunder was bound to have a lasting effect. I knew that I would be extremely hurt if Amelia told me one day that I was crap at running a café.

On top surface we only ever notice the outer shell and if the eyes don't give anything away it takes a very knowledgeable individual or specialist with training to identify the signs of someone's distress. As if on cue Danielle arrived with two coffees and Archie's order of a bacon and sausage roll.

'Enjoy your breakfast Archie, it's good to see you!'

Good girl I thought, it was the sort of encouragement that Archie needed. She went back to the counter taking control of the café. In reality she could run the show by herself.

Dunking my biscuit into my coffee I watched Alfie consume his breakfast as I searched for a solution. I recalled the ten days that the three of us had been travelling the Amalfi coast with Vera and my mum looking after the café. Like a lightbulb flickering into life an idea suddenly appeared.

'You carry on Archie,' I said 'I'll be back in a minute!'

Twenty minutes later my mum walked in through the door wearing her resolution head. Sitting herself down at the table Archie seemed surprised to see a woman around his own age appear before him. She ordered a fresh pot of tea and a plate of toast.

'Hello Archie,' she said 'do you remember me only it's been a while since we last saw one another?'

'Has it?' he replied, still not recognising who she was.

'Why it's me you old fool... Doris Brand from Upper Bottomley Street, you remember.'

I had always wondered what idiot in the town planning department had named the street, more so why we had moved there in the first place.

'Spencer tells me that you've a problem.'

Archie looked across at me as I stood behind the counter then back at my mum.

'The only problem that I have is people sticking their noses into my private life and second that I didn't invite you to my table.' He was less than amused but my mum had dealt with worse on the hospital wards.

'Now that's no way to talk to a lady and you should think yourself lucky that one wants to sit and help you!'

'Help me... how... I'm not barmy or anything?'

She was making progress.

'You're lucky that a lady wants to sit with you. Now consider it fortunate that I have.' That was mum stern when it was needed and determined not to budge. I thought Archie would get up and leave, but he sat perfectly still waiting for the next instalment.

'We need to find that Christmas magic again!'

'Oh that...!' he looked at her blankly, staring straight through her 'it's gone missing, somebody stole it!'

It seemed odd when Archie and myself had been talking he had appeared lucid although down beat, now that my mum was trying to help he seemed confused. I began to wonder if the problem lie with Archie himself.

'What's she saying to him?' Danielle asked as she came over to where I was standing.

Talking almost in whispers I couldn't hear any longer. 'I'm not sure but they've known one another for a very long time. If anybody can help sort out old Archie it will be mum.

They talked for over an hour and as I watched in between making coffee and cutting cake the expression on Archie's face changed sometimes frowning other times almost smiling. For the first time I watched in admiration of my mums nursing skills. Her bedside manner never changed and slowly she had managed to draw out of Archie the real problem worrying him. On the calendar where Amelia had circled Christmas Day I noticed that we had three weeks left.

When Archie suddenly laughed, a deep belly sound coming up from his rounded stomach it was just like he was back to his old self again. I envisaged the manager of Dickens and Harvey's in the High Street being mighty pleased and relieved although I sensed a prevailing wind was about to blow our way, cruelly casting aside the illusion.

'Wow...' announced Danielle 'I thought for sure that we'd be walking the old boy down to see Doc Doland and that he had lost his marbles!'

It was just like Danielle, nothing grey only black and white. I on the other hand wasn't so sure. Archie although calmer was still not his old self. An hour and a half after she had sat at the table my mum came over to the counter.

'Me and Archie are going to pop down to the surgery before it closes Spencer. Archie wants to have a word with the doctor. Have you got that old overcoat out back still rather than have the doctor think that he's just arrived Lapland?'

Slipping into my overcoat, a pair of old trousers and a pair of spare shoes that I had in the bottom of my locker Archie resembled a slightly overweight Charlie Chaplin. Looking at himself in the reflection of the

255

window he smiled although I sensed that it was only half-hearted and that his thoughts were already a good way off from the café.

Putting his costume to one side we wished him well saying that we would see him later but I had an awful feeling that Archie had somehow seen the costume for the last time and as they went out together turning right towards the surgery in Beckett Street I grasped the sudden reality of the situation surrounding Archie's lost magic.

An hour later I took a call from my mum to say that Archie had been put on medication and told to rest at home by Doc Doland. She asked that I pop around to Dickens and Harvey's and explain that Archie was too ill to fulfil his obligation that afternoon. Looking at the wall clock she had also told me that he had been dressed ready to undertake the afternoon sitting at the grotto starting at two thirty. There was an hour and a half to go. I rushed around to the High Street taking the Santa outfit with me.

The long and short of my conversation with the store manager was that there was no else at such short notice to take Archie's place. He tried the agency but every Santa was already working elsewhere. It was after all the busy season. Reluctantly and seeing that Archie was a long standing friend I said that I would stand in for him.

I raced back to the café and told Vera, Martyn and Danielle of my predicament much to Danielle's amusement. At ten past two the store found a damaged pillow from stock which a lady from the household department helped stuff down my tunic. A makeup artist helped add rouge to my cheeks before she applied the false wig, eyebrows and beard which was stuck on with a removable adhesive. Archie boot size was a shade small but curling my toes I managed to get them on. By twenty five past I was ready to face the onslaught queuing outside of the grotto. Luckily I had two female elves to keep control.

Unbelievably and worryingly my first customer that afternoon was a young street urchin named Kenneth, whom I established quickly was Kenneth Dalton. As expected he asked for a football kit and new ball having burst his old one. I told him that I would see what I could do even if it meant I had to buy it. With a frown he was led away from my chair by one of the elves but I heard him pass comment that he thought Santa didn't sound right. I wondered if he had recognised my voice. It was a close call.

That afternoon I met a lot of youngsters of all ages some kind, some not. One little girl wanted so much I thought the list would never end. My worst nightmare however was around twenty five past three when I saw Lola arrive with Amelia. My mum had telephoned Lola to warn her in advance who was standing in for Father Christmas at Dickens and Harvey's and not wanting to miss the occasion Lola had brought forward the surprise so that she could see me in action. Of course little Amelia was happy too not having to wait another week until she could visit Santa.

Putting on my best disguised voice so as not to be discovered Lola sat Amelia on my knee grinning at me like a demented Cheshire cat. Amelia was very confident much to my surprise and immediately she told me her name.

'And what would you like for Christmas?' I asked.

'A baby,' she replied. I almost spluttered when she answered.

'Oh… and would that be a brother or sister?' I looked up at Lola who had her hand over her mouth trying not to laugh.

'It doesn't really matter which as long as the baby can sleep in my room with Angus and me at bedtime and I can dress them up!'

I told that it was an unusual request but I would see what I could do.

'And is there anything else that you would like?'

Putting a finger to her lips Amelia thought about it.

'Maybe a dolls house and another teddy bear, only Angus gets a bit lonely when I am at school and my Auntie Mary and Uncle Thomas told me that I can never have enough teddies or dollies!'

Sensing that a laugh was bubbling down below in my stomach I told Amelia that I would do my very best to see that she got everything on her Christmas wish list. I was about to give Amelia back to Lola when she suddenly put her arm around my neck, pulled herself close to my left ear and whispered *'and tell mummy and daddy that I love them very much!'*

Hearing that Amelia was the best Christmas present that we had ever had.

Around five the curtain fell down over the entrance to the grotto for the last time. Removing the outfit the afternoon had made me appreciate just how hard Archie had worked all these years that he had been Santa and entertaining children and adults alike. It was a rare gift that he had possessed only I don't think many that knew him realised how special. What was also surprising was the bruises I had received from the children where they bashed and bumped into me no more so than Kenneth Dalton.

Had Archie come to the café that day because he needed help or was he just passing, who knows only he could say only he couldn't remember. When I spoke to my mum later that evening she told me that Archie was suffering from the onset of early dementia just as she had suspected. Through Doc Doland arrangements were made with the help of the social services team and members of Archie's family for him to go into a nursing home over Lewisham way. It was a sad day when he left the house that he had lived in since being a boy but he would take with him some of the memories, the good ones of happy smiling children.

One afternoon a week before Christmas leaving Danielle in charge of the customers I went to see Archie in his new home taking a freshly baked lemon drizzle cake that Vera had made especially for him and the other residents. In the large lounge I found Archie sat in a chair beside the window gazing out at a group of children playing football in the park next to the home. He was smiling to himself and occasionally punching his fist in the air whenever they got near the goal.

Ironically my visit coincided with another visitor a Father Christmas who had come along to add some last minute cheer. Listening to Santa tell the residents of his many exploits we reminded of years that had since passed us by when up and down the land Christmas had not been exploited by commercial greed. When Santa told his jokes Archie leant my way and whispered.

'I used to tell them just as funny!' and he did.

Every so often when Archie had a good day he would do a stand-up routine and entertain the others in the home making them laugh, making them sing but when the curtain fell over his memory and he went quiet those were the moments that he wanted to forget, just like the ten year old who had challenged his worth.

As a touching mark of respect for his long and dedicated service the directors of Dickens and Harvey's in the High Street had a framed photograph of Archie placed next to the entrance to the cafeteria so that he would always be remembered. He wasn't wearing his Santa outfit but in years to come even the children would realise just who he was.

That Christmas was a very happy occasion and Amelia had nearly all of her wish list delivered by Santa all except one present the new baby but Lola had a good trick up her sleeve. Putting Amelia to bed one night she told her that Santa had not forgotten about the baby, but that babies took a little longer to make and that if they all arrived on December the twenty fifth then there would be a lot of days throughout the year with missing birthdays. Amelia seemed quite happy to wait until the baby was made. Standing at the top of the landing we both heard her tell Angus and

Shamus, the new teddy that a baby brother or sister would be coming soon.

The Mysterious Red Bicycle

It was there when I opened up early one morning propped against the woodwork of the front window, a mans red bicycle nothing special in design, simply a twenty six inch model with straight handle bars, chrome wheels and thin rubber tyres. We'd had similar left outside before so it didn't concern me that much although I did check to see if there was a name inscribed into the frame which would help identify the owner. Neither was there a manufacturer's registration mark, it seem odd.

I believed the style to be a Raleigh although I was no bike expert. What was immediately apparent was the low pressure in both tyres perhaps accounting for why the owner had dumped the bike outside of the café. I left the bike where it was in the hope that it would be collected sometime during the day.

It turned out to be a very day and it wasn't until I locked the front door that I noticed that the bike had not moved from where I had seen it early the morning. Disappointingly odd was that the owner had not come back to collect it.

Giving the bike a quick inspection it did appear usable except for the low pressure. I thought about calling the police but lost bikes were a low priority on their list of ever increasing tasks. After a few minutes I decided to see Lola instead getting my priorities right. Mary was on her way back having collected Amelia from school and Amelia especially liked Mary collecting her as they always came back to the florist via the swings in the park.

The next morning the red bicycle was still there only overnight it had been turned around, almost certainly by somebody like Kenneth Dalton who seemed to spend most of his waking hours on the streets. The strange thing was that whoever had used or turned around the bike had pumped up the tyres. Going next door to the book shop Bartram was also at a loss as to who the owner could be. I had not seen him in weeks and every time that I did he appeared much older and eccentric. I often wondered how he survived as he had few visitors but the rumour that I heard was that he had come from a wealthy family and the book shop was more of a hobby than a commercial enterprise.

Several customers had also noticed the bike but none had seen it in the area before which made me think that perhaps it was from out of the borough and been used illegally by somebody wanting to get home. Come the third morning I was surprised to see that it was again in a different position only this time a hand written note had been attached to the main frame. It was difficult to say whether it had been written by a man or woman. The note read:

To the owner of the red bicycle,

I hope you didn't mind but I used your bike early evening. You saved me a whole heap of trouble as I was very late for a date with my girlfriend and I knew that if I had taken the bus it would have got stuck in the rush hour congestion.

Turning up for the meal on the bike made my girlfriend laugh and helped set the mood for a very pleasant evening. Whoever you are, your bike saved a bumpy relationship from going down the pan.

Many thanks.

Gratefully yours. Ed.

Over the coming days I could not explain why but I felt obliged to keep the bicycle in good order, sprinkling water over the framework to keep it clean and making sure that the tyres were inflated. Still however there was no sign of the owner. The mystery however became even more mysterious on the fourth morning when I found another note.

Hello.

This has got to be just a quick note as I am in rather a hurry.

I am sorry that I used the bicycle for the whole night, but I did return it as soon as I could. Like a miracle sent from heaven the bike appeared out of nowhere around the corner as I was being pursued by the police. Your red bike gave me the edge and I was lucky to escape. Sorry about the mud splashes.

Joe Long. A lifelong friend!

I have to admit that Joe's note made me smile and I could have done with a bike around the night that I got arrested but that was life, sometimes you got a break other times the cards were stacked against you. Whatever Joe was guilty of the bike had served another purpose.

And so from that morning going forward the tale of the bike became ever intriguing. Some nights the bike would disappear perhaps returning the next day others it would be gone for longer but whatever the circumstances it would eventually find its way back to the front of the café. Occasionally there would be a note explaining why it had been taken but nobody ever claimed the bike as their own.

Of the notes that had been left I had them under the coffee counter. So far the bike had helped save a relationship from going on the rocks, helped a man called Joe avoid capture by the police, assisted with getting an expectant father to the hospital in time to see his baby daughter being born and made good the escape of an illicit lover who had been chased across town by the woman's husband. How the man found time to write the note puzzled me. more recently the bike had attended a funeral at Burwood Memorial Park and then gone missing for a whole week only to come back showing off two new tyres having taken part in the London to Brighton charity event. There really was no telling why or where it could end up when it went missing.

I did however come relatively close to finding out one sunny afternoon when a casually dressed lady took the bicycle up to Claridge's to partake of afternoon tea with a friend. One minute it was there then gone the next. I had kept a vigil throughout the afternoon but when my back was turned for a second it was back with a short note.

Dear owner of this beautiful bike,

We went to tea this afternoon at Claridge's and most delightful it was. We will undoubtedly go again!

Many thanks

Tiffany xx

I was beginning to think that the bike was haunted and being used by ghosts from the past although I did know a tiffany once but that was a very long time ago when I had been a fish market porter.

And then quite by chance the bicycle disappeared for a rather long time maybe a couple of months or more. In a way I felt relieved that we had seen the last of it and things settled back to normal until mid-spring when it mysteriously reappeared overnight much to my dismay. As usual there was another note:

Dear owner of this red bicycle

I hope that my taking your bicycle did not cause you too many problems but I assure you that my need was awfully great at the time. I am living in London as a student and thus do not have a lot of money to spare.

One particular afternoon I received word from home that my father had been taken very ill. Originally from a village called Strakonice this is in the Czech Republic near Prague. I had need of your bicycle to get me to the station and help catch a train. Together we have travelled many miles until I was back home with my family.

Without the use of your bicycle I would not have been there when my father passed away. For the use of your splendid red bicycle I am eternally grateful. One day perhaps we can meet and I will recompense you for the inconvenience.

Yours Alzbeta Grenetza'

Of all the notes that had been left on the bicycle this was by far the most desperate. I was sorry to hear that her father had died but pleased that she had arrived home in time to say goodbye. Looking back it had been many months since the bike had arrived, mysteriously disappeared, then inexplicably reappeared.

Vera thought that the bike had been placed outside of the café for a reason and Martyn who had an interest in bikes took over the maintenance oiling the cogs and keeping the tyres inflated. Before leaving off to go home he always make sure it was in good working order adding a plastic bag which he placed over the saddle if it was raining. On one occasion I had used the bike myself to pop down to the High Street to fetch more sausages from the butchers only I never let on to Lola who thought that I always walked.

Then like it always happens a complete stranger appeared walking in almost at the end of the spring beginning of summer. He was a tall gentleman, had a look of intelligence about him and quite nicely tanned. I could not determine his origin but he was definitely not from these shores. He sat at a table near to the door and ordered two teacakes with an expresso coffee. Under his arm he had brought his own paper.

Danielle took his order over to the table returning moments later.

'The foreign looking gentlemen asked if you wouldn't mind joining him!'

Offering a smile he had the look of an investigator, a private detective.

'You sir… are the owner of this café?' he asked. I nodded that I was.

'Good, then I am speaking to the right man,' he held out his hand for me to take. 'Then I would like to thank you kind sir for looking after my bicycle for me whilst I have been travelling overseas.'

'How do you that it was me who had looked after it?'

He smiled. 'Before coming into your fine establishment I went next door to the flower shop as the bicycle was propped between the two buildings. The lady in there told me that you and members of your staff have been looking after the bicycle during my absence.'

I was astounded. After all this time this foreign gentleman turns up out of the blue and claims to be the original owner of the bike. My expression must have looked suspicious as I let go of his hand.

'My name is Ambati Sharma Kumar and I assure you good sir that I am the owner of the bicycle!'

It was possible that he could be telling the truth although after so long anybody could have made the same claim. After so many months standing outside our café I felt somewhat responsible for the bike.

'Is there anything that will help you identify the bicycle as yours?' I asked.

He nodded, pleased that I had asked.

'That is good that you enquire as there are many thieves in every city. If you would be so kind as to remove the rubber handle covering the end of the handlebar you should find a rolled up piece of paper. On the paper you will find my name and address and a post office stamp honouring the day that it was stamped at the Burwood Post Office in Arden Road. I had the document legalised before I had to leave the country. Please, go check for yourself and hopefully what I say will prove that I am, who I say I am.'

I went outside and did as he asked and sure enough the rolled document was there, duly stamped and unmarked. What further proved his claim was that I had trouble extracting the rubber handle, indicating that it had not been removed in a long time. Going back in to the cafe he had finished eating his teacakes.

'These are indeed the most splendid teacakes and your coffee is better than I have tasted for a long time.'

I thanked him and asked if he could describe what was recorded on the document.

He said. *'My name is Ambati Sharma Kumar and my address is three hundred and thirteen Roland Street, Burwood.'* The post masters stamp should read the twelfth day of December, is that correct?'

He then produced his passport so that I could verify the information. There was no denying that Ambati was the rightful owner of the red bicycle.

'Why leave the bike here?' I asked.

Ambati went on to tell me that he had been a successful part-owner of a grocery store the west side of Burwood but that unbeknown to him his unscrupulous brother's had for months been dwindling him out of the ownership of his shop, stealing his stock and arranging to sell the flat that he owned above the shop. Realising that he was about to lose everything Ambati had used the remainder of his savings which they knew nothing about to take him back to his homeland of Mumbai in India where he knew legal papers would prove that his claim of ownership was without challenge.

Ambati said that he had been cycling past the café late one evening when for some reason or other he felt compelled to get off and leave the bicycle outside.

'I cannot explain it Mr Brand, it just felt completely right. It was my favourite bicycle and I did not want my brothers to damage it or worse whilst I was in Mumbai.'

Danielle topped up his coffee and brought a fresh cup over, whereupon I showed him the notes that had been left. As he read them he smiled and nodded. He was especially pleased by the note that had been written by Alzbeta Grenetza.

'Then I did the right in leaving the bicycle in your safe custody Mr Brand although I am deeply sorry to hear of the young lady's loss.'

I was too. Ambati promised to pray for Alzbeta later at the mosque and I believed that he would. He then re-read the note from Joe Long and the man who had escaped the clutches of the angry husband, they seemed to amuse him 'maybe it serves a purpose for all people,' he said with a wry grin.

'And was your journey to Mumbai successful?' I asked.

Looking pleased with himself he replied. 'Indeed I have legally expelled my brothers from the shop and this country as they could only be here with my assistance. My shop and flat belongs to me only again and along with my stock, my wealth here will hopefully be assured of for a long time to come.

Ambati took a few moments to look at the mural on the back wall.

'This is a good place Mr Brand, a kind place without how do you say it storm, controversy. I would guess that people come here because they like it here. I would like to come here again.'

Thank you, we like it too!'

'Although it is a very fine bicycle and my favourite I feel that it would be wrong of me to take it to my shop or flat. Many have used it for whatever reason and with your kind permission I would like to leave it here for others to use. Perhaps when I come back for coffee and teacakes again we can laugh over other's adventures.'

Ambati was as I thought a clever man who viewed the world with wise eye. Seeing the potential for some free marketing I asked if he would mind Thomas 'Rainbow' Jones signwriting our name on the bike frame offering the reason that it would always find its way back to the café.

'An excellent idea,' he agreed.

Of course I would get Thomas to add the name *Ambati* down both front forks so that people would know who donated the bike.

As good as his word Ambati would come back to the café and order two teacakes and an expresso coffee if only to hear me regale him with more tales of where the red bicycle had travelled and who had used it.

Wherever it did disappear to overnight or during the day people always brought the bicycle back. We put the post office marked document back under the handle bar cover believing that it was unlikely anybody would remove it but only Martyn, myself and Ambati knew that it was there.

To end this tale strange things happen most days at the little red café, oddities that very often end happily, some mysteriously but whatever the reason the red bicycle had become part of our legacy, part of the magic and like a wandering spirit it had a purpose.

A Visit from Pentonville

I recognised the face the second the man walked through the café door and he did the same. Freedom can change a lot in a life but we cannot really disguise how we look. The last time that I had seen Thomas Dreyford or Tom as he preferred to be called was on my last day in prison.

I will begin by stating that I do not normally reminisce over past events and especially regarding the stolen years of my life and the ominous thought of spending a morning in the company of an old lag did not fill me with joy. As Tom walked through the door my expression did little to mask my surprise. Approaching the counter he held out his hand in a time honoured tradition accepting my gesture in return.

'You're a long way from home?' I said knowing that he was originally from Durham.

I just happened to be in the area!'

In my opinion nobody was just ever in the area and not where criminals were concerned. I suggested that we take a spare table suspicious of his visit, leaving Danielle to run the counter. After several minutes she came over with two coffees accompanied by a plate of biscuits. I had been hoping for a short visit.

He thanked Danielle immediately taking from the plate. 'It's been a long time since we saw one another last.'

Not long enough I thought. 'Well things change and I've been busy. Initially I had to get back in the swing of things but after a lot of hard graft, blood, sweat and tears I'm there at last!' I didn't want Tom to believe that my life had been an easy ride.

He looked around focusing on the mural at the back. 'Nice place you have here, you've done well.'

In prison we had shared a cell and inevitably in a confined space you develop an association, some call it friendship although in reality you need a comradery to overcome the feeling of claustrophobia and loss of freedom. I could not help but feel cautious.

'So how can I help?' it was unfriendly and a little direct but I wasn't prepared not just yet to flower it up any not until I had heard his reason for being in the area.

Like a cowboy caught on the wrong side of the reservation he held up his hands to signal a truce.

'Nothing sinister Spence, I promise you, just a bit of business that I thought might interest you.'

Now the alarm bells were beginning to ring. To a habitual criminal like Tom his bit of business could put me back inside. I wasn't interested although curiosity is a human curse and I had to know what he had to propose. I had heard through the grapevine that shortly after my release he had been transferred to Pentonville before he too was liberated, going back to selling dodgy second hand cars, moving swiftly into the upper

274

echelons of the market and dealing in the more exclusive models. Whether it was above board remained to be seen.

'You still selling those Rollers, Mercedes and Daimlers?' I asked.

'That and a bit of scrap.' He replied. 'I've a yard over Essex way where the older ones that I don't sell end up as bed springs or sink tops.'

I have to admit his reply did make me laugh as I couldn't see Tom as a kitchen fitter or bedding exporter.

'So what kind of business did you have in mind?'

He rolled his tongue across the front of his teeth disposing of a biscuit crumb. 'A bit of this and that, importing and exporting as you might call it Spence.'

I knew it, a dodgy dealership and from experience I knew there was no such thing as a free hand up.

'Bringing in and taking out what exactly?' I asked, dreading that he implied drugs.

'Motor parts mainly,' he seemed slightly offended 'what did you think I was implying something dodgy.' He swallowed another mouthful of coffee 'I've turned a new page Spence, I've decided to go straight.'

If ever there was a euphemism understating his criminal intentions Tom Dreyford had just declared as such. I think that he forgot that we had shared a cell together and although being slightly colour blind he could still recognise two main colours, gold and silver.

It was now or never. 'Cards on the table Tom, I am grateful that you thought of me but I'm not really interested. The café does me proud and I have a wife and child to think about these days. I am not prepared to take any risks not for the sake of hurting them and jeopardising our happiness!'

I was surprised that he took it so well, understanding.

Smiling he nodded more to himself than me. 'I thought you might reject the idea, but I couldn't pass by without calling in!'

Passing by indeed, we were around back street of the High Street and close to Convent Garden. You didn't just happen to pass by here unless you fell out of a plane or were dumped by taxi.

'Besides, what do I know about vehicle parts, I can't differentiate a big end from the rear end?'

He sniffed as he put down his cup. 'I was just keeping a promise that I made you when we were banged up. Do you recall, I said that if ever a business opportunity came my way, I would invite you in.' He drank the last of his coffee watching Danielle dart between the tables. 'You've grown very suspicious since you left the Scrubs!'

'Not really but the time inside was a wakeup call. We don't get many chances in life. A couple came along recently and I've grabbed them with both hands!'

Tom nodded, his keen eyes missed nothing.

'What about the lad out back scrubbing dishes, would he be interested?'

I was tempted to look around but looked straight ahead focusing my attention on his eyes. If Tom knew about Martyn he must have been watching the café at some point or seen Martyn and Danielle arrive.

'What about Martyn?' I asked.

'I know that young Martyn Stevens had the good sense to walk away from a robbery down at the High Street. It was a show of good judgement and the two clowns that got caught deserved the sentence they received. Did you know that the boy can drive?'

I didn't, but no doubt Tom was about to tell me how.

'His old man was a stock-car racer, a regular at Haringey and Walthamstow. The boy grew up around fast cars, he passed his test days after his seventeenth birthday. I could use a talent like that popping over to France, Belgium and Germany to help pick up some motors for me. Easy peasy stuff, you know take one out and bring one back. Everything legit and above board and all registered with DVLA.'

And there it was one of the oldest scams around involving a customs and excise loophole. Motoring documents were easy to forge and so good that they could fool the authorities. I had to think fast for Martyn's sake.

'The boy is young and making some real money into the bargain will help him and his girl get a better place.'

277

Tom knew more than he was letting on.

'You too Spence if you came in with me. Having just got hitched and with a young daughter you'll be wanting to move on and get a bigger house. What I am offering is good money for not a lot of work in return.'

I had to hand it to Tom he could talk a good incentive. He had done his homework, been around and made some enquiries. I wondered if he had been next door to *Florrie's Flowers* and spoken to Lola. The thoughts were racing through my head when like a light going on I had the answer. I leant across the table.

'Listen Tom, you and me shared that cell together for a little over two years and in that time we got to know one another quite well, I would like to think that we were friends and that's how it should stay. Your proposition is interesting and would favour both the kid and me and I do believe that everything is above board but I am no fool and although I like Martyn I am not willing to take a risk that he wouldn't foul up the minute we got to customs.

'Whatever his reasons that day for stepping away from the jeweller's job he could do the same again. We both have too much to lose now that we're going straight and with our form they'd throw away the key.

'And say we got to Germany or wherever the foreign police will look suspiciously at a driver as young as Martyn wondering why he was driving a Bentley. To be honest Tom I am too old for this kind of excitement. I had to see the doc recently and he told me that I have a dodgy ticker. You don't want me crashing a decent motor if I had a sudden seizure, would you? Why don't you ask somebody like Toby Watkins or Smudge Jenks only they've both got the ideal credentials for a job like what you're offering?

Turning around his cup so that the handle was over the spoon Tom studied me for a few moments.

'You're a cagey bugger Spence and that's what I like about you and you're always willing to give the other bloke a chance. In the pokey you kept your head low, never upset anybody albeit the screws or the inmates. Are you sure,' he asked 'last offer?'

I held out my hand for Thomas Dreyford to shake and we had ourselves an agreeable understanding knowing that we would never see one another again. He knew that I knew old lags don't ever make a habit of just passing by. Before he left he took one last look at the interior of the café nodding his approval.

'You've done well since the Scrubs. Look after that ticker Spence and good luck for the future.'

Taking back the empty crocks to the counter I watched as he went back to his car which was parked further up the road. Tom was about to get in driver's seat when he was approached by two men looking every inch suspiciously like detectives from the local police station. One of them produced a warrant and asked Tom to lock his car and get in the back of theirs instead. With a wipe of my brow I realised how close I had come to being involved.

I felt Danielle come to where I was standing, watching.

'He was a strange bloke Spence, was he with the church?'

I laughed. 'He would like to think that he could walk on water!'

Talking in riddles she took an order from Martyn promptly passing it onto an office girl who had been waiting. Wink a wink at us both he disappeared out back again.

Danielle watched him leave.

'Do you sometimes Spence I think that there's more to Martyn Stevens than what he lets on.'

I said nothing as it was for her to find out and for me to know.

Reading the newspaper a week later I read about a large scale vehicle smuggling operation that had been busted wide open by Interpol in conjunction with officers from Scotland Yard. Reading down the report I came across Thomas Dreyford who had been named as the brains behind the scam.

Further down the page also two other known names were mention having been caught travelling through Belgium, one Toby Watkins and Smudge Jenks from Wapping. Although there was no way to verify the information the reporter believed that Thomas Dreyford had an off-shore account worth millions. The report stated that the money had been so well tied up in different ventures that it could years to unravel the audit trail in such a complex web of financial dealings. Somehow Tom has secured his pension for when he did get his release papers.

There is an amusing anecdote to end this tale ironically involving a high court judge. Mr Rawson Nicholas who had been on the listing to hear and preside over Tom's case had to stand down because of illness giving way to Her Ladyship Matilda Dobson. During the trial it was established that Judge Nicholas had only recently purchased a Rolls Royce from a Dreyford Motor Showroom and the scam had been operating for the past three. Legally council proved the judge to be the receiver of stolen goods. It just proved that it did not matter which side your bread was buttered crime could so easily ensnare the most innocent victim.

Pushing the door shut and turning around the *closed* sign I watched Danielle and Martyn walk back up the road admiring the flash looking Bentley parked unoccupied against the kerb. They were still very young and had so much to learn but the world was their oyster. Martyn especially will never forget the day that he made the right choice and never would he find out how close he had come to losing everything, mostly his freedom and quite possibly Danielle.

Going back behind the counter to finish off Vera called out to me asking I wanted to partake of our usual afternoon cuppa together, I called back and thanked her.

When I lost sight of them I suddenly remembered back to when I had been Martyn's age, a time when money had little value but meant everything. I realised how foolish I had been. A healthy bank balance still does mean a lot only for different reasons and no amount of fast cars, fancy living could ever replace having a lovely wife, an adorable daughter and good friends.

Pushing aside the swing door I went out back to the kitchen where Vera was waiting silently giving my thanks to the psyche of the café for having once again looked after Martyn and myself.

Off to Paris or Not

The café has gradually been building a good reputation for serving up some of Vera's best cooking along with offering good advice although in principal I believe some individuals already had the answer before they walked through just needing a little encouragement to help them get over the final hurdle.

It would be indecorous of me to give you examples of what they ask whereas instead I can endorse Vera's mouth-watering delights. Anything else should be left to discretion. However of our customers who are happy to disclose what they say many make reference to the unusual sense of calm which invites them in and have them impart of their most inner problems. I too have experienced first-hand how the café can help and been grateful to the presence that dwells within our walls believing that magic is the greater entity.

One such individual who did need help was a young woman who came to us just after a busy lunchtime session. Pulling behind her a large suitcase she appeared vexed and extremely agitated. A polite young man waiting for a take-out order helped her settle herself at the nearest available table.

As she watched him return to the counter I sensed there and then that she had somehow missed the initiative to ask his name and share a few more pleasurable moments in his company although how many of us could say that we have been in similar circumstances only to later ask ourselves *what if I had only...* annoying moments that forever haunt us and disturb our routine.

Danielle took the girls order, a latte with a Chelsea bun.

'I asked and she's off to Paris today,' she told me as I got ready the cup and usual measure of coffee. I could see the green envy in Danielle's eyes as wondered what adventures would be waiting if she were going as well.

I had been once many years back when Sylvia and I had thought we could salvage our marriage remembering how she had wanted to do the tourist bit, browse through Cartier, Louis Vuitton and Abercrombie Fitch before dining along the Avenue de Champs Elysses, taking in the Seine and Eiffel Tower before bedtime. Looking across to where the young woman was sat looking out of the window I couldn't help but wonder how the romantic charisma of Paris had her looking so glum. Maybe I thought she knew of my ex-wife and how she couldn't wait to get back home distrusting all French.

'Have faith Danielle, dreams do come true!'

'Yeah right and pigs fly past the window wearing pink bows.'

With that she went out to the kitchen for some clean cups and saucers. A moment later I heard what sounded like a pained yelp as Danielle hit out and Martyn ask *'what?'* I guessed it would be up to me later to tell him what was wrong.

Pushing the Chelsea bun around the plate with the end of her finger she was obviously not intent of eating the cake moreover ordering the rounded delicacy as a distraction to her thoughts. Going over I used the cake as an excuse to find out what was troubling her.

'Is the bun stale?' I asked.

She looked up somewhat surprised to me standing there. I thought at that point she would burst into tears so I sat down. Taking a napkin from the imitation galvanised buckets that we had on the tables I handed her one.

'I can get you something else if you'd prefer?'

'There nothing wrong with the bun, I am just not hungry anymore!'

Stress or tension, worry and fatigue are all factors that will put us off our food and yet the most important ingredient to keep healthy was good food. Thinking back I recall seeing grown men refuse breakfast or lunch knowing that they had a parole board that morning or afternoon. The mind is a powerful weapon when it comes to the functions of the body. I tried a different approach.

'I hear that you're off to Paris today?'

'I am due to catch an early evening flight to Charles de Gaulle.' She didn't sound enthusiastic about the prospect.

'Is the flight the problem?' I asked.

'No... only now that the day has finally arrived, I am in two minds whether to go or not!'

Doubt *'shall I or shall I not'* one of the biggest hurdles we face in life. Again like minutes earlier when she had missed the opportunity to engage with the young man she had been the victim of her own trepidation.

'Well if the times not right then maybe you should delay the trip.'

'That's not as easy as it sounds. The time is right only I am not sure that I am but until I decide one way or the other I think I'm safer here!'

We appeared to be going around in circles. I took a deep breath and offered some advice as best as I saw the problem.

'Life is full of choices from the moment we wake and whatever options we chose on the day becomes our destiny. We can reflect on what we got wrong but we never really question what we get right. Every day presents a new challenge but that's how life progresses. I really learnt that going with your gut reaction the best way forward. Too much thinking only complicates the issue.'

Of course I had forgot one important element.

'Is there a young man involved?' I added.

She looked down, nodded instantly understating the problem. Men always complicated an issue.

'Now I don't confess to being an expert, but I'd lay odds it's why god created men and women to throw a spanner in the works!'

'It's done that alright. Phillippe doesn't want me to go to Paris saying that my life is here with him and that whatever I can do in Paris I can make happen in London.' She paused for thought 'In a way he is right although Paris is an opportunity that only ever comes around once in a lifetime!'

She noticed my ring and how shiny it looked.

'You've not got any scratches, have you been married long?'

'Five months... the best five months of my life.'

I pushed her Chelsea bun to one side where she could have it later.

'Thing is like you I had to make an important decision, several actually. The only thing stopping me from arriving at the answer was me myself. The solution was easy and there in front of my face I just had to take a leap of faith. Sometimes taking a step back to get things into perspective can only delay the inevitable. The last time I made the wrong choice it cost me big time!'

'What happened?'

'I got divorced!'

She tried to smile, but it didn't really materialise.

'I have a good offer in Paris to work in an exclusive fashion house where they have agreed to put my designs into production. If I turn down this offer I will slamming the door shut on my career forever. I have never wanted to be a name or famous but I would relish the thought of my clothes being worn on the streets of Paris, New York or Milan.

Making sure that Danielle wasn't earwigging I didn't want out conversation to complicate her life. We each need a dream but some are one step beyond reality and for Martyn's sake I could only tackle one issue at a time.

'That's a very tempting offer, I can see your dilemma. And where does Phillippe fit into the equation?'

I had a cheek asking but to sort the problem we needed to lay our cards on the table as I had done in Paris.

'At the moment he doesn't. We argued this morning when he found that I had packed my case last night. I walked out lunchtime without saying goodbye!'

'Phillippe, is he French?'

'No Brazilian. He came to London eleven months ago. We met in a nightclub and from there we seemed inseparable, he moved in with me a month later.'

Those little bells in my head were ringing once again. She went on with her explanation.

'He based his argument on the fact that he didn't want to pick up his hat again and lay it down somewhere new like Paris!'

Phillippe might not have made the connection but I had.

'Do you think that he's being selfish or am I…?'

'More than selfish, your live-in lover is self-centred and only has his own interests at heart. He stacked his deck high this morning almost blackmailing you into staying. At least that's the way that I see it!'

More positive she wiped the tear from her cheek then surprised me by picking up her Chelsea bun.

'He only wanted a roof over his head and a bed to lie, didn't he?'

At last she had got it.

I watched as she devoured the bun and drank her latte. Sometimes it only take a spark to ignite a fire and see the light.

We spent the next half of an hour talking about Paris and I told her about the best places that I thought she could afford to dine. Until she hit the big time she would need to be a little frugal with her money. She asked about Lola and I told her about little Amelia. I said that one day we would take her to Disneyland Paris.

'Then you must come and visit me as well,' she announced, her mind made up. 'I'm going to catch the coach to the airport and arrive in time for my appointment tomorrow morning at the fashion house.'

'Good for you!'

Suddenly there was a determination about her expression, nothing hard just a strong resolve.

'And what Phillippe does is entirely up to him, but I am no longer going to be dragged down by a Brazilian beach bum who can't settle his own ambitions!'

And there it was, doubt had turned to anger which invariably happens to arrive at the point of no return. Whether we get it right or wrong only you can decide. As I told Danielle dreams can become a reality but sometimes they have to be meet at the crossroads, at the right time and the right place.

She paid Danielle for the coffee and cake, kissed me on the cheek and said goodbye, saying that she would send a postcard with her details.

An hour later I saw a frantic looking foreigner peer in through our window then run off down the road, I guessed who he was but smiled to myself knowing that the young woman was long gone. He'd had his chance to stick by her but blown it the moment that he had thought of nobody but himself. He struck me as the sort of man who would lay his hat in many places only never settling in any.

Later that evening I happened to look up at the clock on the mantelpiece hearing Lola read to Amelia upstairs. It was about time that a certain young lady was about to board a flight to one of the most enchanting cities in the world. I wished her well even though I had forgotten to ask her name.

Weeks later Danielle arrived at work with a fashion magazine that her mum had kept back having picked it up at the hairdressers. When she opened it up at the centre folds I immediately recognised the young lady on the catwalk taking the applause. Emily Follingdale had been an unknown name until she had arrived at a fashion house in Paris, but almost overnight her designs had escalated into the halls of fashion fame. Emily's courage had made her change her stars.

A week after the magazine article was published a letter arrived addressed only to *the little red café* where inside there was an open invitation to visit the *Madame Breton Fashion House* where Emily worked together details of her apartment and telephone number. Sometime in the evening I produced the letter to show Lola and Amelia.

'Are we going to visit daddy?' asked Amelia.

'Well...' I replied 'mummy and daddy were wondering what to get you for your birthday, but we had a long hard think and decided we had best wait until we went to Paris only we did hear that a certain Mickey Mouse has a Disney shop at his theme park where there are lots of toys. We thought you could choose your own present.'

Our plan was greeted with a squeal of enthusiastic delight.

Before she went up to bed Amelia sat on the sofa with Lola where together they went through the holiday brochures that I had brought home along with Emily's letter. Amelia was so excited she found it hard to contain herself knowing that her birthday was only a few months away.

'Is that instead of my garden party?' she asked.

'No...' smiled Lola 'you will have your party and as promised we will still invite all your friends from the home.'

I wrote back to Emily Follingdale and thanked her for the letter and invite stating that we would let her know the details of when we were due to arrive.

A Public Health Inspection

The dreaded letter arrived one Monday morning with Ted our postman taking great joy in recognising the logo stamped across the top right corner of the envelope.

'Looks like you'll be getting a visit soon from the public health inspector,' he said, the obvious delight creasing his cheeks either side of his nose making him resemble a mouse.

Vera arrived as I was about to shut the door. She noticed the familiar official envelope in my hand having seen a good many before.

'Don't they have anything better to do?' she asked stretching her back as she made her way through to the kitchen.

'Like everybody else they have a job to do!' I replied, a feeble attempt to humour her.

'Well I do object to their poking their nose in here and why can't they do it elsewhere. I have a whole kitchen and larder to clean besides cook and bake.'

'Delegate,' I suggested. 'Martyn will need to learn what's required and the experience might prove useful for the future.'

Vera let the tension ebb from her aching limbs.

'You don't have many good ideas but that's one of your better ones. The other was marrying Lola and adopting little Amelia!'

Vera loved being known as Auntie Vera to Amelia.

Ignoring her usual banter I read down the details of the letter.

'They will visit anytime within the next five days.'

Danielle and Martyn met with the same information when they arrived and Vera wrote a note to order Martyn some catering clothing so that he looked the part. Danielle could wear what she normally did out front of house, a tee-shirt, trainers and jeans.

'Who is this Mr Arnold Armstrong?' asked Martyn, digesting the requirements as laid out in the form attached to the letter.

'Our area health inspector. A nice chap really, a little overweight although a stickler for cleanliness and hygiene. You'll know when he arrives because he always wears a three piece pin striped suit, with a gold chain dangling from the waistcoat pocket to the third button up. Looks a bit like a beadle. Considers himself to be a gentleman and don't be fooled by the scent of his aftershave, Armstrong will have the drains up if deems it necessary'

Martyn looked at Vera and whispered 'what's a beadle?'

'Charles Dickens.' She replied.

Martyn nodded although I believe he was none the wiser.

'Has he...' he ran his finger down the list of possible fines 'ever slapped a prohibition notice on the cafe?'

'No, although the last time he was here he found a dead mouse behind the freezer which earned us a return visit. We had a ginger Tom who lived in the yard out back and it was he who had pushed the mouse through the air vent, why we've never found out. Our saving grace was the ginger bugger tried to do the same when Armstrong was back visiting. We've since put a strong mesh over the vent.'

Vera put a solitary digit in the air 'his wife suffers from bunions which is a very sore subject with old Armstrong so watch what you say to him about wearing the right footwear.'

Monday and Tuesday passed quietly without any sighting of our pinstripe official but come Wednesday lunchtime with the queue almost out of the door Arnold Armstrong promptly walked in and around back of the counter rubbing his hands together. He had on the same silly grin that I had he wore on his last visit.

'Well here we are Mr Brand always a pleasure to see you!' he extended his arm to shake my hand but I stepped back not to be caught out as I was serving customers.

Putting a tick in the box he grinned again. 'A good start, always maintain the best possible levels of hygiene when serving the public.

He stood to one side and observed until the queue had gone down to just one or two late arrivals admirably watching Danielle flit between the tables and who surprisingly had on a white catering jacket over her tee-shirt. The jacket was spotlessly clean despite having delivered and collected a good many lunches. I saw him tick another box, so far we were doing alright. When trade was less busy I shook his hand then washed my hands in the side beside the Fracino Contempo. Another box ticked.

'It's turned out nice again!' I announced.

Arnold Armstrong walked back over to the window and looked up at the sky.

'Nice, although I suspect that there's an odd cloud of doubt about!' Typical of the man who could find a speck of dirt in a raindrop.

'Have you been busy?' I asked wondering where he wanted start.

Pulling his fob watch from his waistcoat he checked the time.

'The clocks always against me Mr Brand, never enough time to get around all the premises on my list and so little window of opportunity to make time for my dear wife.'

I wanted to ask about her bunions but so far we had got off to a good start.

'Still...' he smiled 'I've always space left in my diary for the little red café!'

Arnold Armstrong was the archetypical council official, armed with a case load of forms many that you never understood, a pen in his top pocket and a glint in his eye.

At six feet two with a mop of fairish auburn hair, a paunch fighting against the buttons of his waistcoat and his ever present rounded rim glasses he made a formidable figure. Danielle always thought of Arnold Armstrong as a university professor rather than a hygiene sanitary inspector.

The afternoon had started quite well until another bell chime had me look around and to my dismay see Gordon Proudfoot, the Environmental Officer for Burwood Council walk in. We also knew one of another from the fish market when Proudfoot was out earning his spurs. I wasn't sure why but I looked back at Arnold Armstrong hoping for some kind of support. With two of them on the premises I could feel my knees buckling. It was like a pincer movement that had been strategically planned.

'Mr Proudfoot has recently transferred to our office and he will be taking over my position soon when I retire. I invited him along today as I thought your café would be the ideal establishment to break him in gently.'

I looked at Proudfoot and smiled, the one that he didn't need was breaking in gently. Like a bull with a thorn stuck in his rear he could charge at anything red, green, yellow or blue. Behind me I saw Danielle disappear momentarily into the kitchen to warn Vera and Martyn. She returned almost immediately grinning at Arnold Armstrong.

'How is Mrs Armstrong's feet' she asked.

I felt the earth open up yet not swallow me whole. Expecting Armstrong to mark us down on the form he had always liked Danielle and I think secretly he had a soft spot for her charm and innocence.

'She's getting along,' he replied 'thank you for asking and you look very smart!' It was another tick in the box.

He introduced Gordon Proudfoot to Danielle only I dared not look up.

'You sound like a descendant from one of those Red Indian tribes!' she announced Danielle.

I looked for a place to hide only nothing presented itself to me. To my surprise Proudfoot took her remark in good heart, he laughed and held out his hand for her to shake.

'Nothing quite as grand. My family heritage originates from middle England although my particular strand hail from the Scottish Highlands. And you?' he asked.

I don't know how Danielle had achieved it but she had the two of them almost eating out of her hand.

'Local she said. My family originate from the workhouse, well least I think my great-nan did. Do you fancy a slice of lemon drizzle cake and a coffee before you start looking around?'

Within seconds both officials we sat at an available table and I was ordered behind the counter to make the coffees whilst Danielle cut the cake extra-large.

Taking their coffees over Proudfoot seemed interested to continue his conversation 'you have an interesting set of forenames name Mr Brand, a throwback from the golden era of the movies?'

I watched Danielle wipe the edge of the plates with a napkin before she brought them over. Armstrong ticked another box. She had him wrapped around her little finger.

'Entirely my mother's fault.' I told how the names had come about.

They both looked very impressed when Danielle served their cake.

'Some mothers have a seriously wicked sense of humour when they register our birth. Mine named me Gordon Lightfoot Proudfoot.' He held up his left hand as he cut through the cake with his fork in the right 'and yes, she did have a thing for the Canadian born singer.

Standing beside the table Danielle was captivated by their names.

'You Mr Armstrong sound like an astronaut and you Mr Proudfoot like you are the chief of a war-faring tribe. I wish that I had an interesting name like you both have.'

She excused herself and went out into the kitchen to help.

'What an interesting girl,' said Proudfoot 'quite extraordinary for somebody so young!'

They insisted on paying when they were done whereupon Proudfoot suggested that they start with the stockroom having read the report about the dead mouse. When the three of us went through to the kitchen I noticed that Martyn was missing.

'Where?' I mimed at Vera as Proudfoot went inside the stockroom furiously ticking down his clipboard

Vera sidled over and whispered *'he's out back keeping the cats at bay as they were starting to gather around the bins!'*

Those darn cats were the bane of my life at times and why I wondered did they always appear when the public health inspector was around.

Closing the stockroom door, he then began inspecting the kitchen. Standing in the corner Vera had her arms crossed across her chest holding a rolling pin. I wanted to laugh and cry at the same time.

When Martyn suddenly reappeared he had a long scratch down his right forearm the war wound of an altercation with a large ginger Tom. Proudfoot recommended a biological wash and some antiseptic cream leaving the wound open to let the air do its job. To my surprise he advised that Martyn stay out of the kitchen He was a lot different to when I had known him at the fish market.

Seeing that the first aid box had adequate provision he added another tick.

'Cats can be an infernal nuisance around the back of restaurants and cafes, eating houses and in the home. We have two at home and they're always going for my ankles!'

He carried on walking around the kitchen looking under shelves, around the back of the cooker and inside the large fridge freezer.

It was all that he said on the matter as he watched Martyn bath his arm then add the cream, ticking another mystery box.

Pulling a wrapped package from the back of the fridge freezer he gave it an almighty sniff. I thought it odd because we never had fried fish on the menu.

'Do you mind,' said Vera 'that's my supper, I put it in there this lunchtime as it was safer than anywhere else!'

Arnold Armstrong could no longer contain himself he started the laugh with me joining in followed quickly by Danielle, Martyn and finally Proudfoot and Vera. Wrapping the fish very carefully he replaced the package where he had found it and then ticked his form. Armstrong took himself out front where he needed some fresh air.

From there hence Gordon Proudfoot invited Vera to show him different aspects of the preparation area and cooker that he had on his list, embarrassed that he had almost ruined her supper he was more lenient than I had expected him to be.

We passed the inspection with flying colours, the first time ever. I was immensely proud of Vera, Danielle and Martyn. I would make it up to them later. Leaving Proudfoot to sign off the paperwork I went back out front where Arnold Armstrong was looking out of the window.

'I hear from sources that you tied the knot recently Mr Brand,' he offered his hand and congratulated me.

'And adopted a little girl,' I added.

His smile was genuine.

'Well you've a lot to look forward too then and Mr Proudfoot, has he any comments to make?'

'We passed without any hitches!' I tried not to sound overzealous at the result as it could mean that we cut some corners.

With that said Gordon Proudfoot appeared. He also added his blessing and his hand.

'You've a nice clean café Mr Brand and I would be pleased to visit again only perhaps not officially but just for lunch.'

I told him that he was welcome anytime. Sometimes a little white lie doesn't hurt.

'And you Mr Armstrong, what are your plans now?' I asked.

'We are moving on from Burwood perhaps to a little place by the sea. Mrs Armstrong rather likes Bournemouth, a nice sandy beach.'

I wished him well rather pleased that he was going. Today's visit being his last to the café had mellowed his approach but in the past he could be a tyrant.

Coming past the window I saw Lola head for our door. She smiled at the men then looked at me.

'Have you any suggestions what I can do about the cats out back in the yard,' she asked 'they nearly scratched poor Mary's arm!'

Martyn held up his 'they got mine instead.'

Gordon Proudfoot produced his card and handed it to Lola.

'If you would permit me to have a look perhaps I could help.' He was certainly different from the fish market visits.

'I'd be grateful,' replied Lola 'we think it's the smell of discarded *gyposphila paniculata*!'

'Ah,' said Arnold Armstrong raising a finger 'more commonly known to gardeners as 'baby's breath' it emits a pungent aroma that smells like cat-nip, hence the problem.'

'Then I will be only too pleased to assist to see how best we can address the issue.'

He would advise a better assortment of bins which he arranged with the refuse department. Two days later they arrived supplied with keys.

Whilst Gordon Proudfoot was with Lola I sat and talked to Arnold Armstrong. He told me about his wife's bunions and how the cooling waters of the bay would help soften her soles. He told me about his love of gardening and how he intended growing his own vegetables. When

Lola came back she talked to Arnold about flowers both sharing a common interest.

That afternoon the barriers had come down and really Arnold Armstrong and Gordon Proudfoot were just ordinary men with an important job to do. No longer would we fear a visit from the public health inspector but moreover assist them. Of course having Danielle and Lola around was bound to help sway any discrepancy.

Over the coming years we saw Gordon Proudfoot annually but his visits were always a pleasure and at the end of a visit we would all sit down and hear of his escapades when visiting other premises in the borough Lola cleverly had him arrange the café visit to coincide with a visit to the florist to check on the feline problem but also knowing that it was around the time of his wedding anniversary. In a way we were killing two birds with one stone or as Proudfoot would put it, ticking all the boxes.

Life can be a funny old covenant, we arrive and we do our best in the in-between bit then leave when our time is up. Problems like a dead mouse, a feral ginger tom cat and dead flowers are menial compared to the greater scheme of things.

Every so often when the sun is shining I wonder if the Dorset coastline did help improve Mrs Armstrong's bunions although undoubtedly the warm climate would provide Arnold a bumper crop of vegetables.

A visit to see Doc Doland

Mid-Spring had arrived bringing in a warm, welcome breeze blowing in from the east. The days of grey skies, below zero temperatures and flurries of snow were now a mere memory which in time would be forgotten.

Although I lived in the big city my interests extended to keeping pace with rural events happening in the country following the progress of the farmers who toiled ceaselessly to feed us. A concern was how global warming was affecting the crops and the seasons.

Television documentaries went some way to help explain the difficulties that the farmers and cattle had to overcome but when the food landed on our table our interest would quickly change to filling our stomachs.

Embracing the warmth in the sunshine and hoped that it was widespread across the British Isles and that lambs were frolicking, cows resting and pigs wallowing in gooey mud, events that had not changed down the centuries.

The sunshine was a welcome respite having endured rain for the past three days, leaving behind an unsettled feeling of what lie ahead. However today everything seemed different, fresher and more alive. Spring had arrived.

Vera on the other hand arrived moaning that her washing was still damp although I did try to explain that she had left it on the line for the past seventy two hours. As a precaution she had with her umbrella not trusting the predictions of the weather forecasters on the radio. Pointing the tip of the umbrella at my chest, she warned.

'One more word out of place Spencer Brand and you'll spend the morning at Doc Doland's as he surgically extracts this!'

Pushing aside the front door I let her go first and watched he head towards the kitchen. We had known each other long enough to appreciate when a moment of quiet time was an essential necessity. Once the radio went on and she started to hum to the music her mood would change.

After a quarter of an hour and ten minutes humming I tempted fate going through the swing door.

'Fancy a nice cup of rosy lee?' I asked.

'That would be very welcome,' she still wasn't her normal self and something amiss appeared to be soaking up her thoughts 'I'm all behind this morning and it's Cedric's fault as he decided to stay out all night last night. The bugger does what he likes occasionally and I've no idea what he gets up too!'

I could tell Vera wasn't amused and I assumed her moodiness to be lack of sleep. A minute later the bell over the door chimed announcing the arrival of Danielle and Martyn. Like a fresh spring breeze she waltzed into the kitchen.

'Mornin'… sunshine at last,' Danielle announced 'this should bring the customer back today!'

She was the eternal optimist always bright and cheery, always so full of life. Martyn on the other hand was always a little more reserved and no more so than this morning, why was evident. Looking at Danielle her appearance had changed dramatically overnight and instead of the normal straight down to the shoulder style her hair had been pinned to look like the spout of a pineapple. We exchanged looks but said nothing. Vera however was having none of it.

'What's have you done to your barnet,' she asked 'it looks like you've taken a fast spin in the washing machine!'

As tactful as ever I could see dark clouds looming. It did look off all spikey and not sure in which direction it should settle but worse still were the ends which had been dyed in red and orange. To me Danielle resemble a large orange with lumps of cheese attached the type that you'd find as nibbles as a wine and cheese party.

'I'm not afraid of criticism,' she replied hanging her coat on the peg 'it happens to be my new look!' she gave us a twirl although the back was no different to the front.

'Blimey,' said Vera 'you look like you're on fire!'

'It's a fashion statement,' and that it was. Danielle looked to where Martyn was slipping into his cooking overalls. Since the visit of health inspectors he had got used to wearing the white tunic. 'Of course as usual he's not sure!'

Vera came to Martyn's rescue. 'I can't say as I blame him. My Cedric came home looking better this morning!'

I closed my eyes expecting World War III to begin but Danielle had soaked up the sunshine on the way into work and she wasn't to be down-hearted, whatever anybody had to say.

'I got the idea from a fashion magazine that Emily Follingdale recommended.'

I was somewhat surprised. 'I didn't know that you kept in touch.'

'Oh sure, replied Danielle 'we ring and write to one another all the time. One day I'm going to Paris with or without Martyn!'

Standing by the door to the store Martyn gestured his response by raising his palms. When she went to use the cloakroom Martyn felt it was safe to comment.

He whispered to Vera and myself *'between us, it's like waking up next to a hedgehog.'* I laughed although I hadn't meant too.

Turning the bacon under the grill Vera was coming back to top form.

'The gypsy's would bake hedgehogs in mud over the campfire, somebody should do that to that girl this morning!'

Closing the door of the cloakroom behind her Danielle reappeared. 'Who's having a campfire... are you thinking of going camping Vera?'

Intervening I told her that Lola and I were thinking of taking Amelia one weekend. I hinted that we had best go out front where the bell had chimed once if not twice. As a parting gesture she told Martyn that the hairstyle would grow on him and if it didn't there was always the settee. Young love could be so entertaining.

Now as you would expect our regulars were postmen, off-duty nurses and men from the council depot, each one a public servant, ordinary hard working individuals with an opinion and interest in the world about them. Taking up her station behind the counter Danielle filled the Fracino Contempo with fresh water as I went to serve the tables.

'Who's the disaster behind the counter?' asked the dust crew at the corner table.

I felt myself cringe screwing up my cheeks daring not to look behind towards the counter and the door.

'It's a trial fashion statement!' I muttered under my breath.

'Bloody hell Danielle,' called out one of the men' my young daughter took a troll doll to bed last night. You must have slipped into the room and modelled yourself on it!'

The peel of laughter didn't help one bit. I tried in vain to take the orders but the men were having none of it. I needn't have worried myself because Danielle was already equipped with a response.

'Well Fred Eames... it's lucky for little Daisy that she takes after her mother as any resemblance to you would have the poor girl howling.'

The same old Danielle, tough as old boots and ready to give back what she took. Other times she could as soft and as compassionate as you'd expect of a girl her age and especially around Amelia she was especially protective and loving but not where dustmen were concerned.

The laughter had Vera poke her head through the swing door to see what the commotion was about. It told her that it only Fred Eames getting the double-barrelled version from Danielle. Just like the weather Vera changed her stance on the matter, ever the protective mother of her flock.

'One day Fred Eames you might want to remember that I'm cooking your breakfast out back!'

It was enough said and Vera had effectively got the point home. At last I took their order before going on to the other tables.

Soon after things settled and trade was normal for the start of a new week picking up a regular heartbeat and enjoying the company of some of the local elderly residents that was until around mid-morning when Mary suddenly burst through the door and asked that I accompany her next door.

I was around the other side of the counter and next door before the door to the café had closed. I found Lola sitting on a chair out back in the preparation area. Her normal radiant glow was like the colour of the rain clouds that we had all become accustomed too of recent and her breathing was a little fast.

'I am alright,' she said allaying my fears 'and I did try to stop Mary coming in to fetch you but she was gone before I could move.'

Stroking Mary's arm to show my appreciation I wasn't having none of it.

'Mary did the right thing and we're lucky to have such a loving, caring friend!'

'I've checked Lola's pulse and its racing Spencer,' Mary looked anxious.

Feeling her forehead she was a little warm despite her pallor.

'Do you hurt anywhere?' I asked.

Lola looked at me and then Mary.

'I don't hurt anywhere you big oaf. I had to vomit then sit down after, it really is nothing to worry about Spencer, I promise you!'

Now the ladies amongst you will no doubt have already guessed the reason for Lola taking it easy after having visited the cloakroom at the rear of the florist but men being men would miss a whirlwind in a storm if it wasn't right in front of them.

'I want Doc Doland to give you the once over and make sure that's nothing more serious.'

Both Lola and Mary laughed.

'You make it sound like I'm due at the garage for an MOT. I assure you Spencer that everything will be fine and will run its natural course.'

I was still missing the point but I did insist upon going and so leaving Mary to run the florist I hailed another dustcart working in the road to take us to the surgery. Much to Lola's insistence that going would be a waste of the doctors and her time we mounted the cab of the dustcart.

Pushing aside the door to the surgery we waved to Bert and his crew as they gave us the thumbs up.

'Am I missing something?' I asked my mind doing somersaults inside my stomach. Lola frowned and told me that I would soon catch on.

Sitting in the reception Lola's colour had turned a nice flesh tanned pink and her eyes were once again sparkling. Although I don't confess to being any medical expert I was going through the list of possible causes that I knew that could make her feel faint. When they called her name Lola stood and gave me the option.

'You can come in with me or I can tell you why when I come back out!'

Looking around the waiting room and at the faces of the old biddies occupying the other chairs I didn't want to sit there all by myself so I went in closing the door of his consulting room behind me.

Lola explained her symptoms to Doc Doland who looked over the top of his glasses at first her then me. When he looked at me he made me feel a little uncomfortable as though I was to blame for Lola's condition.

'I will examine your wife behind the screen Mr Brand, perhaps you'd be kind enough to sit there quietly for a couple of minutes.'

It is quite amazing how muffling that screen can be plus their whispered conversation as I tried hard to hear what they were saying. When Doc Doland reappeared to wash and dry his hands he had a smile on his face. Writing out a prescription he handed it over to Lola and advised that she get plenty of fresh air and sunshine.

'Is that it?' I asked expecting something else although I knew not what.

'Come on Spencer,' said Lola taking my hand 'I'll explain what on the way back!' She thanked Doc Doland and apologised for having taken up his valuable time.

Outside the surgery she suddenly looped her arm through mine and pulled me in tight.

'Do me a favour...' she asked 'promise me that you'll never change, only I love you just the way you are.'

I remembered our church vows taken in St Mary's when Father Michael had mentioned *in sickness and in health'*. Walking back to the café and florist I was still none the wiser, not until Lola stopped us walking. She kissed me then held me close.

313

'Cio' che e' buono Spencer perche' sis ta per diventore padre.'

Amelia had taught me one or two Italian words and phrases but she was much better than me.

'I need to go see Robert Styles?' I asked.

'No you fool,' she laughed 'you are going to be a father and Amelia is going to have either a brother or sister to play with!'

Wise men say that special moments descend from heaven like a thunderbolt and grab hold of your heart, her news did precisely that. Scooping Lola up my arms I raised her inches from the ground and spun her round before realising the delicate condition she was in realising that another life was growing inside of her.

The walk back to the café was slow and careful. I wanted to know what to expect, wanting to know that I could cope. Suddenly in a moment our world and Amelia's had become enchantingly magical.

Turning the corner we waved at the dustcart as it drove past seeing four happy smiling faces only this time I gave the thumbs up sign much to their delight.

Placing a *'back in ten minutes'* sign on the door of the florist Mary closed shop and joined us in the kitchen next door where Lola announced that she was pregnant. The tears and cheers, kisses and hugs filtered through to the customers out front and when we went to celebrate our news they too could no longer contain their joy.

Vera pencilled a circle around the New Year give or a take a week or two telling Danielle that whatever the baby would start the next year just nicely. Later that afternoon Lola and I collected Amelia from school stopping off at the swings where pushing her back and forth we told her the good news. Jumping down from the swing seat she ran into our arms and together we cried again seeing her so happy and in nine months' time Amelia would help choose the name for her baby brother or sister.

From the park we had two very important visits to make where we allowed Amelia to tell her grandmother's about the happy event.

Lying next to Lola as she slept soundly I thanked god for his wisdom in bringing to me Lola and Amelia and now a baby. As a family we had been blessed with happiness and love and I prayed that night that it would always be so. The morning sickness and other times of complaining of when her back ached or her feet were swollen, including the unusual food cravings were all part and parcel of the happy event. With each passing day I became more adept at what I needed to do although surprisingly enough Amelia was always on hand to put me right where I did something wrong.

At night I would follow a shooting star, make a wish and pray. There would be more visits to see the nurse at the surgery but at least I could say that I was wiser now than I had been the day that we went to see Doc Doland.

The weekend after announcing our news Danielle had had enough of washing and spiking her hair every day allowing the colour to wash out naturally much to Martyn's relief. Come Sunday when we could all relax I found Amelia in her room talking to Angus and Shamus telling them how the baby was coming and going through a list of names that the three of them had thought of for the baby.

An Unexpected Customer

Sometimes having caught sight of a customer as they walk through the door you can tell almost by instinct what they will order as their eyes fall longingly on a certain cake or pastry inside the display case. That's the easy part, the second is their choice of table, however and by far the hardest is third knowing what they are thinking.

It was like that the day that Alfred Buggins walked in. He arrived with a distinct purpose in mind although perhaps not in his right mind for Alfred albeit aged ninety two had in his possession a pistol, a rather remarkable relic from the First World War but nonetheless it was convincingly real and almost certainly loaded.

Why he decided that the little red café should become his hostage zone only Alfred could answer that conundrum. The one thing I was grateful for looking up to the heavens was that he had walked past the florist shop.

Perhaps to begin this mysterious tale it might be best if I offer some background history which will hopefully throw some light on the challenging time ahead.

Born in the back room of a fine Georgian terraced three storey house in the academic and professional district of Bloomsbury in the year eighteen ninety seven, Alfred Buggins was the son of Beatrice Buggins, seamstress and Benjamin Buggins the miller. Alfred however had little time for schooling preferring to spend his time learning a trade and making good quality furniture.

Maturing into a rather handsome young man he was ready for the call for volunteers, signing up with the Kings Royal Rifle Corps to defend his King, his country and Kitchener. With fearful unease his parents could nothing to prevent their eighteen year old son from joining the war effort and getting aboard the train leaving for Buckinghamshire where he was to be billeted learning the basic rudiments of fighting and warfare. By October of the same year he found himself as part of the military theatre on the Macedonian front.

The futility of war needs no introduction but suffice to say that through death opportunity present Alfred with a command of his own and as a battle weary lieutenant he had successfully brought a lot of his detachment home, having received only minor scratches himself on barbed-wire.

Awarded for his gallantry Alfred had once told me that medals were only forged in the blood and bones of those who had died. He saw no glory in reward whilst other lie buried under the mud.

On the rare occasion that he would visit we would share a pot of tea together, talk about football and his Arsenal, his love of furniture and his beloved family but hardly ever the war and his exploits. I think the memory of his lost comrades haunted poor Alfred.

By the time that he had fought the second campaign and returned home as Captain Alfred Buggins, he was adamant that he would never ever again pick up another firearm in anger so it was a surprise when he walked into the café brandishing a loaded firearm.

Alfred sat himself down at a table out of sight of the door and asked that I call through anybody from out back. One by one Danielle, Vera and Martyn sat at a table near to where Alfred had made himself comfortable. Laying the gun on the table he asked Danielle if she would make him a pot of good strong hot tea.

As Danielle stood up, she asked 'and your usual teacake?'

Lining up opposite behind parked cars the emergency services were beginning to take a strategic defensive. Fearing for his safety I sat at the table beside the window directly in their line of sight.

'Are they outside,' he asked 'the police?'

'They're there Alfred and soon the rooftops will be swarming with marksmen.'

Unperturbed he breathed in deep and apologised for any inconvenience that he might be causing. I saw Stephanie Steele take up a position behind the crime scene tape that had been quickly looped between the lampposts to keep back the onlookers. I had hoped that Lola and Mary had been led to safety as the tape was attached to their rainwater down pipe. The police didn't bother with Bartram and his book emporium as it had been shut for the past week.

'It's looking a little like the Wild West out there Alfred, the Calvary are in position and there's no sign of the Indians!' I remembered as a boy stamping on the wooden floor during Saturday morning cinema when the projectionist had put on a good cowboy.

Alfred nodded as Danielle brought over his tea and two teacakes.

The old soldier sat quietly weighing up his options.

I pondered as I sat close by my old friend what was going through the man's mind. The recipient of a Distinguished Service Order for outstanding bravery, Alfred was a man of upstanding honour and courage. He had miraculously survived two vicious campaigns and retuned home a hero to his wife Mabel. Putting the past behind they had raised their family in Fitzgerald Street and seen their sons and daughter forge a life for themselves in a competitive world.

At eighty eight Mabel had sadly passed on to pastures green the middle of last year a loss that Alfred had never believed would happen wanting to be the first to go. He told me shortly after the funeral that Mabel had been the backbone of the family.

Polishing off his teacakes Alfred wiped the crumbs from the front of his jacket.

'Doc Doland come to see me end of last week. I thought it was a social visit but it turned out that he and the children were concerned that I was losing touch with reality. I'd be the first to agree that I do not understand everything that happens nowadays but at least I'm around to see it happen unlike a lot of my comrades that never got past their twentieth birthday. It was suggested that I leave my home and enter a residential retirement home where I would be expected to live out his days with people my own age.'

And there we had the reason for the siege although I wondered who it was that had alerted the police as there had only been the four of us in the café besides two customers when Alfred had walked in and the middle-aged couple were still present. Vera suddenly stood up and walked over to Alfred's table sitting herself at the seat opposite his.

'That's the problem with the younger generation of today Alfred,' she began 'once the skin turns leathery like a worn out lizard they want to put us on the scrap heap. I'm staying here and so are you!' It brought a smile to Alfred's cautious face.

Looking over to where the couple were silently in admiration of Alfred respecting his dilemma they politely turned down his offer to leave the café, wanting to show their support and solidarity to the old soldier and Danielle had said that it was too exciting to leave.

Expecting the arrival of a police negotiator we passed the time drinking tea and coffee sharing a freshly baked lemon drizzle cake. I told Alfred about Lola, little Amelia and the baby that was due around New Year. Congratulating me Alfred pulled out his wallet and passed across several photographs that went everywhere with him.

The first was of his lovely Mabel and when she had been a young woman working on the land at a farm out Bedfordshire way. The second of their wedding taken standing beneath the arched doorway of the church and the third of their eldest son Reginald who had been named in honour of a brave soldier that Alfred had fought alongside in the conflict at Macedonia, catching a hail of machine gun fire that by rights should have hit Alfred. Reginald Munch died later that afternoon but the young lieutenant was determined to keep his memory alive. Another captured the family before the children had come along with Mabel his brother George and Alfred's younger sisters, Alice and Dorothy. The last was more recent of his children, his grandchildren and great grandchildren. Studying each image I looked at the faces of the people in them happy and carefree unaware of what life would throw at them.

'I am not angry with them,' Alfred said as I handed back the photographs 'just disappointed that they didn't include me in their decision. I know that I am finding things hard since Mabel went but I am coping. They forget the time when their mother had to go for convalescence after she'd had a hysterectomy. It was me who cooked the meals, washed their clothes and made sure they slept easy every night. I kept house and none of them ever wanted for anything.'

Vera suppressed his embarrassment by handing over a paper napkin.

'She was a grand lass my Mabel and always on the move never sitting down for more than a minute at a time. Even when she hit eighty seven and the last year of her life, I begged her to take things easy but despite

Doc Doland's insistence she continued at the same pace.' He placed his hand over Vera's 'I think she knew the end was in sight.'

Vera nodded only Alfred had an unexpected surprise to deliver.

'It don't get any easy lass, that's for sure. I know how hard you suffered after the piano player passed away!' Danielle was listening in as curious as ever. She looked over at me but I shrugged my shoulders much to Vera's relief.

The moment was interrupted by the sound of a loud-hailer somewhere outside.

'In the café, this is the police. Come outside and give yourself up and we can talk about your actions!'

Typical police I thought lacking any empathy and allowing a six foot two, hairless, brainless ape to use the megaphone.

'Don't you do anything of the sort,' Vera ordered 'you stay where you are until Spencer has had a word.'

I looked across my jaw dropping, me have a word. Two things that had the hair on the back of my neck rise was anything in a uniform and the other a loud mouthed copper.

Pushing my head through the gap in the door holding a white handkerchief I waved at Lola and she waved back which was a good sign.

'Alfred is not prepared to talk to anybody not until his family arrive. Until then you might as well arrange refreshments for yourselves. We have enough stock in the café to carry the siege on through the night if needs be!' With that said I closed the door, much to the surprise of man on the megaphone.

Alfred looked concerned. 'I can't be here that long,' he said 'only I've got Tiddles to feed at six and tonight is cooked fish.'

Danielle put Alfred's mind at rest suggesting that if it came to it, she would slip out the back way, take his key and feed the cat then come back afterwards. There was no way that she was going to miss out on the excitement.

'I will not surrender until my sons and daughter agree not to put me in a home. That decision might seem thick-skinned but if I give up my independence I give up my will to live.' He looked around at the faces in the café. 'I might not be able to hold up this gun for long but I am no fool and I won't be swayed neither by any false promises.'

Sending Lola a text I asked if the police had contacted the sons and daughter, she responded stating that the police wanted to know if Alfred would release his hostages soon. I told her that we were making a stand on Alfred's behalf and would be staying. If it was good enough for Alfred's platoon at Macedonia, then it was good enough for the battle at the little red café. Lola replied as I knew that she would 'Okay... Love you!' From my seat I saw a bald head behind the cars sag, his resignation losing faith for a quick resolution. Five minutes later Lola texted that the family were on route.

A minute passed and the megaphone asked if they could talk direct with Mr Buggins?'

This time Vera went to the front door determined to answer the police request. 'No you can't... he's safe in the trenches here and until the family arrive we have nothing to say.' Making sure that Michael Parkin captured her best side she replaced the loose strands of hair tucking them behind her ear. Closing the door she fisted the air. 'That'll give the buggers outside something to think about!' Going back over to Alfred's table she gently patted his shoulder. 'We'll get through this together or go down fighting!'

Half an hour after Vera had closed the door I saw two men and a woman exit a police car. I told Alfred that his sons and daughter had arrived asking if he was ready to face them.

'I've faced worse.' He pushed the pistol over to Vera. 'You are just like the company soldiers back in nineteen eighteen facing the enemy. I would have been proud to have gone into battle with any one of you!' Looking at the door of the café he saw his family arrive. He looked at me 'I'm ready!' he said.

Vera disappeared quickly dropping the pistol down the front of her pinny. When Alfred had initially arrived she had been making pastry for an apple pie, in the kitchen she placed the gun in the pie dish placing a thick topping over the firearm hiding the ridges with some fancy pastry designs.

As Danielle let the arrivals in Alfred whispered 'what about the gun, I'll be in trouble for that?'

Furtively I looked around replying 'What gun, it was all hearsay and whoever told the police got it wrong.' I winked 'Vera's sorted the problem and once this is over, we'll get it back to you!'

Alfred suddenly clutched his chest and I thought that he was about to suffer a heart attack but instead of falling forward he sighed and breathed calmly.

'Mabel just let me know that she's still by my side, she often does that in time of trouble!'

Inviting the middle-aged couple out back for an impromptu cuppa we gave Alfred and his family the freedom of the café to talk through his dilemma. There were no raised voices, probably a few tears and an understanding that had been missing as happens from time to time. It doesn't mean one side loves the other any less but that a misunderstanding can create a ridiculous rift. When Reginald came through to the kitchen to say that everything had been resolved we all went back out front.

Shaking each of our hands we were surprised by how strong his grip was. He kissed Vera on the cheek and thanked her whispering something in her ear although none of us heard what although I guessed that it was about Cyril. Whatever he said it made Vera smile and puzzled Danielle all the more. Giving me a salute I saluted him back.

'You know I have always liked this little café of yours. There's something here that beats and that's why Mabel came to help!'

We watched as Alfred led his family across to the police line where the crowd cheered and applauded. Reginald talked to the inspector on the megaphone and squared everything suggesting that there had never been a gun involved and it wasn't so much a siege as a stand for one man's human rights. I watched the police driver take them home believing that we had unfortunately seen Alfred for the last time.

As the car drew away people lined the street acknowledging the old soldier, young and old alike he would always be a hero and not just from an era gone past but a hero of our time.

The inspector and his cronies came into the café to question us but we all stuck to our guns and said pretty much the same as Reginald Buggins had. When they searched the premises they obviously found no evidence of a firearm just an apple pie sitting on the side ready to be baked in the oven.

I told the police inspector that because of the recent rain Alfred had brought with him an extendable umbrella to offer some protection. To the uninitiated it might had resembled a firearm but then that was the fault of the manufacturer not a ninety two year old captain with a distinguished service.

When the police dismantled the cordon Lola and Amelia came over with her aunt Mary.

'Did the old man hurt you daddy?' Amelia asked, concerned that I might have been frightened by the ordeal.

I knelt down and pulled her into me gently explaining.

'Alfred was just a very old soldier fighting one more battle darling, a battle that he was determined to win. He didn't hurt daddy because we are friends and sometimes friends have to stand together!'

Amelia would not understood a word of what I had said but it didn't matter as long as I was safe. She pulled a painting from her rucksack to show me, a painting that she had done that afternoon at school of an angel sitting on a cloud with a rounded sun at her back.

'It's really lovely Amelia,' I said 'a beautiful painting and we should pin it somewhere in your bedroom where it can watch over you, always!'

It was a beautiful painting reminding me of the photographs that Alfred kept in his wallet of Mabel and his family. I believed him when he said that Mabel had come back to help that believing that the spirit in the café could well be an angel, who knows.

A month after the visit from Alfred Buggins the old soldier fought his last battle and laid down his sword with his family by his side including his great grandchildren. Reginald came to tell us about his passing stating that although it was very sad they were all relieved because he was once again with their mother. Vera gave me the pistol that she had kept hidden. I in turn gave it to Reginald.

'This gun kept your father alive throughout two terrible world wars. I think you should keep it somewhere very safe in honour of his extraordinarily remarkable life.'

Reginald took the pistol wrapped in a brown rag. He shook my hand and thanked us all before walking back to his car and his own family.

Alfred Buggins was one of the bravest and most honourable men that it had been my privilege to know. In memory of his battle that day we had a plague made for the wall of the café, it reads:

In memory of his last great battle, Alfred Buggins, Capt., Kings Royal Rifles. A hero to the last.

A Birthday to Remember

First came the sunshine creeping slowly above the chimney tops like a sleeping dragon rising from the night followed by the euphoric chirping of the birds although the most important wake-up call was yet to come, Amelia. Lying in bed we were already awake aware that the day would be full of excitement, boundless energy and perhaps a little apprehension.

When Amelia came racing into our room bringing with her Angus and Shamus she took two great strides before leaping onto the middle of the bed climbing in between Lola and myself, kissing us good morning before settling her two teddies my side moments before she gently lowered and placed her head on Lola's abdomen listening for the baby. She would tell us that she could something moving about although at this early stage I guessed that it was probably nothing more than Lola's stomach gases.

'Do you think the baby knows that I am listening?' she would ask.

'Of course darling,' Lola would reply 'and baby is thinking that's my big sister out there and soon I will be coming out to play.'

Watching the two of them chat and talk about the baby I accepted that as a family we loved one another but there did exist a very special bond between Lola and Amelia, a girly thing. It was inevitably going to happen as Amelia spent so much time with Lola and Mary in the shop on a Saturday and after school each day coming into the café for the odd snack and to see Vera, Danielle and Martyn. Naturally I didn't feel any envy of the love between them as it was pleasing to see that Amelia had settled so well into a routine and accepted the house as her home but more importantly Lola and myself as her mummy and daddy.

For weeks Amelia, Lola and Mary had been planning the birthday and garden party that we had promised. Danielle had been making small table decorations, taking ideas from fashion magazines and Vera said that she would bake the cake leaving Martyn and Thomas to volunteer their services and help collect the tables and chairs from the church hall, setting them up in the garden. Each evening I had been outside stringing up a line of lights stretching from the top of the kitchen window to the end of the garden, across the fence and back up the other side ending with a loop in the small apple tree beside the rear dining room.

When I switched the lights on to test that they all worked Amelia went along the line counting the different coloured bulbs making sure that there was equal greens, blues, reds, yellow and orange. She was a funny little girl and in her bedroom everything had a place to lay, sit or stand and woe betide anything that wasn't. Lola told me that it was probably the only way that the children's home could operate daily keeping a proper control of children, toys and keeping bedrooms tidy. I hoped that one day Amelia would leave something out of place if only for her own peace of mind.

Suddenly realising that today was her birthday Amelia peered down either side of the bed searching for signs of any wrapped presents and cards but she saw none. Lowering her head onto Lola's chest she looked but Lola cuddled her closer still so that she could kiss the top of her forehead and whisper in her ear.

'Mummy and daddy were just going to sleep last night when we thought that we saw a fairy walk along the landing. She had all of your presents in her arms... I think she took them downstairs.'

In a flash Amelia was out of the bed and heading for the front room leaving Angus and Shamus behind. Lola and I put on our dressing gowns and took a teddy each knowing that they would be needed downstairs.

In a flurry of paper tearing and opening of envelopes the moment of dejection had turned instead to exhilaration and joy. Spreading her presents in a circle she had them spaced in equal importance. First she had a new dolly that talked from Mary and Thomas, a set of colouring books from Vera, a children's make-up set from Danielle and Martyn and from Nana Capella a brightly coloured new dress, shoes and cardigan and from my mother a collection of games for under tens.

From Lola and myself I wheeled from under the stairs a dolls pram where inside the cot Amelia unwrapped a number of smaller gifts containing a trinket box, a box of sweets and a new bedtime story book. The last box however contained a snow globe of the Eiffel Tower. Amelia looked at us both slightly puzzled before shaking the glass orb, watching the snow cover the tower wondering why we had given her something so peculiar in the middle of May.

'Look under the pillow of the pram,' Lola hinted.

Finding another envelope Amelia carefully peeled back the flap extracting three airline tickets. Reading through the details her smile began to grow and grow.

'We're going to Paris…' she squealed jumping up and hugging us both *'I'm going to see Mickey Mouse!'* The surprise was much better than we had both imagined and the day had only just begun.

Lola and Amelia showered then got dressed in readiness for the adults who were due to arrive and help prepare the sandwiches, jellies and savoury treats. After doing the same I went back downstairs in time to hear the doorbell ring only to find Amelia already there as pulled open the front door to see my mother there with another parcel in her hand. Amelia kissed her nanny then raced back into the front room where she had in addition to her birthday presents a beanie hat with flowers, a matching scarf and gloves.

'I hear that you're off to Disneyland soon so you might need those as the evenings can be a little fresh abroad!' Putting them on Amelia tried them for size much to my mums delight.

The next bell to sound was Nana Capella who also arrived armed with another gift. A little girl's handbag where inside Amelia found a small purse containing a number of euro coins.

'You'll be needing them to buy something nice in the Disney shop!'

Sitting beside Lola we watched as our daughter nestle herself between her two grandmothers enthusiastically showing them both what she had received before their arrival.

Amelia was growing in stature every day, gaining confidence surrounded by people who loved her very much and the transformation from when we had first met her at the café was simply amazing. Of course when the bell continued to chime she was first to the door first greeting Vera, Danielle and Martyn in the same manner repeating herself countless times although nobody minded because this was her special day. But when Mary and Thomas arrived she eagerly pulled them into the front room much to the amusement of everybody where encompassed by us all Amelia Brand had her family all in one place taking centre stage.

Soon after midday Arnold engaged the brakes of the double decker bus parking outside the house moments before a steady stream of happy, smiling children entered going through to the kitchen and then the garden out back followed by Carolyn Johnson. An additional surprise minutes after their arrival were Stephanie Steele and Robert Styles. I made a mental note to talk to Robert later.

Amelia was delighted to have the children come to her birthday party and see so many friends once again. Thomas did his usual disappearing act accompanied by Mary returning half an hour later dressed as a clown although his hair I noticed on this occasion was straight instead of a mass of curls. The women organised the serving of the food as the men helped pull streamers and inflate more balloons some which had a funny noisy screamer device which when released would whizz around in the air before deciding upon which child to land.

I thought that seeing Amelia so happy some of the children would have been a little envious of her circumstances but looking around the garden I didn't see one unhappy face. No doubt the party was going to be a social event every year which would be interesting to follow as the children grew older.

Alone and together Carolyn Johnson took the opportunity to speak to Lola and myself expressing her gratitude and how pleased she was to see Amelia so happy, stating that at one point Amelia had insisted on her going upstairs where she was proud to show off her bedroom then have Miss Johnson see the airline tickets for Disneyland and Paris.

Mama Capella, my mother and Vera sat at a table set aside for the adults talking to one another having never seen so many children in one place. I wasn't party to their conversation but I gathered from Lola that the party reminded them of when they had been young girls dancing around the maypole before joining in the festivities that followed.

That day the garden party lasted until five in afternoon when Carolyn Johnson thanked us for inviting all the children to our house and Amelia's party, whereupon with Arnolds help we somehow managed to stand, be seated or sit on the grass everybody together to have our photograph taken, a beautiful reminder of a wonderful May occasion.

Putting Amelia to bed that evening with Angus and Shamus by her side she looked not only exhausted and happy but content. We asked her if she had enjoyed the day to which she replied.

'It was a very good day mummy and daddy although I wish baby could have been here too to have joined in the games and eat jelly and ice-cream!'

We wished her goodnight and kissed her lovingly on the forehead, telling her that the fairy from the night before had heard what she had just said and that she would undoubtedly convey the message to the angels. Leaving her bedside light on low we pulled the door too and stood outside on the landing.

'Having this baby means everything to Amelia. I just hope that in time she realises that there could be more!'

I took a peek back in at Amelia who was already asleep then pulled Lola in close to me before kissing her.

'Just how many are you planning on having?'

She laughed. 'Oh... I don't know, maybe enough to fill a garden.'

That Magic Moment

Having experienced a very good summer a deluge of snow that winter was not surprising arriving overnight as most of us slept in our beds. To Amelia's delight it was still there when she woke. Jumping out of bed she had promptly pulled back the curtains and whooped with joy at the sight of the crisp white blanket that was covering the garden, trees and bushes.

No matter how many times you experience snow as a child it is as magical as the time before although the fun can be short lived if you don't get outside before the sun peeks between the clouds and turns everywhere into a mushy mashed potato.

Making sure that she had the warmth of a decent breakfast inside her stomach we let Amelia loose on the back garden where like a demented goblin she ran one way then another chasing the falling flurries creating patterns in the snow beneath the branches, until she decided that she would lay down spread her arms and legs wide to create a snow-angel. Snow was a child's paradise.

Sitting at the window seat Lola watched Amelia and I as we scooped up bucket loads of fresh snow gradually moulding them together until we had the assemblance of a rounded body followed by a ball-shaped head and finally a pair of size twenty feet. Cutting in half a fallen branch we made arms adding a parsnip for the nose and a lump of coal for each eye. Standing we admired our efforts.

'Do you still use your old football scarf daddy?' Amelia asked thinking that it would add the finishing touch quite nicely to our frozen sculpture.

Minutes later I returned and together we wrapped my patriotic red, white and blue scarf around the snowman's neck.

'Best we don't tell nanny that the snowman has my scarf only she knitted it for daddy.' Giggling mischievously she dotted three more lumps of coal down the front giving the snowman a fashionable overcoat.

Tapping on the window Lola invited us back indoors having seen the colour of the sky change to a bluey white suggesting that another cold snap was on its way. I made the invite all the more exciting promising hot chocolate and a toasted bun. We banged the loose snow from the soles of our boots and went inside not a moment too soon as a heavy fall dropped from the sky overhead promptly hiding the feet of our snowman.

'Was that good?' asked Lola as she supported the large lump protruding out front of her maternity dress.

'It was mummy although daddy said that we should come in because he was getting cold. I do think he needs some thicker socks to keep his feet warm!'

I grinned, our eight year old daughter was no longer the shy, retiring coy little girl that we had picked up from the children's Home. Amelia had developed again gaining confidence, enthusiastically engaging herself around the house, looking after Lola and the baby making sure that both were comfortable whatever time of the day.

Like a midwife she would check at least three or four times a day on the baby's progress, clenching her hands tight with excitement when the bump moved and every night before she went to sleep she would ask if her baby brother or sister was due that night, disappointed come the next morning when nothing had materialised. Silently I was as disappointed.

Boiling extra milk to stir in the hot chocolate I eavesdropped their conversation as they discussed the gender of the baby with Amelia stating that the odds were stacked in favour of a girl as opposed to a boy, a good indicator that she wanted a sister instead of a brother.

Whispering in Lola's ear when she thought I couldn't hear, she said *'they've got funny bits, I know because I saw them when I was at the children's home!'* Lola looked over at me raising her eyebrows.

It was about the only time that Amelia had mentioned Saxon House besides the day of her birthday when she had waved goodbye to the bus load of departing friends. Putting the empty saucepan in the sink I made sure that Amelia's chocolate was an acceptable drinking temperature placing Lola's within reach of where she sat.

Lola had flourished fast expanding bigger than a helium balloon and despite several hot curries and warming stews we still had no appearance from the baby.

At *Florrie's Flowers* Mary had insisted that Lola stay away arguing strongly that a draughty and often wet shop floor presented a dangerous hazard to both mother and child. I sympathized knowing that Lola was climbing the walls at home but in return for her state of immobility I received the odd scowl and threat that I was never going anywhere near her again.

With time approaching fast Mama Capella would arrive before I went to the cafe and as arranged my mother would deliver and collect Amelia from school. Vera had volunteered to take over the running of the café but Lola was happy more than happy to have me out of the way and not fussing around.

I did pop in now and then to see Mary although I need not have bothered as she had everything under control with Thomas doing most of the heavy work. It was nice to see Thomas as we rarely got the chance to catch up with one another as his commissions and attendance at various art events kept him so busy. He did tell me that with his new found fame he had managed to rent a good medium sized studio where he could paint in peace and store other works of art. With each sale his popularity spread.

Mary too had come a long way since leaving St Michaels Convent and possibly some of the nuns might have questioned what she derived from arranging flowers, potting bulbs and watering earthenware pots but Mary would convincingly reply that at last she had found inner peace and love with two men, Thomas a very talented artist and second with god.

When Amelia was safely tucked up in bed I would talk to Lola about Mary managing the florists whilst she was at home with the baby. At first Lola said that she would take the baby to the shop but in time she accepted how impracticable it would be realising also that perhaps it would present Mary the ideal opportunity to demonstrate her home grown talents.

Having never been around anybody close who was pregnant, I could not help but be concerned and over the past few months I had noticed my weight dropping significantly whereas Lola was adding on the pounds. Having gone down a size in trousers I had also added another two notches to my belt. Lola however told me that I looked younger and healthier so perhaps some good had come from the stress of the being an expectant father.

With Amelia's help we had sorted, washed down the walls and prepared the spare room in readiness for Thomas to add his mark and turn it into a nursery, although Amelia wanted an assurance that eventually the baby was going to share her room. Lola and I also found it rather amusing that she deemed it necessary to sort through some of her older clothes and toys putting them in the spare room for when the baby was older. More surprising was when she said that the baby could have Shamus if it didn't have a teddy of its own.

Between our mothers both had made sure that Lola was well stocked with baby clothes, knitted all-in-ones and bedding for the cot. And with just a week to go Mama Capella camped down in Amelia's room being close at hand in case the waters broke whilst I was at work. Of course Amelia loved it sharing everything with her nana.

In between various other duties Amelia would take me around the supermarket explaining what mummy did or did not buy. Other times to give mummy time to rest and take a nap we would visit the park, wade through thick snow or slide down a long steep slope.

Surprisingly Lola agreed to Amelia having a few friends over from the children's home so that she could have some quality time with children of her own age instead of just being around adults all the time. I was concerned that the noise would be too much for Lola but Carolyn Johnson was on hand to keep all four of them under control. I had unintentionally noticed also that Lola had formed quite a friendly association with Carolyn Johnson and after the birth they had arranged to meet up for lunch.

Packing the three children into the car I made sure that they were safe to travel as Amelia waved from the window. It was good that she saw her friends and enjoyable for the others too.

At the café Danielle had several sweep stakes under way, guessing the baby's weight, the name, date and time of birth. Without Lola knowing I had five pounds on all three sweeps. And Lola had already been given lots of gifts from the baby-shower gathering two months before the happy day but all week as the day got closer different customers had been arriving bearing small gift boxes and packages, leaving some with Mary and others with me.

Vera had baked a big fruit cake for the occasion and made Amelia a smaller version in the bargain not wishing to have her feel left out. Thomas had promised to paint a family portrait when the baby was able to sit up and Danielle had crocheted a blanket for the car set. I didn't know that she could crotchet but apparently during our honeymoon my mum had taught her the basics and from there on in she had mastered the craft herself.

For those of you readers who have experienced such an event you will understand that despite all the planning and preparation things rarely go smoothly. A baby has an agenda all of its own coming when they are ready and not when you demand that they make an appearance not unless a medical intervention becomes necessary.

Cursing and turning, unable to find a comfortable position Lola would be aware of Amelia around swearing in Italian, muttering under breath when the pain was severe although Amelia had become quite proficient in her mother's and nana's native tongue. Quite out of the blue one evening Amelia suggested that I sleep on the settee to give mummy the double bed to herself so that she and baby had room to manoeuvre.

However and don't say that I didn't advise against it... the afternoon before the calendar suggested that the baby was due Mama Capella and Lola decided to take themselves off to Dickens and Harvey in the High Street believing that I was close enough should the waters break. And naturally as expected whilst checking the price of a post-natal dress Lola was aware first of a twinge then another until she felt the moisture run down the inside of her leg. A knowing look at Mama Capella had her mother singing for assistance.

The shop manager was all for calling an ambulance but Lola was insistent that I should be on hand at the birth so instead she breathed deep regulating control of her contractions like we had been shown in the antenatal classes. They managed to walk to the café before she grabbed my hand tight and through gritted teeth told me that the baby was coming.

I too wanted to call for an ambulance but Mama Capella told me that there wasn't time so with Martyn's help we pushed together several tables and Danielle gave them a quick wash-down. Vera supplied fresh towels as Martyn ran to get Doc Doland. Still gripping my hand Lola looked deep into my soul.

'Never again Brand,' she exclaimed as the contractions came thick and fast.

Standing next to her daughter Mama Capella laughed 'I had three daughter's Lola, the second is much easier!'

It was not quite the encouragement that Lola wanted to hear.

'Mamma mia il bambino sta arrivando,' she screamed as she held the huge bump and looked at me with daggers in her eyes.

I somehow managed to release the grip on my hand heading for the phone behind the counter stating 'I'm calling the ambulance,' but before I could dial Lola screamed at me once more.

'Spencer... the baby's coming NOW!'

Bundled to one side Mama Capella and Vera took over command, shielding Lola from preying eyes using large table cloths they methodically saw to Lola and the baby. I called the ambulance regardless who arrived around the same time as Martyn and Doc Doland. Danielle supplied warm water and fresh towels as Mary came rushing in from next door to assist.

I did ask what I could do to help but received a resounding *'nothing'* in reply before being told to stand next to Lola and support her head.

Amidst the furore my mum arrived with Amelia having collected her from school. Amelia immediately wanted to know what was happening behind the sheet. When Lola heard her daughter's voice she asked that Amelia be brought around so that she could be present when the baby was born.

With a minute to spare holding her mummy's other hand Amelia saw her baby brother born and I lost fifteen pounds on the sweep stake. Doc Doland did what was necessary with the umbilical cord then handed the rest over to the ambulance crew swaddling the baby in fresh linen.

When Mama Capella laid her new grandson on Lola's chest Amelia started to fret when she heard the baby cry but Lola encouraged her daughter to gently stroke the baby's back and soothe his coming into the world. It was a bewitching moment that I will never forget for the rest of my life. A magical moment in a magical place. Looking up at the ceiling I knew somewhere my father was looking down upon us all.

I embraced Lola then Amelia, Danielle and Mary, Mama Capella and my mother then Vera, who said 'he's beautiful although thankfully he has his mother's looks.'

Vera was right and our son did look Lola, thank heavens.

'He is amazing... a miracle,' I announced as Lola smiled back gently stroking the back of Amelia's head.

'And what do you think of your brother?' she asked.

'He's a bit little to play out in the snow, but I suppose he'll grow!'

Either side of the sheet burst into laughter including Amelia who didn't quite know how she had caused the moment but that was another of her enchanting character traits, always so innocently funny. Suggesting that I hold the baby Lola looked up at me with a smile.

'He's ours Spencer... every bit of him, like little Amelia!'

We let Amelia hold her brother although she gave him back fairly quickly believing that he might break if she held onto him too long. In time she would hold and cuddle him for long periods whilst together they watched the telly.

Standing aside so that the paramedics could take over Lola still had time to tell me the names that the three of us had agreed upon *Antonio John Alfred Brand.*

Each befitting of a little boy who had his great grandfather's name, another belonging to a brave soldier and John because he was Amelia's favourite character from one of her bedtime stories. In time when she understood I would let her know that John was also my father's name. And in time Antonio would relish the fact that Alfie Wilson was not only a known writer but an adventurer too.

Much later we would look back and reflect that in all the hullabaloo that afternoon the café was the best place to have brought our son into the world. It was where we had first seen our beautiful little daughter and so appropriate was that Amelia was there to see her brother born.

Things happen for a reason although we don't always realise it at the time. And neither brother nor sister would ever want for anything, not with a loving mother and father, two doting grandmothers and five aunties, Vera, Danielle and Mary living in England and two in Florence. Lest not forgetting that they had many others dotted across Italy plus two very protective uncles in Martyn and Thomas. In time other babies would be born and expand our big family unit but there would always be sufficient love to go around.

Amelia and I went with Lola in the back of the ambulance where the maternity doctors and nurses at the hospital weighed and gave Antonio a clean bill of health. Later that evening we were allowed to come home with the midwife coming to visit first thing in the morning.

Just for the record Thomas won the sweep. Antonio had been born at five minutes to four, weighing in at six pounds and four ounces, quite a healthy weight or as you modern mums would rather have it recorded two point nine kilogrammes.

Word soon got around that we had a new addition to our family and with the ringing of the doorbell Amelia opened the door to Robert Styles and Father Michael who came to give their blessings, Stephanie Steele to report on the happy event and how I don't know but even Alfie Wilson sent his congratulations all the way from darkest Africa, as did Carolyn Johnson and the children from the home.

The next morning assisted ably by Amelia, Lola and the midwife bathed her brother although Amelia refused to wash his extra bits. Fussing over him she never left his side much to the delight of Lola and myself. In the years to come Amelia and Antonio would build a snowman together. Weekends were always hectic with many visitors filling the house but as a family we wouldn't want it any other way.

Lola did as promised staying away from *Florrie's Flowers* allowing Mary the chance to blossom and surprisingly without changing very little sales at the florists boomed. It wasn't that Lola had done anything different prior to her pregnancy it was just that Mary had found her niche in life.

Mama Capella took herself off to Florence taking with her a full photograph album of her new grandchildren and my mother too decided that it was time for a holiday going to Brighton with Vera where they intended doing a lot of shopping and playing bridge.

During her absence Martyn ran the kitchen and proved himself to be a damn fine cook getting praise not just from Danielle and myself but many of the customers as well.

On the second Sunday in March we had Antonio christened and Amelia blessed in both faiths with Robert Styles and Father Michael doing their bit. Amelia was extremely pleased about the event as she had a new dress and shoes brought by Lola for the occasion.

And so good people the time has arrived to end this chapter and finish the book with just one last statement to make. I am a very lucky man. I have the most beautiful and loving wife, who is mother to our two wonderful children. I am fortunate to own a magical little red café who without good friends to help run it I could not take all the credit for its success. We have amazing customers who become friends too and without whom this book would not have been possible.

Life has turned out good for me despite the odd hiccup but I am excited about the future and the prospect of meeting many more interesting people. If by chance you are in the area and feel that you could do with a pot of tea, a coffee or a slice of Vera's lemon drizzle cake, why not pop into the cafe and say hello.

Goodbye for now, dear reader!

Vera's Recipe for Lemon Drizzle Cake.

Best served with a nice cup of tea or coffee, whatever the time of the day!

Cake Ingredients:

- 1½ large eggs

- 87.5 grammes (3 oz.) self-raising flour
- 87.5 grammes (3 oz.) caster sugar
- 87.5 grammes (3 oz.) softened butter
- ¾ level teaspoon of baking powder
- ½ lemon, finely grated for the zest

The Lemon Icing:

- 50g (2 oz.) granulated sugar
- Juice of ½ lemon

You will also need:

- 450g (1lb) loaf tin, greased and lined

Method

- Preheat the oven to 180º Celsius or gas mark 4.
- Beat together the eggs in a large mixing bowl, add in the flour, caster sugar and butter, the baking powder and the lemon zest until you have a smooth consistency. Turn out ingredients into the prepared tin.
- Bake in a pre-heated oven for approximately 35 minutes or until golden brown. The texture of the cake should shrink away from the side of the tin and be springy to the touch.
- Whilst the cake is still warm, make the lemon drizzle topping. Mix together the sugar and lemon juice, then when ready pour over the warm cake.

- Leave to cool before loosening the sides, lifting from the tin and placing on a cake stand or plate.
- Fill the kettle and switch on.

Note: If you should ever be in the area please do pop in because you are always welcome at the little red café and do let us know if you enjoyed the cake!

Printed in Great Britain
by Amazon